UNCONQUERED SON

Book I of the Imperial Chronicles

THE COMING YEARS WOULD TEST THE COURAGE OF CITIZENS AND SUBJECT PEOPLES, OF LEGIONARIES AND SLAVES, OF THE MEN AND WOMEN OF THE EMPIRE; AND DETERMINE WHETHER THE NATION CHOSEN BY IMPERIUM WOULD FULFILL ITS CALLING: TO RULE OVER ALL THE WORLD.

—Primo Alleus, national historian, writer of *The Imperial Chronicles*

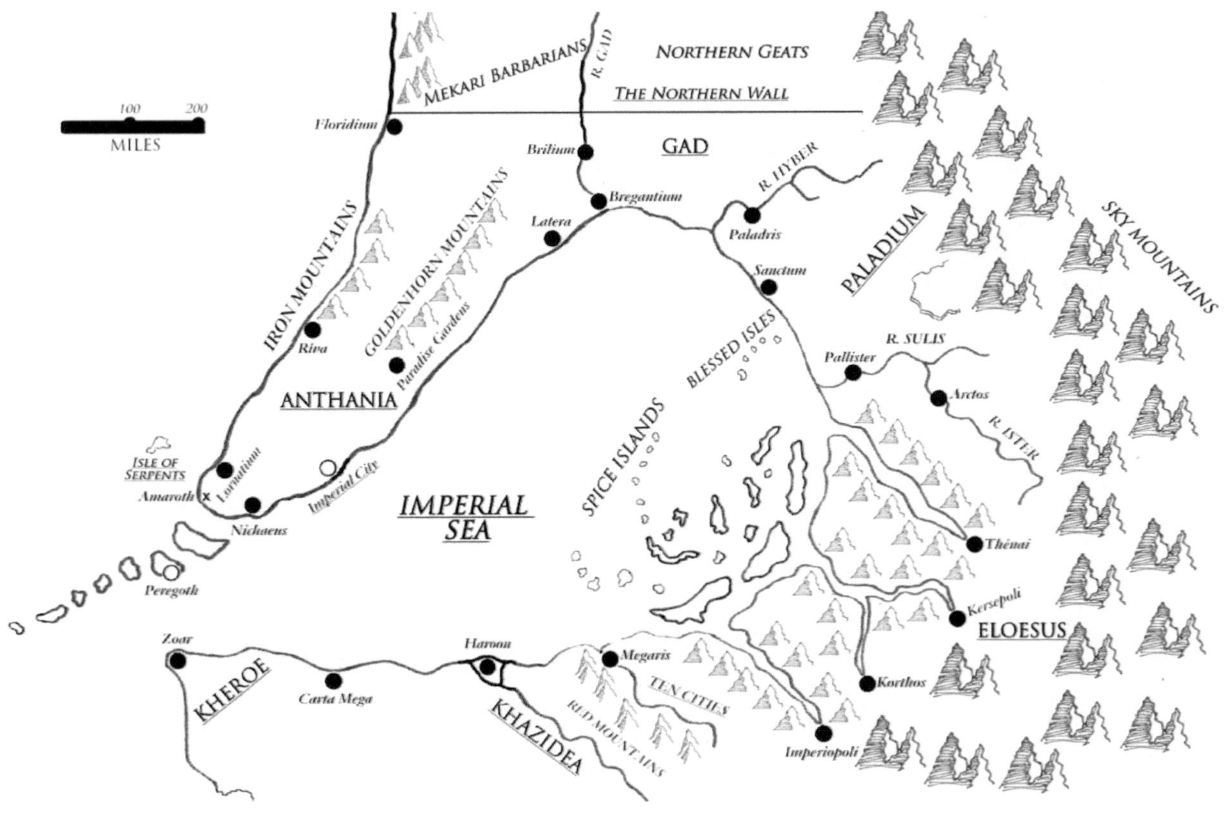

KHEROE
Zoar
Peregoli
ISLE OF SERPENTS
Amaroth
Lormation
Nicluens
Carta Mega
Imperial City
IMPERIAL SEA
ANTHANIA
IRON MOUNTAINS
Riva
Floridium
GOLDENHORN MOUNTAINS
Paradise Gardens
MEKARI BARBARIANS
R. GAD
KHAZIDEA
Harmon
BAD MOUNTAINS
TEN CITIES
Megaris
Latera
Brilinte
Bregantium
GAD
THE NORTHERN WALL
NORTHERN GEATS
SPICE ISLANDS
BLESSED ISLES
Imperiopoli
Kaethos
Paladris
Sanctum
R. HYBER
PALADIUM
Pallister
R. SULIS
Arctos
R. ISTER
Kerepoli
Thenai
ELOESUS
SKY MOUNTAINS
MILES
100
200

Imperial City

<table>
<tr><th>WARDS (LABELED)</th><th>THE CITY: ITS SIGHTS AND WONDERS</th></tr>
<tr><td>

a. Armory District
b. Kings Terrace
c. Maxima
d. Villa Regis
e. Bulus Wharf
f. Market District
g. Canyon Row
h. Newmarket
i. Mud Bottom
j. Meridia
k. Mystia
l. Villa Mares
m. Loud Surf
n. Perrine
o. Gaboline
p. West Limes
q. East Limes
r. Terrentian
s. Majorian Markets
t. The Strand
u. Meletus
v. Urubus

</td><td>

City Bounds: *No legions may enter. It is the law.*
Wagontown Settlement: *A Haunt of Halflings.*
Dualmis: *An island across the sea.*
Imperial Harbor: *A wonder of the world.*
1. Imperial Square: *The Imperial Palace, the Council House and the Hippodrome, among other wonders.*
2. Campus: *The city's most ancient boundary.*
3. Imperial Arena: *Glory. Honor. Blood.*
4. Walk of Triumph: *See the nation's heroes and be amazed.*

</td></tr>
</table>

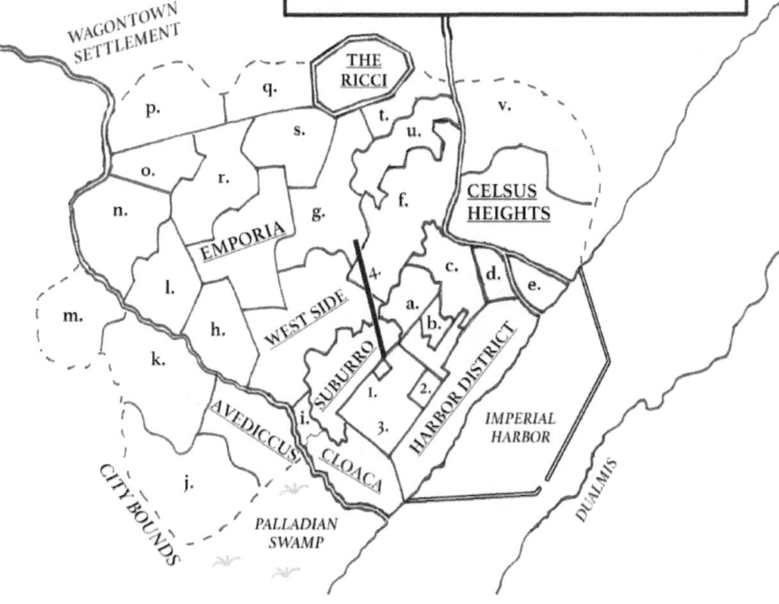

PROLOGUE:
THE DARK-EYED TWINS

Lucento-Valens Adamantus, Legate

The dark coach careened toward the legionaries. Hungry silver ghosts flew out the windows and around the wheels. The rebels had taken the heavily-fortified city of Dubaquis, proclaiming that Yblis—lord of the underworld—viewed all people as equal, in death.

Lucento—the bloody *leader* of the Seventh Anthanian Legion, veteran of a hundred wars—shook in his boots. The black coach and its hungry ghosts rode toward the last remaining legionaries. Out of an original five thousand, Lucento could only make out a few dozen still alive.

Dark storm-clouds had formed over Dubaquis, yet no rain came down. The rebels had shattered the aqueducts a week ago, and the parched citizens had let them in. Like demons or dark undead, it seemed they only entered a place with an invitation.

The dark coach rammed into the front lines. The hungry ghosts came with it. The soldiers' faces melted like wax. Screams rang out. The front lines turned and trampled each other. Yet the loudest noise, to Lucento, was the beating of his own heart.

The black coach continued its hellish ride. Lucento bolted to the right, through the legionaries as they trampled each other, knocking people over before they could knock over him. *The world is wild, and only the strong survive.*

At last he reached the edge: a stone ridge that extended from the nearby mountains. The black coach, by the grace of the gods, had gone the other way. Lucento hopped toward the ridge. He clutched the rock, but scratched his hands and fell back into the screaming mass. He glanced over. The black coach turned the other way—toward Lucento. The ghosts swirled around it, eating the men's faces. On the rocky ground, a legionary begged for help.

"Help me up!" he screamed. "Help me up!"

Lucento leapt toward the rocky ridge again, but again failed to gain a handhold. He slipped down, cutting himself and opening a small wound on his hand. "Damn it all!" he screamed. "Hieronus help us!"

Yet the god of justice and just war seemed to be on the side of the rebels. The coach rattled through the army, impaling men on its spiked wheels.

"Help!" the legionary on the ground screamed.

"Forgive me, Hieronus!" Lucento cried, and, using the wounded man as leverage, leapt over the rocky ridge seconds before the black coach skidded next to it, slaughtering all in its path.

Panting and trembling, Lucento staggered across the black earth. Though it was day, the dark clouds overhead turned all to night. Dubaquis was a remote city on the edge of the Iron Mountains. Help was many leagues away. Yet if he ran north, perhaps he could escape the rebels. Perhaps, if he ran many miles, he could reach Novica. Perhaps, if he kept running…

A blue spear of lightning flashed in the distance. A deafening boom of thunder roared across Dubaquis. Rain began, at first a drizzle and then a downpour.

I'm too old for this. I'm too old for war.

He ran as the dirt turned to mud, as the rain soaked his tunic. His sword, a standard Imperial issue, had once given him security. Now, it felt worthless against these forces of the underworld.

Lightning flashed again. A band of rebels ran across the road. Some of them were mortals. And of these mortals, almost all were escaped slaves. Their rebellion against their condition was understandable. Unacceptable, yes, but understandable. Yet they did not realize that they played with fire. The lord of the Underworld cared nothing about them. And when they were finally defeated, the

Empire would torture and kill them all.

"Defeated?" a little girl's voice said, echoing through Lucento's mind.

"Defeated?" said a little boy's voice.

Lucento turned his head. On the paved road leading toward Dubaquis proper, the leaders of the rebellion stared at him. The boy, Fabius, and the girl, Marcia. Ten years old, both born on the thirteenth of Anthanos. The Dark-Eyed Twins.

The girl spoke without moving her lips. "No more slaves. No more poor. No more Knights. No more Augusts. Just darkness. Just darkness. Just darkness."

"Just darkness," the boy said silently.

With dark, dead eyes they gazed at Lucento. His neck-hairs stood on end and he backed away from them; but they followed him off-road, onto the damp ground, stepping forward slowly with their little feet.

The boy, Fabius, spoke again in Lucento's mind. "No more slaves. No more poor. No more Knights. No more Augusts. Just darkness. Just darkness. Just darkness."

"*Stop!*" Lucento cried.

"Just darkness," the girl, Marcia, said.

Lucento's fear at last planted his feet on the ground. He stood there, shaking, as the twins walked toward him.

The last thing he saw was a shapeless, many-fanged face tearing toward his neck; and a hand dragging him into a black abyss.

The last thing he heard was, "Just darkness, forevermore."

PART ONE

CHAPTER ONE:
BAD NEWS

Claudio-Valens Adamantus

When the news reached Cipium—the Adamantus family ranch—Claudio's mother, Catalina, sat down at the kitchen table and poured herself the last of the white wine.

The golden medal of service and the Imperial standard across the coffin were no consolation. Catalina no longer had a husband; he no longer had a father.

"I'm sorry, mother."

"Do not be sorry." Mother's voice was strong. "We must get through this as we always have; we are of the knightly class… defenders of the Empire…" She broke into sobs.

"Damned rebels," Claudio growled. He fought tears of his own. But expressing emotion was unacceptable as an Imperial Knight; and his mother needed his comfort. She needed a strong rock against this tempest.

"I knew he was too old for war, but he didn't listen," Mother wept. "He didn't listen to me."

"I will avenge him."

"No!" Mother sobbed. "I will not lose you as well. You are my only son, and all your sisters have married…"

"Then I will not avenge him. I will do as you wish, Mother."

"I love you, Claudio. Remember that."

That night, as the setting sun painted the horse ranch in bronze colors, Catalina, Claudio, and the family servants decided on the time and place for the funeral. The honorable Lucento would be buried the next day at the family ranch, near the horses he loved so dearly.

The priest—a devotee of Hieronus, god of justice and just war—sprinkled the corpse with oil. "Hieronus, take Lucento Adamantus into your home. He has lived an honorable life, and was just in all his dealings. May his eyes look forever skyward until the end of time."

They laid the wooden shell into the deep pit as Catalina sobbed and Claudio held her. Once the servants began shoveling dirt, they headed back to the ranch house. Along the road they walked. Mother's sniffling continued, and Claudio, by grace of the gods, was able to hold his tears in.

The sound of galloping echoed through the air. Not unusual for a ranch; but it came from south along the road, not where the horses and foals were. Claudio looked back. A man in the purple-sashed white tunic of the Imperial court rode toward them.

Within seconds he had reached them. "Signore!" the man called out. "Are you Claudio-Valens Adamantus?"

"Yes," Claudio stated.

"I am so sorry for your loss," the man said.

Claudio said nothing.

"If you have not heard, the emperor has passed on."

Catalina gasped.

"His will was read last week. The Imperial Council has conceded to the will and Giton Seánus Algabal now sits on the White Throne."

Catalina gasped again, but Claudio held his reactions tightly in check. Giton Algabal—a distant relation of the emperor—had moved to the Imperial Palace with his mother three years ago. Rumors had already reached Claudio that Giton was the most cowardly, evil-hearted pleasure-seeker the Councilors had ever seen. In truth, he was barely of Imperial blood at all; his father was a barbarian from Khazidea, and his mother was half Easterner and half related to the emperor. Yet the Council held no real power to go against the emperor's will. The Council, really, had no powers at all.

"Signore?" the man said, breaking Claudio out of his stunned silence.

"Yes?" Claudio said calmly. "Go on."

"Your family is among the most revered of the knights," the man continued. "His Undying Glory is hosting a grand reception on the seventh of Odens to celebrate his coronation. He wishes all his senior knights to attend... I extend the invitation to you as well, signora."

"I do not think we will be able to attend," Catalina said.

"Forgive me, signora, for giving you counsel. The emperor does not easily forgive slights... if at least one of you does not go, he will have a long memory of that throughout his reign."

"I will go," Claudio said abruptly.

"Very well," Catalina said. "I shall mourn in private. But it is necessary." She nuzzled her head into Claudio's shoulder, dampening his shoulder with her tears. "Go, pack your things." She looked up at the rider. "Tell the emperor to expect my son." She whispered in his ear as they walked toward the ranch house: "Be careful."

He set out early in the morning with a handful of servants. He did not ride in the carriage, where all his things were; a knight rode horses, by definition. He would ride until he was saddle-sore, and beyond.

By late afternoon, they reached an immense wooden sign along the main road:

THE PATH OF TIDUS
FORT MARTELLO... 55 MILES
AURELEA... 75 MILES

The sign listed more towns and cities below, but at the bottom, Claudio's destination was written:

Imperial City... 531 miles

He sighed at the distance. Two weeks' travel, if all went well. He would grow saddle-sore indeed.

CHAPTER TWO:
A STRANGE GIRL

Marcus Silverus

Marcus Silverus wanted a huge house on a private island, a pleasure barge, nightly parties on the ocean, and a harem of beautiful women like the southern Padisha Emperor. Right now, all he had was a crammed room in the Imperial Palace and an annual salary of twelve hundred gold pieces. Not enough to buy a private island, unless he saved for years. And Marcus Silverus spent every last penny he made.

As he looked out his sixth-story window onto the light blue waters of the Middle Sea, the mansion-lined island of Dualmis reminded him of his lifelong ambition. Somewhere out there in the bright seas, there was an island for him.

A few fathoms below lay the garden. There, fig trees grew in abundance. He looked down and noticed a stranger there. A girl wandered through the gardens. She wore a dark red, ragged cloak. Obviously she was neither of the Knightly or August Class. So what was she doing in the palace?

Marcus could not resist curiosity. He could not resist much.

The girl was muttering to herself and Marcus couldn't discern her words.

"Are you all right?" Marcus asked and walked over to her.

She was muttering something about Peregothius, founder of the Empire. Marcus removed her hood. She had bright red locks of hair. Her lips were full and colorful. Her eyes were a light, lush brown, complementing her even face well. She was beautiful. But her muttering and inability to respond indicated this girl's stark, raving madness.

"What's your name, girl?" Marcus said gently.

"The Trifold Goddess," she said. "The Mother. The Great Mother."

"Is that your name?"

"No…" She looked away. "My name's Tivera. What's yours? Don't answer!"

Marcus laughed, not knowing how else to react. She must be a street-rat that somehow made it into the palace. She would not fare well if Antonio, Marshal of the Imperial Guard, found out.

"They're after me," Tivera said. "They're all after me. I need help." Her eyes darted this way and that.

"Who's after you?" Marcus ran a finger along her cheek, and realized she was cold and shaking.

"Mother. Father. They are going to beat me again. Don't let them beat me again."

Marcus stifled a gasp. He put his arm around her shoulder. "Relax. It's going to be okay." If the Guard found her, she would be escorted back to her abusers. "Come with me."

He would take her to his room. Marcus knew himself as a drunkard, a partier, and a man of loose morals; but he also knew he had a heart.

Marcus took her into his small bedchamber. "Are you cold?" He offered her a blanket, but she recoiled.

"No!" Her eyes darted about wildly. "I can warm myself. I am an augur…"

"An augur?" *Unlikely.*

She opened her hands, in both her palms, twin white lights grew in size.

Marcus shuddered. Magic never failed to frighten him; it seemed so out of the norm. But this magic was strange. "You create light… not wind, like the augurs. Maybe you are a magus… are you from Fharas?" She didn't look the part.

The lights vanished. Tivera covered her ears with her hands. "Don't say it! Don't say it! La-la-la…"

If she is an augur, then she is an insane augur, Marcus thought. Power and insanity was not a good combination, as he learned from the history books.

He forced her hands off her ears. "I must take you to the Augur Collegium and see if they will admit you."

"Mother and Father will find me," Tivera whined. She started shaking again. "Please don't take me there."

"The collegium will not deliver you to your parents," Marcus said calmly but firmly. "I will ensure it. Now come with me. You're better off at the collegium than here, I tell you."

Marcus looked into Tivera's eyes and saw innocence, pure innocence. Anyone who wanted to harm this poor girl was a wicked person indeed. Somehow, because of her frailty he felt obligated to protect her. If the collegium would not take her, then he would take her in. If she ended up on the streets Marcus would never forgive himself.

The streets of Imperial City had grown less dangerous than a year ago, when Emperor Julio Seánus banned wheeled vehicles from entering at daytime. But light quickly faded from the sky, and soon night would set in. Marcus could not count the dangers of the night streets: murderers, muggers, wild dogs, chariots rattling through narrow alleys.

But he led Tivera as she whimpered, holding her quivering hand. The Augur Collegium was just a short walk away from the Imperial Palace. They passed the Imperial Hippodrome, several grim gray apartment blocks, and finally reached the collegium itself.

Above two propped-open wooden doors, etched on a stone lintel, was the collegium's motto: "On the Winds of Fortune, We Speed to Victory."

Tivera's whimpering reached a peak. "I don't want to go in."

"Tivera, it's for the best. It's better than starving on the streets… being murdered in the darkness."

At the phrase "murdered in the darkness" she shrieked. Marcus steadily led her through the propped-open wooden doors and entered the famed Augur Collegium.

They passed into the greeting room. On the colored marble was the insignia of the Augur Collegium: two crossed torches upheld by two hands. Against the wall was a desk, and behind it sat a man, obviously an augur. On his head, he wore a white-winged leather cap. In his hand he held a long, plain wooden staff. At once he stood up, and bowed. "Marcus Silverus, Guardian of the Wine Cellar."

Marcus flushed in embarrassment at the miniscule title, but the augur's eyes obviously held reverence… reverence, perhaps, for *any* Imperial title, even the lowliest of them all. "I come to admit this girl into the collegium. She is a magician, an augur, but she creates light."

The augur's eyes widened. "You cannot call her an augur if she does not wield the power of Wind. Light! That is strange; it is not seen much in magicians. Perhaps, among the magi of the south, but maybe not even among *them*." In an instant, his eyes lost their wonder. "Now do not be insulted, my signora, but many try to worm their way into the collegium without having real power. Let me see your handiwork."

"Show them," Marcus urged her.

"I… No! No!" she mumbled.

"Tivera," Marcus said sternly. She didn't know what was best for her, or how vulnerable she was on the streets. "Show him."

"Ah… all right…" She stretched out her palm and a small, wavering mote of light appeared, growing larger until it shone as an incandescent orb. The light relaxed Marcus, put his soul at ease.

The augur's eyes lit up with fascination. "Ah! Yes! Yes, I am sure we would be interested in seeing her." He smiled. "Will you join the Order of Augurs, my signora?"

"I—I don't know," Tivera stuttered.

"I will take that as a yes," the augur said. "In matters of faith… do you pledge your faith to Animon, the Wind Lord, and his twin sister Celera the Quick-Footed?"

"No," Tivera said with startling clarity. "I worship Mira, the Trifold Mother."

The whom? Marcus never heard of such a deity.

"It is no matter," the augur said. "We will accept her."

Marcus wasn't sure he liked the look in the augur's eyes, but he knew intellectually that Tivera would fare better here than in the streets.

"Come with me, Tivera."

She looked at Marcus like a sad dog abandoned by her master. As Marcus left the Augur Collegium, he—for a reason he did not know—fought guilt.

CHAPTER THREE:
SLAVES REBORN

Silvestro Matteus, Legate

The mission verged on suicide: succeed where the Seventh Anthanian Legion failed. Conquer the rebel stronghold of Dubaquis, where the best of the legions had perished. Yet Silvestro would not enter with the same bravado that proved to be the Seventh Anthanian's doom. He would use actual strategy when he attempted it.

Three thousand soldiers marched in Silvestro's legion: two thousand, five-hundred common legionaries; three-hundred Imperial Knights; and a two-hundred strong auxiliary force of archers from Eloesus.

A fearsome force, one that could conquer and people the whole world; and yet, the Seventh Anthanian—almost twice as strong—had broken upon this rebel stronghold like water crashing against rocks.

As Silvestro rode with the Knights, he surveyed the region. This was Anthanian central valley, on the edge of the imposing Iron Mountains. Here, the sun baked the uncultivated yellow grass, and the rarer, arid fields of wheat. It was hot like southern Anthania, perhaps hotter, but without the respite of the sea. You could not strip your clothes and cool off in the water. Water, here, was a precious commodity.

The weather had been sunny and blue-skied, but now—the last leg of the journey—a dark spot hung in the distance, and just looking at it sent a shiver up Silvestro's spine. Perhaps it was a cloud, but if it was a cloud it was an evil one. A man practiced in the art of divination may tell Silvestro more; but until recently—until just a few days ago, when the rumors started to reach him—he had not believed in that art or in underworldly powers.

A rider appeared in the distance. The black, hooded cloak he wore flapped in the wind. He held the reins with black gloves, and wore black boots over his feet. His horse was gray and sparse of hair, sickly and—if the showing ribs were any evidence—malnourished. Around the man's left sleeve was a red band.

Silvestro halted and signaled the people behind him to stop. He hollered, "What do you want?"

"My name is Achaeus," a voice rasped from behind the hood. "Once I was an Eloesian slave, mistreated by my domino. Now I have been reborn as a Son of the Underworld."

It took monumental effort for Silvestro to speak firmly. "Achaeus, you are an Eloesian slave. If you feel you have been mistreated by your master, could you not have taken it up in court, rather than joining a cult? It is illegal to badly mistreat a slave."

"You don't understand, do you?" the voice rasped. "There is no hope for slaves in the Empire; there is no justice. Only in Yblis, God of the Underworld, will we find our justice. And then, in Him, it is the rich and the powerful that will have no hope."

"Show your face!" Silvestro roared and swept his standard-issue Imperial sword out of its sheath.

To his great surprise, he removed his hood to reveal a bloody face, scarred beyond human recognition. "In Yblis there is no ugly or beautiful. There is only Him."

"Soldiers?" Silvestro roared. "Javelins!"

"I came here to help you," Achaeus said. "I came to warn you, because if you go any further, you march to your doom."

"Launch!"

A dozen javelins soared through the air. Most hit the ground around Achaeus and bent over. The last of them sank into Achaeus' chest and out the other side. His horse bucked onto her hind legs and whinnied, then turned around and galloped back toward Dubaquis, off-road toward the black cloud. The limp body of Achaeus did not fall from the saddle.

As they continued down the road it became clear to Silvestro that strategy—and perhaps, a strange strategy—was necessary. His wife, on the rare weeks he spent at their small home in the foothills, told him of her great faith in Luos, god of light. That he protected the weary and the lost against the evils of darkness and shadow.

Perhaps, even if it were not to Luos, they might make an offering to a god. Perhaps, to all gods; and perhaps that would break some of the underworld lord's power.

At the next open field Silvestro ordered the legion to make camp. He would have to make preparations. He would have to plan, to understand the enemy, and to sacrifice.

He sent two legionaries, Donato and Piero, to go spy. He sent one cohort to go seek out a cow for sacrifice. Then, watching the legion set up their tents along the field, he paced the grounds nervously. The words of Achaeus hung over him like a raincloud. *I walk to my doom,* he thought. Yet if the rebellion was not decimated, the whole Empire would grow unstable. It was his duty as a citizen, and if he died in the attempt then it would be an honorable death.

Soon enough the cohort returned, wrangling a steer by its horns after retrieving it from a nearby ranch. Yet before Silvestro could turn his mind to sacrifice, Donato came sprinting back to camp, screaming, "Piero's been captured! Piero's been captured! We have to go save him."

"Calm yourself!" shouted a centurion named Horatio. "We will do no such thing."

But Silvestro could see the desperation in Donato's eyes. Piero had apparently been his good friend. "Don't give orders for me!" Silvestro snapped at him. "I will take a century. In fact, I will take *your* century, Horatio. You will come with me, and we will find Piero."

"Thank you! Thank you, signore!" Donato looked uncharacteristically bare of armor; only a linen undershirt and breeches for sneaking. In his effort to move quietly, he had discarded his standard-issue helmet and hauberk.

Horatio and Silvestro exchanged glances. Horatio's eyes held a trace of a glare, but even he was too honorable to argue with his commander.

Silvestro led the century on foot. The journey to the black cloud took a long half hour off-road through fields of dry, golden wheat. The farmers dared not complain; they feared the legion. But even they had to worry about the black cloud and the bad tidings from Dubaquis.

In time, they reached the area underneath the black cloud. The twilight turned to night. The rolling wheat was gray, and all color was a pale shadow of what it once had been. It seemed they entered into a world of the dead. A chill breeze blew in from the dark gray, now-visible Iron Mountains, turning everything in its path cold.

It was silent here, yet not silent. Despite the lack of spoken word, it seemed that underneath the pervasive quiet, a low moaning arose: a strained sob of the restless dead.

Silvestro broke the silence. "Follow me!" he said with a firmness and command that surprised him. He moved forward, sword extended, walking quietly.

At last, through the tomb-gray fields of wheat, the black walls of Dubaquis appeared. Silvestro had no doubt that the stone structures were once light gray underneath a sunny sky. Now they formed a black shape over the horizon.

Silvestro marched forward, and his soldiers followed a few steps behind. He made it halfway through the wheat fields leading up to the black wall, and then stopped. He turned around, looked into Donato's eyes, and asked, "Where did he go missing? Was it beyond the wall?"

Donato shook his head. "It was near the gate," he whispered.

"A man in a black hood ran after him and I ran back to camp."

Coward. Silvestro did not say the word, but it was true. "Take me to where you last saw him," he said.

Donato nodded and gulped. Then he took the lead.

They were perhaps a hundred yards from the gate. The low, constant moaning of the dead grew clear, so that Silvestro knew the noise was not just in his head. Above the city and below the dark steely skies, disembodied white ghosts flew this way and that. Perhaps they were the source of this strained, painful cry. It dawned on Silvestro as he crept through the wheat fields that his skepticism was no longer valid; with his own eyes, he saw the spirits of those long-dead. People did not just perish and turn to worms like the Thenoan School of philosophy taught; they lived on in agony in the underworld, under a constant mournful sky.

Silvestro looked around him. A figure appeared in the distance. A man in a black hood stood there with a red band wrapped around his sleeves; yet this was not Achaeus. This man was a bit shorter and thinner.

"Stop!" Silvestro hissed. "*Javelins.*"

The clanking of metal echoed through the air.

"See that man?"

A few murmurs of assent.

"Launch!"

The javelins went flying. Almost instantaneously, the figure drew a shield from his back and crouched, blocking the projectiles like a turtle-shell. One javelin glanced off the shield; another stuck into it and bent over, rending the thing useless in close combat.

"*Charge!*" Silvestro roared.

The soldiers ran at the hooded man, but the hooded man did not give chase. He remained perfectly still and as they grew closer it became apparent he was unarmed.

They were almost within range of cutting him down when he shouted, "I can give you Piero." But the voice did not sound like a man's.

"*Halt!*" Silvestro snapped, and the soldiers stopped immediately. "Surround him so that he may not escape."

The man lowered his hood, and they realized it was not a man at all. A woman stood before them with a thin, pale face and long brown hair tied into a ponytail. "I can bring your friend back to you. And if you strike me down, you will only have yourselves to blame for your doom."

"Weapons down," Silvestro snapped. He peered at her, observing her sickly pallor. "You are a woman."

"In the eyes of Yblis there is no man or woman, rich or poor, August or common."

"A philosophy many would take to, and even I—admittedly—can see the attraction in," Silvestro said. "But it is clear, judging from the darkness you spread and the atrocities you've committed, that your message is demonic in nature."

"To call Yblis a demon is the ultimate blasphemy," the woman said. "He is a god, and an angry god that lives beneath the others' feet… but he is nevertheless a god."

"What is your name?"

"Kyra," she said. "Once I was an Eloesian slave, serving a cruel master that beat me every night. Now I have been reborn in Yblis."

"You poor thing," Silvestro said. "It is illegal in the Empire for a master to mistreat his—"

"Ah, yes." Kyra cut him short. "You told that to Achaeus too. Quaint." She looked into his eyes. "The Empire will fall. The rebels will take Imperial City, and a hell-mouth will swallow it. The emperors have committed crimes against nature."

That, Silvestro said, *is both untrue and treasonous.* The Empire had created long-lasting peace through the region. Peace through strength, as King Peregothius said.

"Do you want your friend?" Kyra said. "You will have to enter the City of the Dead alone. Only Silvestro the Imperial-blooded. Even the children of Yblis take oaths seriously, and I hereby make an oath not to harm you. By coming here you have shown your mettle. Come with me, Lord Silvestro; I know your name, for my god has told me."

"Very well." Silvestro looked back at the hundred-and-one men behind him. "Wait for me."

Heads stuck to the black gate, impaled on spikes. Silvestro shivered. Slowly it cranked open. He had hardly taken one step when Kyra thrust a foul-smelling cloth over his mouth. He slipped into unconsciousness before he could catch a glimpse of the city.

CHAPTER FOUR:
THE WHITE THRONE

Julia Seánus Algabal, Empress mother

"You aren't even an Imperial!" the traitor said as the Imperial Guard grabbed him by the arms.

It was half-true, Julia knew, but it didn't matter. The former emperor, Julio Seánus, was her uncle, and she, his last remaining relative. Her son, Giton, was now emperor. Her ex-husband, Urunam Algabal—dead for many years—would have been proud. Giton's position was mostly due to her; but Urunam still would have been proud of the child.

And thus, in the spacious circular meeting-room of the Council House, she sat in the Yellow Seat. Giton sat in the White Seat right next to her, elevated high above everyone else. Twice in this long day of meetings, Giton had fallen asleep and only his dear mother dared wake him.

The traitor screamed as the guards dragged him off. A councilor named Galvano stood up and unraveled a scroll, reading the next matter of business on this very long meeting-day.

"A letter from the governor of Eloesus," the councilor said. "A number of my people have begun setting up shrines to living emperors. I find this unsettling, as the emperor is said to be first among equals, and I seek your permission to ban this new 'Imperial cult'…"

"Ban it," Julia said. "The emperor is not a god. My son is not a god, and there are to be no temples to him."

Bruesio, an old councilor, stood up. "My good emperor, I suggest that you bash all the temples down and flog any members of this new 'cult.' Put it on the list of proscribed cults, and arrest those responsible. We cannot have our Empire tainted with these southron ideas of emperors being gods."

"It could instill respect," argued Karo, a younger councilor in his thirties.

"No!" Bruesio hissed. "He is wrong. Surely you agree, emperor. What do you think, emperor?"

In the ensuing silence, a snoring became evident. Julia looked up, peering high into the White Seat, and saw that her son had once again fallen asleep. She flushed with embarrassment and poked him repeatedly until he awakened.

"What? What is it?" Giton grumbled.

"Do you think living emperors should be worshipped as gods?" asked Councilor Galvano.

"Oh, well… I don't know." Giton wiped his eyes. "Is it dinnertime yet?"

A few frustrated sighs echoed through the room.

"I think you had best get some sleep," Councilor Bruesio said with a hint of a sneer. "Then we will reconvene when you are awake and fit to give commands."

That is not the way to speak to an emperor, Julia thought. *Or the son of a* bel, *though they do not respect that title here.* She stood up. "I am sorry, councilors." She jerked Giton's purple gem-encrusted robe, and growled, "Come with me."

In their private room, the anger developing in Julia finally released itself. "How dare you, boy! Sleeping during a meeting with the councilors… you're embarrassing me, and you're making these stodgy Imperials think you're incompetent."

"If they think that, I'll just have them killed. It's nothing," Giton said.

She looked into her son's brown eyes. She could see a little of her uncle in him, the fiery emperor who inspired the council. She needed to awaken that very fire in her son. She needed to turn him from this slothful, negligent teen into a powerful and determined Commander of the Empire. "Listen to me," she said. "You must stay awake in these meetings… you must *inspire* people. The emperor is not a god. He is not immune to swords and poison. You must project strength, and wisdom, and *command*."

"Easier said than done," Giton said.

"No," Julia said. "Every talent is a skill that can be learned; it comes easier to some than others, but it can be learned. I must get you a teacher in oratory…"

Someone knocked on the door and Giton leapt to his feet. He ran to the door and opened it, revealing a young woman in the clothing of a Khazidean belly-dancer: a skirt that went far above the knee, a bare waist and a paper-thin midriff. Giton embraced her. "Sabin!" he said.

Julia fumed silently as Giton ran away with her through the door. *You can teach oratory,* she reflected. *But you can't teach determination. And without determination he will never learn.* She shrieked quietly. If only she had borne Urunam another son… one that had cares beyond bedding girls and guzzling wine to the point of drunkenness.

She stood up. "Why?" She wrung her hands. She felt like throwing something.

A figure appeared at the door. It was Antonio, Marshal of the Imperial Guard. He was trustworthy and indeed had been very helpful to Julia. He was the one who forged the emperor's will, and now received a secret monthly sum from the Empire's coffers.

"Antonio!" she said. "I am so glad to see your face."

Antonio's return smile was grim. "And I am glad to see yours, signora. But I have ill tidings."

Julia's heart sank in anticipation of the disappointment. She imagined the worst thing that could happen in the world… Giton dying. She braced herself for that, and now, she supposed, she could not be disappointed.

"The councilors will take a vote next week. Councilor Bruesio has accused Giton of incompetence."

Julia sighed, and it seemed her whole soul—all her energy—

left her. She fell back onto the couch and began crying. "The damned bastard Bruesio… I hate him. He must die. In the south no one can disrespect a king. And in the Eloesian kingdoms of old, before the Imperial pigs invaded, a group of pathetic old men couldn't depose the sovereign. What a backward land this is!"

"I advise you not to speak like that, signora." Antonio crossed the room and sat down next to her. "It is indeed grave tidings, but we must not act rashly."

"I want to kill Bruesio."

"That would alert suspicion, and you would be the only suspect."

Julia glared at Antonio and noticed—in his steel breastplate, his chainmail skirt and thin blackish hair—how wise and commanding he looked, in such complete opposition to her son. "Perhaps I should arrest the whole council."

"Better yet," Antonio said, and brushed Julia's long hair, "you could pay him to cancel the vote."

"Perhaps," Julia said. "Gods know that a single piece of furniture from this room would sell for a thousand gold pieces. And yet, though you advise against it, my heart's desire is to have them *all* arrested, every last one of them. The fate of the Empire should not be in the hands of those incompetents."

"Maybe you speak truly, that they deserve it." Antonio smiled. "But you must remember, my Julia, that the people of the Empire are not like those of the South or East. Because they vote in the councilors, they have an illusion of having power. The free men and women of the Empire think they are actually in control of their lives."

"Then the people must not be so prideful," Julia hissed. Realizing that tears had begun to flow, she got off the couch, crossed the room, and fetched a napkin. "They must be taught respect. And my son—*you know?*—my son truly is incompetent. I would not admit such a thing to anyone besides you, Antonio. Even I have times of weakness." She wiped her tears with the napkin. "Still, he is the emperor. They should not have such power over him."

"True, signora, in the South and the East," Antonio said, "but not in the capital. I fear you must play by our rules, and gold coin can go a long way."

"How much is necessary?" Julia said. Suddenly the tears made her feel self-conscious. She was a proud Imperial matron—a widow, but the Empress mother—and no one should see her in such a pitiful state.

"A thousand gold pieces is enough for any sane man to do anything," Antonio said.

"Then go," Julia said. "It angers me that it is necessary. I don't trust those councilors, and I know they will vote against my son. So go… offer Bruesio the money. Gods, what a barbaric land this is."

CHAPTER FIVE:
DUTY

Claudio-Valens Adamantus

For fourteen long days, Claudio-Valens rode down the Path of Tidus. With the bronze peaks of the Goldenhorn Mountains always to his left, he passed village after village. By the fifth day, the distances between the villages had shortened. By tenth day, the baked yellow grass had given way to roads, densely-packed apartment blocks, and houses. Like a herald of something greater, this suburban sprawl hinted at the glory of what was to come.

At last the fourteenth day came, and Claudio passed through the Arch of Conquest that marked the entrance to Imperial City. Once inside, Claudio rode in the shadow of the towering apartment blocks. On one of the bare brick-faced sides, an advertisement for the Imperial Arena had been painted: "Glory, Honor, Blood—Two tickets for five silver." Another came right after it: a picture of a woman in a brassiere and skirt, and the words "Lady Ciutta's Den—Third Building on Straight Street—Enter and Enjoy." Claudio immediately looked away, feeling a stab of shame at his countrymen.

The city swarmed with people. A pack of urchins bolted past Claudio as they chased a dog, laughing all the way. A pair of Fharese noblewomen in white gowns approached cautiously from the other direction, their faces hidden by blue veils. A wealthy eastern couple—dressed in purple and glittering with jewelry—pushed through the crowd with a gaggle of slaves, even as they shouted complaints about the "squalor" and "ugly buildings." More familiar to Claudio, a band of legionaries—on temporarily leave, apparently, and identifiable only by their military capes—stumbled down the way, reeking of alcohol.

The city drew men and women from the four winds.

The Empire itself was much the same, a disparate group of people united by a single force: the proud and intellectual, if useless, east; the rustic, unlearned north; and the west, kindred in blood and vision. Five parts, five peoples, all governed by one.

"One Land, One Vision, One Emperor," Claudio found himself muttering the Empire's motto under his breath.

Soon he reached Imperial Square. The people here were clustered even tighter. Merchant stalls lined the perimeter. On the north side was the hippodrome, and beyond it the towering White Palace with its colonnades, domes and immense columns. At once he made his way there.

The guards recognized Claudio and let him into the palace, explaining that he made it just in time for the celebration, that it had been moved back a day and would start tonight at sundown. Hearing this Claudio immediately went to his private quarters—a small marble-floored room on the seventh (and highest) story of the palace. The sun was already dipping below the horizon. Hurriedly he asked a servant for soap and a washing bowl; his skin was caked with dirt and sweat from the long journey, and his smell was less than pleasant.

He remembered that—at least partially—the reason he came was to scope out this new emperor, to see if he fit the exemplar of Anthans, first of the emperors. If he didn't, he would need to report back to his mother with the grave news, and perhaps do something else.

In time he scrubbed all the dirt from his skin. He donned his nice clothes: a felt hat, a fine tunic of scarlet cloth and short woolen breeches. He glanced at himself in the mirror and adjusted the hat a few times. His unruly brown hair refused fit into the right place. Such fine clothing was not seemly for a man of the knights' class; it was showy and against what his father Lucento had taught him. But the Augusts and the Imperial Family had, in recent times, taken to excess and showmanship. It was improper for a wholesome Imperial, but, alas, it was necessary for Claudio to dress like this.

He waited until the sun had mostly set before he exited the room.

Inside the grand hall, Claudio realized he was the most humbly dressed of all the partygoers. The men wore silk tunics of rich forest green and dark purple. The women wore billowing dresses of samite, dyed sky blue or flame red and woven with gold or silver thread. Claudio even caught sight of an Imperial woman in southron belly-dancer clothing: in an orange veil, a short skirt and a tight red midriff.

I, Claudio thought, *am about ten years behind the current fashion. No, make that a hundred.*

"Ah, Signor Claudio!"

He turned around to find a balding old man in a green, silver-embroidered tunic and form-fitting trousers. The purple sash around his chest identified him as a councilor.

"Don't you remember me?"

"Ah, yes!" Claudio said, and froze, biting his lips as he realized that no, he really didn't.

"Councilor Bruesio… how could you forget him? No one can!" He was clearly drunk, and the wineglass in his hand lent credence to Claudio's guess. "The last time I saw you, you were a child. Ten years old, at most, and the son of the most famous legate in the Empire."

The collective noise of the chatter got to Claudio and he remembered just how truly inept he was in situations like this. He put on fake smile and tried to project an air that said, "I am *so* happy to be here." Then he said aloud, "I hear there's a new emperor."

"Yes, yes," Bruesio said. "That is what the whole celebration is about, after all." He laughed and took a sip of wine. "I like him very much. He is *such* a good ruler."

Claudio saw dishonesty in Bruesio's eyes. He was wise to speak well of him in public; yet self-serving dishonesty always sent

Claudio's blood boiling. "I must go," he said, and walked off. Claudio could taste Bruesio's stunned silence in the air as he walked away.

The party went on. The crowd grew collectively stupider as the racks of wine slowly emptied. Claudio had a glass of his own, though he never liked the taste of the stuff. He chatted as little as he could—a silent figure, for the most part, throughout the night, and the lack of acknowledgment did hurt him. But he was not a councilor or even an August; just the son of the most famous—and now deceased—Imperial Knight.

Eventually the identity of the new emperor became clear: a young man, about Claudio's age, swarthy, with jet-black hair, wearing a white-and-purple robe studded with gems; and—Claudio noted—completely and utterly drunk. What little glimpses Claudio caught of him through the hours included his grabbing women and making lewd gestures, making filthy jokes and cementing it in Claudio's mind that this young man had two purposes in life: sex and drinking. The imperial office was just a means to that end.

Late in the night, Claudio was stunned to see the girl in southron dress approach him. She tore off her veil, revealing brown eyes and light, sun-kissed brown hair. "Hello," she said. "What's your name?"

"Claudio."

"You're awful quiet." She smiled, flashing a set of bright white teeth. "Want to know a secret?"

"Erm—"

She was beautiful. "I'm not August. I'm not even of the Knightly class. I'm a girl from Lady Ciutta's den, nothing special, just a whore from the west side. I don't know why I'm telling you this but I think I can trust you."

Her breath reeked of alcohol. Claudio felt duty-bound to take her back to her place of work. "How did you get in here?" he whispered.

"I snuck, and I climbed. The security precautions aren't as strenuous as people say…"

The Imperial Guard would kill her if anyone besides Claudio found out. "Miss, you need to get out at once. You're very lucky I'm the one you told."

"I knew I could trust you."

Glass shattered somewhere. A few gasps echoed through the room.

A shrill woman's voice called out, *"Someone tried to murder my son!"*

The girl was gone.

Claudio rushed over to the scene of the commotion. Julia Seánus covered her eyes with her hands. She shrieked, "Someone handed my son a glass of wine, and Leon tested it, and *look at him now!"*

The bodyguard—Eloesian by the look of his face and a slave by the look of his simple brown clothing—lay on the floor in a seizure. In his still-shaking hand he clutched the stem of the shattered wineglass.

"I knew some people didn't like my son!" Julia hissed. "Well I won't let you kill him! He's my son, gods damn it all. *He's my son!"*

"Calm yourself," said the councilor from before, Bruesio. The event seemed to have wrenched him from his drunkenness; in fact, it seemed to have sobered almost everyone. In the corner, next to his mother, Emperor Giton stood shaking, face white with fear.

Finally he said something, "Once I find out who did this, I'll have him peeled!"

Claudio spent the night in his room pondering. Things were not well in the White Palace, and he needed to get to the bottom of it.

The strange night seemed a blur to him. But despite his reservations he knew he was needed. An assassination attempt on the emperor was rare, even with such a devious and—dare Claudio think it—incompetent boy on the White Throne.

"Yes, I am needed," he said aloud as he stared out into the lights of the city and felt the cool breeze of the sea. Tomorrow, he would write a letter to his mother. He would stay in Imperial City because duty called.

CHAPTER SIX:
BAD DREAMS

Marcus Silverus

Ever since Marcus left Tivera at the Augur Collegium, it seemed a demon plagued his dreams, filling his mind with nightmares. He dreamed of sharp pains, of strange tools, weird pictures and dark grins. He dreamed of sadistic laughter and painful instruments, poking and prodding waking him up in the middle of the night, when the moon was still out.

Even what little ceremonial duties he had to perform as Guardian of the Wine Cellar seemed stressful. He had not gotten a good night's sleep in many days. Fatigue was all he felt.

His racing thoughts ended and he realized it was a sunny day, and he was eating the noon meal with his friend Niccolo.

"Hello?" the tan, blond-haired young man said, in a tone that indicated Marcus was the stupidest person on earth. "I said my friend Jacopo is having a party at his father's mansion on Dualmis. Are you coming, Marcus? It's tonight."

"I—I don't know."

"Come on!" Niccolo sounded angry. "What is *wrong* with you lately? You used to go to every party in the city!"

"I don't feel myself." It was true; all he could think about, lately, was Tivera. Perhaps she was sending him a message through his dreams. She was, after all, an augur; a strange augur, one that had the power of Light rather than wind and speed.

"It's Dualmis. It's an elite party. There will be *girls*." Niccolo said the last part through gritted teeth. He slammed his fist down onto the table, shaking the little scraps of beef that remained of their meal.

"Sorry, Niccolo… I don't think I can make it. I'm sick."

"That's right, you're sick," Niccolo sneered. "You've lost it, Marcus. You've lost your charm. You've become boring." He stood up and threw three silver coins onto the table. "That should cover me." He stormed off.

Some friend Niccolo is, Marcus thought. But he realized he didn't care, as he wandered the streets just south of Imperial Square. He knew where his legs were taking him: to the Augur Collegium, to Tivera.

Soon enough the collegium stood before him. Above the lintel, there were words: "On the Winds of Fortune, We Speed to Victory."

A woman's voice spoke from behind him.

"Septimo! Did you hear? Someone tried to assassinate the emperor!"

"No! Surely not!" a man answered.

Strange. Marcus, in his few interactions with Emperor Giton, found him relatively unsuited for the position, but not worthy of assassination. Especially not just weeks into his reign. Then again, a sense of apathy had fallen over him. All he cared about was rescuing Tivera, and he had lost a friend because of that.

He tried to enter the collegium but a staff blocked his path. The bearer of the weapon said, "The public is forbidden entry."

Marcus backed up a step, then glared. "Do you know who you talk to? I hold an Imperial title. I can go wherever I please."

"What do you want?"

"I want to speak to Tivera. In fact, I *command you* to let me speak with Tivera."

The augur's expression soured. "I do not know of any Tivera. In fact, I don't know what you're talking about at all."

"*Let me in,*" Marcus boomed and pushed toward the gap in the doors.

In the span of one second, three things happened: the tip of the staff knocked Marcus on the mouth, knocking a tooth loose; the shaft hit him in the chin, and the augur shoved him all the way down the steps and into the street.

"We move with the speed of the wind," the augur said. "Remember that when you try to fight us."

Grabbing his mouth as it flared with pain, Marcus stood up. He cast a quick glance behind him and saw a crowd had gathered to watch. "The Silveri do not give up easy," he said, repeating his father's words as he wiped his mouth. His fingers came out dripping with blood. He grasped the hilt of his sword with his right hand, then questioned the wisdom of battling an augur. Marcus wasn't a terrible swordsman, but augurs possessed powers of wind and speed, and someone who "wasn't terrible" was certainly not a match.

Up on the top of the stair, the augur smiled proudly. "'The Silveri do not give up easy.' That is what you say. It's a quaint saying. Unfortunately, 'not giving up' does not mean 'claiming victory.' Besides, I've heard the only thing the Silveri do not give up on is drinking."

Marcus swept his sword fully out of its sheath. "I can have you arrested."

"Can you?" The augur laughed. "What is your position, again? You said you had an Imperial title. Your name is Marcus Silverus, no?"

Marcus nodded his head brusquely.

"Guardian of the Wine Cellar, then."

A few people in the gathering crowd laughed abruptly, but quieted down when Marcus glared back at them. He glanced to his sword, noticing it was a standard military issue, nothing special. For a second, shame filled him. He looked back up at the augur and felt disarmed by his words, even though Marcus held a slicing weapon of steel and the augur wielded a long wooden pole. He could not let the people see an augur talk down to a man with an Imperial title, even if it was Guardian of the Wine Cellar.

Yelling out, he charged up the stairs and swung hard at the augur, who in turn blocked with the butt of his staff and whipped around to strike Marcus on the head. He thrust his hands forward and a gust of wind blew Marcus down.

Marcus fell down the stairs and hit the street with a thump, grunting in pain. As he stood up, he said, "You'll pay for this."

As he left he couldn't help but hear the snickering of the crowd. He flushed red in shame.

Soon he reached Imperial Square. The sun was at its highest point in the sky, and many had gone indoors to escape the heat, leaving the area less crowded than it usually was. Near the edge, Marcus made out the figure of Antonio, Marshal of the Imperial Guard. Even from a distance he recognized the thin blackish hair and stern grey eyes, the steel breastplate and long red halfcloak.

It dawned on Marcus that Antonio, most trusted of all the public officials and an honest man to the core, was authorized to issue warrants. In fact, he was authorized to do much of what the emperor and the councilors could do. Perhaps he would issue a warrant for Marcus to enter the Augur Collegium; and hopefully, gods willing, not ask why. To say he was doing it to rescue an insane homeless girl would be silly.

Marcus quickly crossed the distance between them, feeling slightly self-conscious about his bloodied mouth and bruised body. But he hailed him and said, "Greetings, Lord Antonio."

Antonio smiled. "Marcus."

"Erm, well, this might sound silly, but I was wondering if you would issue a search warrant for the Augur Collegium." Marcus bit his lip.

Antonio raised a brow. "Why?"

"I think they might be doing something illegal."

"I'm afraid you'll have to take it up with a judge," Antonio said. "I can't go issuing warrants left-and-right."

"Antonio, please." Marcus put on his best desperate face.

Antonio's half smile pursed into a solemn line. "Perhaps, you can tell me more…”

“There is a girl I know. She is an augur that went for training. She’s been sending me letters—” *Not dream signals. Good call.* “—and they are doing horrible things to her.”

Antonio sighed quietly. “All right, Marcus. The collegium is one of our best military resources, but if you just go get her, then that is fine. I will inform them in advance, so they can be ready for you tomorrow morning.”

Not his first choice. “All right,” Marcus said.

More nightmares assailed him that night, worse than ever before. Three times he woke up in his bed, covered in sweat. He was awake at dawn, and he went into the collegium as soon as the sunlight illuminated the city streets.

When he reached the collegium, several augurs waited for him in the entrance.

“Marcus Silverus?” one said.

Marcus nodded.

“You are free to search the whole perimeter.”

Marcus looked at them untrustingly. “Where is she?”

“Who?” said one of the augurs, a blonde woman and perhaps the leader, judging by the gold medal hanging around her neck.

“Tivera. The girl I brought here.”

The woman laughed. “She ran out and escaped into the streets. Scared of ‘Mother and Father,’ that they were going to come after her.”

“Who are you?”

“You may call me Maestra Fiora. I am Steward of the Collegium in Maestro Bachio’s absence.”

“Very well,” Marcus grunted, and pushed past them with

more force than was probably necessary.

He searched all three stories, going through every room one by one. The marble floors and the furniture were immaculately clean. The glass windows that looked out into the courtyard were wiped to perfection. The lecture halls, some filled with young would-be augurs and some completely empty.

But there was no sign of Tivera. Still, something didn't sit right with Marcus. Something had happened to her, whether outside of the collegium or within it. And he did not trust Maestra Fiora, or any of these augurs.

He went through the rooms again, searching every corner, moving aside tables and chairs. He had, perhaps, spent an hour there, when a noise echoed through the hall: a whimper—*"Help me!"*

It was coming from the wall. At once Marcus felt around the stone bricks, and at last found a latch. He pulled it with all his might, and the false barrier fell through.

And there was Tivera. Poor, innocent, insane Tivera. Eyes bulging in fear, her hands were tied fast with rope. She lay on a hard wooden table. Next to her—in the corner—vials, beakers and jars were packed tightly in a wooden shelf. They had been experimenting on her. Immediately, Marcus drew his sword, and hacked at the rope. It was thick, but with each slice a few strands came loose until finally it burst. He hacked the ropes off her legs, but as soon as they came loose, he felt a presence behind him, and a gust of portentous wind.

As Tivera clambered to her feet, whimpering, Marcus whipped around—seething—and saw an augur in his winged cap. He slashed in a hard cross-cut, but in a second's lapse the augur's staff was in position, blocking the sword.

Marcus felt the pain before he realized the staff had struck him. Then it struck him again.

"*Ai!*" Tivera wailed. She thrust her hands out before her; a thin beam of light went through the augur, cutting through his flesh. Blood poured from the newly-opened wound.

The augur would surely die.

Marcus grabbed Tivera. She had committed a crime—the murder of a citizen—and Marcus was complicit. But even if he were free of guilt, he would stand with Tivera, get her out of danger before a judge sentenced her to death.

They fled together out of the Augur Collegium. Together, Marcus would hire a ship to ferry them to who-knows-where. Together.

CHAPTER SEVEN:
TABLES TURNED

Silvestro Matteus, Legate

When Silvestro opened his eyes it was morning. For some reason, he expected to wake up in his small home in the foothills with his wife cooking eggs. That could not be further from the truth. The sky was dark and grey, but without rain. Around him was a city of black stone, its houses and homes burnt to ash and in the center of it, a gap in the earth so deep he could not see the bottom.

And Silvestro was in a large cage, behind black prison bars. Behind him, dozens of men—perhaps captives—lay shivering in the cold damp of the morning, wearing nothing but their undergarments.

They had taken his sword and his armor. *The rebels.* Last night, the rebels captured him. Yes, now he remembered. The woman, Kyra, captured him. He remembered her pale, deathly face, and shivered. He grasped the bars, and a chill ran through his body as the cold metal touched him.

The gap in the center of the city. Could it lead to the underworld?

"I'd get away from there," a voice said from behind. Silvestro turned around. A man was talking to him, a burly man who looked like a legionary. "They don't like it when you touch the cage. They'll think you're trying to escape."

"Well maybe I am." Silvestro relinquished his grip on the prison bars. "What is this place, anyway?"

"Once it was Dubaquis. Now they call it Doom," the man answered. "The rebels dug that pit. Spent days digging it, said it's at a fault in the earth, a big crack. They say if you fall in, you'll fall a long time 'til you hit the bottom."

Silvestro frowned. "And you? What's your story?"

"I am—was—with the Seventh Anthanian."

The air grew chill. A sense of hopelessness fell over Silvestro like a great shadow; then he realized the source: a few hooded rebels walked in from the left, black cloaks flowing in the constant wind. One held a scroll in her black-gloved hands, and she read from it, "Noldo Oneus, it is time for you to answer for your crimes."

"My turn." The legionary stood up, looking into Silvestro's eyes like a reprimanding father. "Don't give in to their mind-games. They will torture you, but never deny the glory of the Empire."

Silvestro keeled over and retched as the man was led out of the gate. He guessed these rebels took 'torture' seriously. He stood back up, nonetheless still filled with nausea, and peered into the baleful grey sky. The ghosts of the tortured dead still swirled around it, and Silvestro knew he had been transported to hell.

The other prisoners did not want to talk like Noldo did. They sat there whimpering, giving short answers before they hid their faces with their hands.

Silvestro pondered how he could escape. There truly was no escape. The bars were of solid iron. Above him, arches upheld a weight of stone. Behind him there was no door, only earth. He fell to his knees and prayed to Luos, God of Light that his wife worshiped so dearly.

"Luos, save me from this darkness!" he whispered.

"*Get up*," a voice croaked. Above him, beyond the bars, was a man in the black hood uniform. "I'll cut you if you do not obey."

Silvestro stood up.

"You offend me, and you offend Yblis." The man pushed a latch on the door. It opened. "Your prayers to Luos will go unanswered. And you will pay… you've cut in line, and you'll get your punishment first, before these others."

A few behind him sighed in relief.

This is my chance, Silvestro thought. He bolted through the wide doors, hearing the scythe whistle as it cut through the air and the shredding of linen as the curved blade sliced through his undershirt. He sprinted through the city under the dark, portentous sky, looking for a gate, looking for any way out. Finally he saw the gate, and it was open.

But dozens of black-hooded rebels stood in his way. He turned, looked back. Dozens stood behind. *I'm surrounded.* He lifted his hands in surrender. "I surrender!" he called out.

Two black-gloved hands restrained him and forced him, in view of the others, to a large alcove in the stone wall. There, bound in rusty chains against the black stone, was Noldo, the legionary from before. He groaned in pain, still alive, though judging by his cries he didn't want to be.

Opposite him, behind a stone lectern, a man in a black hood read his sentence. "Noldo Oneus, tribune. Kept alive after the battle with the Seventh Anthanian Legion after the others died—all to ensure you would answer for your crimes. Your slave came with you, with the legion. She escaped in the battle. We freed her. She is one of us, now. She said you beat her, Noldo Oneus. You mistreated your slave."

"I might have hit her, once," Noldo said. "I regret it."

"Not good enough," the hooded man said. "Flay him alive."

A few rebels stepped out from behind Silvestro. In their hands, they held whips with thongs covered in broken glass. Immediately they set to their task. Silvestro shut his eyes as the whips dug into Noldo's skin, as he was, indeed, flayed alive. When his tortured cries stopped, Silvestro looked away, not wanting to see his bloody body.

"Next," said the man behind the lectern.

Noldo's body hit the floor, and they pulled it aside. One of the rebels wrangled Silvestro into position. Silvestro grunted as the rusty, chipped chains dug tighter and tighter into his chest. *This is it. I'm going to die. Let it be for the glory of the Empire.*

"Silvestro Matteus," said the man behind the lectern. "Leader of the Thirtieth Kersepolan Legion, formed in Kersepoli in 1094. I have no crimes written down for you. Your legion waits for you a few miles away. They are surely confused."

"What do you want from me?" Silvestro roared. "Gods! Kill me if you're going to kill me. You won't get any crying or whimpering from me."

"I have no punishments for you," the hooded man continued. "Perhaps it is time for you to speak with Fabius and Marcia."

The infamous Dark-Eyed Twins soon stood before him, so quickly it seemed they flew there. They were pale like corpses, young—ten years old, at most—with dark shadows under their eyes.

The boy spoke. "Will you lead your army against the emperor?" he said. "Will you join the rebels and conquer Imperial City and free the slaves?"

"Never," Silvestro said. "Glory to the Empire!"

Fabius's gaze darkened. "Would you rather die?"

"Yes," Silvestro said.

"For many ages," Marcia began, "the Empire has captured slaves. You say you have laws against mistreating them, but no slave would dare go to court. Our master beat us almost to the point of death. Then we found Yblis. Don't you understand? Don't you feel sorry for us?"

"After what you've done, I could never feel sorry for you."

"Jerk the chains tighter," Fabius ordered.

The rusty bands tightened with almost rib-crushing constriction. Silvestro let out a wheezing gasp.

"The Empire is bad," Marcia said. "The Empire is doomed."

"Treason," Silvestro wheezed. Around him the darkness seemed to increase, like a heavy cloud all around him. The tightness of the chains made him dizzy.

"The Empire will fall, and the world will rejoice," Marcia continued.

"If the Empire does fall," Silvestro said, "then it will only be because of traitors like you."

The little girl's eyes lighted with anger. "Whip him."

The first glass-covered thong cracked on him, excoriating his forearm. Silvestro's entire body sang with pain. "Long live the Empire!" he screamed.

"Take it back," Fabius said.

"Never," Silvestro said. "Long live the Empire, and forevermore!"

But Silvestro did not give in to the subsequent skin-shredding lash, or the three dozen that fell after it.

His flayed, bloody body hung tight in chains until they threw it in the hell pit. But even in darkness it lay as a testament, a sacrifice to the Empire.

CHAPTER EIGHT:
TROUBLE IN THE SOUTH

Antonio Laureana

The Imperial Council would vote on the emperor's incompetence tomorrow. Tonight, Antonio would offer Councilor Bruesio the thousand gold pieces to cancel the deal. *I have the whole Imperial Court in my hands,* he mused, as he looked out onto the blue sea.

But a ship was sailing in from the south. Judging by the gold eagle insignia on its red sail, it was a government ship. Its swiftness indicated its intent as a messenger vessel. At first he thought it might bear an important message, but quickly discounted it; it was probably minor, announcing a small shortage of grain or olive oil.

He could not have been more wrong. The messenger, an Eloesian sailor, looked left and right in an attempt to avoid eye contact. "I am afraid I bear bad news. Very bad."

By a stroke of fate it was Bruesio that had come down to the entrance hall with Antonio; no surprise, of course, as the "emperor" delegated almost all of his duties to others.

"Tell us the news," Bruesio demanded.

"Archamenes, Padisha Emperor of the South, has invaded Eloesus."

Antonio's heart sped up and a sensation of falling briefly overtook him.

Bruesio had gone white. "What do you mean? We have a longstanding truce with the southron emperor."

"He has broken it," the sailor breathed.

"Gods!" Bruesio cursed.

"He has an army," the sailor continued. "Ten thousand men. A thousand Invincibles on the front lines. The magi... they're worst of all, wielding powers of flame."

"I will address the people," Bruesio said. "Antonio, perhaps you should stand guard in case the crowd gets anxious and tramples me."

Antonio nodded.

Bruesio looked to the messenger. "Now tell me all you know."

With the rest of the Imperial Guard, Antonio accompanied Bruesio to the Imperial Square and the lectern on the High Podium. The bells rang and a crowd soon gathered before them.

In a shouting voice, Bruesio began his speech. "We have just received news that Archamenes of the Fharese Empire has crossed into Eloesus, burning as he goes. The Ten Cities of the Fertile Vale now call Archamenes their king."

The crowd roared in anger. "Death to Archamenes!" a man in the front cried. His long hair was lined with gray and what few teeth he had were yellow. *Poor lout*, Antonio thought. *Impoverished, perhaps diseased, and all he can cling to is the fact that he is an Imperial.*

"By Lorenus, God of the Sea, and by Imperium, Spirit of the Empire… *Archamenes will go no further!*" Bruesio roared, turning red and shouting with such command that a chill ran up Antonio's spine. "The Emperor Giton will not stand for this, I assure you! I have word that the Hand of Imperium will speak at sundown. But let it be known in all your hearts that this deed will *not* go unpunished. The armies that swarm before them will be without number. Our ships will blockade their ports, and our augurs will be upon them with the swiftness of the wind and the power of Imperium. I swear to you, we will bring back Archamenes' head to Imperial City and thrust it upon a pike for all to see!"

The crowd roared both in anger in excitement for what seemed like minutes. Bruesio turned, and Antonio followed him up the walk to the palace.

Antonio called Bruesio to his chambers. His room in the Imperial Palace was small, as were most in that house of hundreds. But he had furnished it finely with the money he received every month from Julia Seánus: silk drapes, silk clothing, fine soft beddings, and exotic wood furniture.

"Signore, I have a business proposition for you," Antonio said. "Take a seat."

Bruesio looked at Antonio suspiciously as he sat down on the teak bench. "And what is it?"

"You are voting on the emperor's incompetence tomorrow, correct?" Antonio said.

Bruesio nodded. "I hope it to be a seamless transition to another emperor, as long as the Guard does its duty and honors the will of the Council."

The indirect accusation of dishonor did nothing to Antonio. "Well, Bruesio. What would you say if I offered you a thousand gold pieces to change your mind?"

"A thousand gold pieces?" Bruesio scanned the room, as if to look for spies. "This isn't a trap, is it?"

"Of course not," Antonio said. "I have word from a benefactor that if you keep Giton on the White Throne, he… or she… will pay you an entire thousand gold pieces."

Bruesio nodded slowly. "Once I see the money, I will do as you say."

Antonio read the gold-lust in Bruesio's eyes, and smiled.

CHAPTER NINE:
A STRANGE LAND

Julia Seánus, Empress mother

In late afternoon, Antonio arrived in Julia's room.

"It is done," he said. "Councilor Bruesio has canceled the vote of incompetence, citing a changed perspective."

"Good. I can finally breathe again," Julia said as she brushed her hair in the mirror. "I still do not forgive him."

"Do not hold a grudge," Antonio said. "It doesn't help anyone."

"Do not *lecture me*, Antonio," Julia hissed. Her blonde curls simply wouldn't fall into place.

"Did you hear of the invasion? The Padisha Emperor—"

"Yes," Julia sneered. "And my son's plan of action will be announced at his speech tonight. Yes, he will actually give a speech himself. I advised him in this matter."

"What is your course of action, if I dare ask, signora?" Antonio said.

Julia finally gave up on her stubborn hair and set the brush down. She swiveled in her seat to face the leader of the Imperial Guard. "You will hear it tonight. Now leave me, Antonio."

He walked away and eventually his footsteps faded to nothing.

A huge crowd had gathered in Imperial Square, as many as could cram in hearing range of the High Podium. Trumpets pealed as the Imperial family—Julia and her son the emperor—made their way to the lectern. The Imperial Guard, in their red halfcloaks and steel armor, stood watch along the perimeter of the podium.

At last, as the sun set over the western hills, her son spoke. "People of the Empire," he said, golden circlet twinkling in the light,

"I promise you, peace will come again. The balance will be restored and you will soon return to your old lives, as they were. The Empire will remain strong."

A few cheers echoed through the air. Julia smiled.

"Being half-southron—my father was a Khazidee—I know how their minds work." Hushed silence. "I have offered the Padisha Emperor a large sum of money to keep him at bay. Peace will return!"

The crowd roared, but as it became deafening and overwhelmed her son's speech, it slowly donned on Julia that they were angry.

Why are they angry? Surely they want peace! Julia wrung her hands. These Imperials were a strange lot, so proud and so ungrateful.

A stone flew from the crowd and nearly hit Giton.

"Calm down!" Julia screamed.

More stones flew. "Traitor!" someone in the crowd screamed above the roaring din.

"Traitor?" Julia was aghast.

Antonio walked up to the lectern and took Giton's hand. He led her son away, and told her, "It is best if we leave."

"I will send out soldiers to kill them all," Julia growled.

"Send out soldiers to block off the palace, but do not kill them," Antonio said.

Julia did send out soldiers. From her upper story room, she watched as several hundred of the dogs died, until their roars finally stopped in the night hours. She did not understand these Imperials. But one thing she knew: they would learn to respect their emperor.

CHAPTER TEN:
THE VISITOR

Emperor Giton Seánus Algabal

Giton awoke in the middle of the night. A shadow hovered above his bed. As his eyes adjusted, he made out the figure of the young man at the party. The Imperial, about his age… the knight, the son of the legate Lucento. "H-hello!" Giton stammered.

The knight held a sword in both hands.

He was handsome, Giton noted. Had he come into his room like a worshipper unto the priests of Atman? The knight, his Celestial Visitor, and Giton, the Godling priest?

"What do you want, friend? Wine, perhaps?" Giton asked.

"No." His booming tone seemed to shake the walls. "I've come for something entirely different."

"Love?"

The knight laughed coldly. "If I had any love for you—which I don't, not at all—my love for the Empire would infinitely outweigh it."

The knight pitched back his sword, and before Giton could react, drove the cold metal deep into Giton's chest. Giton choked, unable to scream or speak, unable to inhale.

The knight yanked out the blade, his eyes void of mercy. As Giton's veins opened, the knight wiped the blood off his sword on the dry side of the bed. The life left him. The knight stalked out as silently and coldly as he had entered.

The life slowly drained out of Giton; and in time, he was dead.

PART TWO

CHAPTER ELEVEN:
VENGEANCE

Claudio-Valens Adamantus

Claudio kept a low profile in the ensuing mad days. The Imperial Palace, as expected, spiraled into a frenzy; the Imperial flock no longer had a shepherd. Without a strong commander, the bureaucratic council had taken charge, even as the news reached them that the Fharese army conquered Ten Cities and pressed inwards toward Imperiopoli and Korthos.

Through it all, no one suspected the true assassin: Claudio, son of the famous legate Lucento. Respect for the emperor was paramount, and had been instilled in Claudio at a young age; yet Lucento had also taught his son that he should never revere the emperor more than the Empire. Claudio knew that, in Heaven, his father beamed with pride.

The fourth day after the assassination dawned. The air still was cool, and a few clouds rolled in from the sea. Claudio already resigned himself to another quiet day, waiting for things to run their course.

Someone knocked on the door. Claudio rose and crossed the room. An open door revealed Councilor Bruesio with the purple councilor's sash. "Claudio-Valens Adamantus."

"Yes?"

"The Council has argued over this issue for a few days… We are all in shock after the assassination, and doing our best to recover from what has happened. But the threat in the east remains…"

And now you will make me emperor. Claudio laughed under his breath. *Unlikely.*

"The army of Archamenes is about ten thousand strong," Bruesio said. "We are lucky to have you here. You are the son of the legate Lucento. We have nominated you to Grand Legate. You will have, in your power, three legions: a force of twelve-thousand men. Do you accept?"

"Absolutely," Claudio said without hesitation.

"You must drive them away from Ten Cities and the southern vale, and make arrangements so that they will never incur so far into our territory again. We are assigning you to the legion because they respected your father, and they respect you. It is your chance to prove yourself."

Claudio nodded. "I will do my utmost for the nation."

The letter to Mother would aggravate her indeed. But even she understood and respected duty; and duty called.

As soon as Bruesio left, he set to writing it:

Dear Mother,

I am so very sorry to tell you this. I know you wanted me to stay at home, and live a quiet life on the ranch. But Hieronus, God of Just War, has different plans for me. I regret to tell you that I must face the barbaric Emperor of Fharas. But if I live, and I believe I will, then I will return to you. And if I die, you will have the ranch; and I will have what I've always wanted, honor.

—Claudio

He sent it with a letter-carrier, who departed at noon.

Late in the day, a military advisor took Claudio into the boardroom and explained the logistics of the counterstrike. One three-thousand strong legion was already stationed in Imperiopoli, waiting for the others. One was in Gad, near Bregantium, about four-thousand strong. The last of them, about five-thousand strong, was stationed near Imperial City. This left several legions in Gad, and a full legion in Nichaeus, to protect the Empire in the others' absence.

The Empire controlled the sea, and had for hundreds of years. With vicious boarding tactics they subdued the triremes of the ancient Eloesians; with liquid fire they burned away the dhows of the Fharese. In great galleys, they would transport the Imperial City legion; and another, separate fleet would ferry the Bregantium legion to Imperiopoli.

Meanwhile, another fleet would blockade the port of Haroon and forbid any ships from leaving. All trade was frozen with the Fharese Empire. Once the army was out of Eloesus, the advisor said, it was up to Claudio to make sure such incursions never happened again.

I won't stop there, Claudio resolved.

The next morning, they would set sail.

Claudio awoke before first light. When the sun finally rose over the sea, hundreds of ships—transport-galleys and war-galleys both—greeted him. Dawn cast her glimmering pink light on the square sails, all bearing the war-eagle of the Empire. Like an army of the sea they filled the harbor.

Down below the palace, the legion made a procession through Imperial Square, carrying their armor, helmets, and weapons in hand. Not an official procession through the Walk of Triumph, but a practical one. Yet still, the thousands and thousands of soldiers went on without number as they walked down the way, and it seemed in Claudio's mind—and perhaps in the minds of all who watched them— that there existed no larger force in the world. Soon these legionaries would filter into the transport galleys, and then—with Claudio-Valens Adamantus on the flagship—they would sail to Eloesus to fight the Empire's enemies; and there was nothing more Claudio wanted in the world.

CHAPTER TWELVE:
THE DEPARTURE

Marcus Silverus

Finding ships proved a difficult proposition. Though Marcus raked in a tidy sum of money each month, he, without fail, spent it all. But right after Tivera—that foolish girl—murdered the augur, he had run to his room and gathered every last penny. In all, he counted silver coins worth about five gold pieces, give or take a few pence.

At this time of the year, large freights sailed in from Haroon and the lush Khazan River Valley, transporting full cargoes of grain to the hungry citizens of the Empire. They, of course, had to sail back to their home port, and Marcus could likely find a ride with one of those.

Yet going to Khazidea, home of a strange people, was something Marcus would do only as a last choice. Rumors had reached Marcus about that far-off land; their king and queen were brother and sister, and some of their priests—unlike the Imperials—held vast political power and were wealthier than most nobles. Gods should not line men's coin-purses; priests should strive for higher goals. Yet who was Marcus to reprimand them? He lived first and foremost for himself… until now.

He eyed Tivera, trembling and murmuring about her parents and about the augur. He wondered what they did to her, and why the augurs experimented on her. But it was not worth worrying about until they were safe on a ship.

One by one he searched the ships docked in the port. There was a fleet of pleasure ships planning to sail around the coast to Nichaeus and, from there, to Peregoth—birthplace of the Empire— and to the various historic sites on the islands of Imperial District. The captain, however, said he would charge twenty-five gold pieces; a price Marcus could afford, perhaps if he saved his money. But alas, he did not.

In the end a difficult choice was forced on him: go to the strange land of Khazidea, or take up with another ship bound for Bregantium. Marcus would not mind going to Bregantium—by all accounts a pleasant small city—but it was the crew that filled his mind with doubts. The captain was a large man, with iron thews of arms and scars running the length of his body. He was swarthy; Eloesian, perhaps, or just kissed by the sun.

The man's name, as Marcus soon learned, was Perga.

"I promise an easy journey, as the winds allow," he had said. "And, as long as you help me with whatever I need, I'll let you ride along for one gold piece."

Marcus had walked away, then deliberated for an hour. He did not trust this Perga; but Marcus truly had no choice. If he refused, Tivera would be put to death, and he would be thrown into jail. He would not allow either of those things to happen.

And so he walked back to Perga and told him, "I'll go."

Marcus led Tivera on board *The Sea Dragon.*

The poor girl was mumbling incoherently. "I don't trust them… don't trust… won't trust!"

But Marcus put a hand on her shoulder. "It's okay, Tivera. We don't have a choice… It will all be okay."

Around the eastern shore of Anthania, the water reached a remarkable depth. Strange fish—poisonous sea jellies, octopi, squid, and more—often washed up on the beaches, or ended up in fishermen's nets.

Perga gave Tivera and Marcus a tiny room below deck. Huddled there, they had felt the first movements of the ship disembarking, and now, they careened with the ship as it plowed through the waves. It was nearly pitch black, but Marcus held Tivera's hands to console her.

"It's dark," Marcus said, "but soon we will leave in the light, and we'll be in Bregantium. And from there, who knows what will happen to us?"

"Light," Tivera said. "Light…"

A dim spark appeared, casting light on the hands that had drawn it up. It grew in brilliance until it was a white luminescent orb, and the room was bright: as bright as broad daylight.

"Perhaps you shouldn't do that." Marcus frowned, though the light was a comfort in the dank darkness of the ship. "Look at all the trouble it's gotten you into. And me, too."

"No?" Tivera sounded shocked. "No light… No light." In a moment's span, the brilliant orb faded to a spark, and then to nothing. Again the pitch blackness took over.

Marcus shut his eyes, noticing no difference; then, he let the movements of the ship and the creaking of wood soothe him to sleep.

When he awoke, he had no idea whether it was night or day; below deck, all light was absent. For a moment he longed for the light that Tivera had brought him. He stood up and shivered. He opened the door a crack, and saw a bit of light filter in.

Gulls cried out overhead. Tivera was sleeping. He walked up the stairs and climbed onto the deck.

The brightness of the sun and the celestial orb's low position proved that it was morning. The skies were bright blue. To Marcus's left, land was visible: clusters of population, with houses, temples, shops and shrines; and large expanses of golden wheat-fields, olive orchards, and walnut groves. He had no idea where they were. But a fair wind was blowing, and the ship cut through the waters at a swift pace. The men aboard left the oars unattended, letting the sails do the work.

Perga approached him. The sailor, with his black beard and scarred face, was as crass and uncultured a man as any Marcus had seen. But he greeted Marcus with a smile. He was friendly and he had not yet done anything to earn distrust; and that was the important thing.

"My good signore." Perga smiled. "The winds have favored us greatly today. It is as if Lorenus, god of the seas, is blessing our journey. Or perhaps an augur is in our midst, guiding the winds to our fortune…" He laid a hand on Marcus's shoulder. "But that's not likely. The gift for augury is rare; the hand of magic is fickle, and chooses few. I am sure neither of you two have any such gifts."

"No, we don't," Marcus lied. "We are as average, as ungifted as people come." He smiled.

"That is good," Perga said. "The world needs the labor of common men; else, who would trim the hedges in the gardens of the rich? Who would till the soil and feed the Empire's great cities?"

Marcus chafed at the comment, but managed to keep silent. He was not common in that sense. His hands had no blisters, and he knew nothing of manual labor. But would he, soon? "I am common as dirt," Marcus told him nonetheless.

The constant rocking of the ship had begun to make him nauseous. They had only been at sea for a day. But the day was bright and warm, and it was good to be outside and bathe himself in light… though, on reflection, he realized that Tivera's light had comforted him even more than the sun.

Days went by at sea. When required—and it was often— Marcus helped the sailors to the point of exhaustion. They braved choppy waters and minor storms, but for the most part fortune had favored them. But Marcus, unused to long journeys such as these, grew more and more seasick with each passing day.

To his left the land rolled on; from the densely-packed megalopolis that ran from Imperial City to Nichaeus, the area became steadily more agrarian. By the fourth day of sailing, the majority of land was farmed: rolling hills covered in wheat; walnut groves and olive orchards; and cattle ranches where plants refused to grow. It was noon of the fourth day when Marcus—for the first time in his life—caught sight of the Goldenhorn Mountains. Named for their rich stores of ore, the peaks reached great heights. To the east of them—and soon, in Marcus's plain view—was chaparral heathland, dry and bereft of water, where nothing useful to man could grow.

On the galley sailed, hugging the shore for the most part and never leaving sight of the heath-covered waste. The air grew oppressively hot, and sweat slicked Marcus's skin; and Tivera's as well, when she left her room below deck, although that was rare.

Halfway through the fifth day, a large bay opened up in the shoreline. A few boats sat there idly, tied to primitive docks. To Marcus's surprise—and not without alarm—Perga barked orders for men to land there.

Tivera, climbing up from below-deck, cried out something about continuing to sail.

"What are we doing?" Marcus tried to sound assertive, but he knew these sailors outnumbered him. "I thought we were going to Bregantium!"

A wicked grin crept over Perga's lips. "You thought wrongly. We are going to Tarso."

Marcus had heard of Tarso, though he had always considered the name fodder for stories and nothing more. A city of pirates, escaping the wrath of the Imperial army by reason of its seclusion. He put a hand around Tivera's shoulder, and told her it would be all right.

CHAPTER THIRTEEN:
GRAVE TIDINGS

Bruesio Lornodoris, August

The issue at today's meeting was what some now called the worst crisis in hundreds of years. The White Throne sat empty, the Fharese Emperor invaded Eloesus, and a mysterious rebellion began in the north. The Empire, Bruesio knew, was in peril.

All thirty councilors were in attendance, packing the seats of the Council House. The White Throne sat empty; with the death of her son, Julia Seánus retreated into her personal chamber and hadn't left in days.

Bruesio, Speaker of the Council, walked into the middle of the circular marble floor and shouted, "Men of the Council, I greet you. Long live the Empire, and long live the emperor."

"Long live the Empire," the other councilors chanted in unison, "and long live the emperor."

Bruesio spoke loudly. "Claudio-Valens Adamantus has gone to fight Archamenes with a force of twelve-thousand men and twelve augurs. If he has even a little of his father in him, the soldiers will respect him. His family's patron god is Hieronus; and I have told the high priests in Sanctum to make sacrifices on his behalf."

"I do not like that boy," grumbled Councilor Fabiano. "Nor did I like his father."

"That is your loss," Bruesio said coolly. "Now the first matter of business is this: I believe in the power of the Council. Yet an empire as vast as ours must not be ruled by thirty bickering men. We must elect a regent—just for now—to manage the affairs in this difficult time."

"And I suppose you will be the new emperor," sneered Councilor Karo.

"Truthfully, I would not be averse to such a responsibility,"

Bruesio said, "but I will not nominate myself. For I am modest, as rare a trait as it is these days. We need a ruler experienced in the military… someone who will project strength and be well-liked—and reassuring—with the people."

"Governor Marcusio," suggested Councilor Juliano. "He has done well in ruling Gad, and served a while in the Nichaean Legion."

"I would never vote for him!" laughed Councilor Karo. "He lives in Bregantium, that backwater town, and all he's ever known is Gad. He would not know how to rule an empire so large, and Imperial City wouldn't take him seriously."

"The people of Gad are wild and rebellious. He knows how to deal with trouble," Councilor Juliano argued back.

"Silence!" shouted Bruesio. "We need a military leader, someone practiced with the sword, who leads charges and guides from the *front*… someone whom everyone knows as a great warrior, and a wise leader."

The doors of the Council House flew open and in their wake stood Antonio, Marshal of the Guard.

An answer to our worries, Bruesio considered. *Perhaps he is just what we are looking for.*

"Councilors," Antonio said, "I bear bad news. A rider came from Dubaquis, the rebel city. The gates have opened and an army has poured out. He says it is like they are from Hell itself. A dark coach rides in front and destroys all in its path, just by virtue of its presence. I suggest we send the Nichaean Legion to crush them and make an example. They must be taught a lesson."

Bruesio turned to the twenty-nine councilors before him. "Members of the Imperial Council, Augusts all… I move that we place the Empire under martial law, with Antonio Laureana as regent for a period of six months. All against it?"

Numerous hands went up. Bruesio counted them: fourteen.

"All for?"

Bruesio again counted the hands: fifteen.

"I cast my vote for it. By a vote of sixteen to fourteen, the resolution is passed."

Bruesio looked at Antonio. A stunned expression had fallen over his face. "When is my coronation?"

"There will be no coronation, nor will you wear the Imperial Circlet," Bruesio said. "It is in our law, and shows the *temporary* nature of the position." Yet Bruesio knew it was a precarious situation; under a state of martial law, much power was given to the emperor, and, therefore, the regent.

CHAPTER FOURTEEN:
STAGE EXIT

Regent Antonio Laureana

Antonio sat down on the purple-cushioned White Throne. Never once in his life did he think this would happen. In fact, he was rather content pulling the strings of the Imperial court through his dealings with Julia Seánus. But now he was temporary ruler over the provinces, and the source of his power was the White Throne itself.

Antonio called for a court messenger and said, "Tell Legate Arsinio to leave Nichaeus and face the rebels."

With that bothersome task done, he could focus on what he always wanted. Yes, he had respect for the serious, intelligent and—dare he mention it—old and infirm Emperor Julio Seánus. As much respect as was needed for the Council to like Antonio, at least. But Antonio liked Emperor Giton's view of Imperial office; an opportunity to explore the limits of power. For lack of better terms, Antonio liked women very much, and—for all his recent aggression—the Padisha Emperor knew how a ruler should be treated.

He would respect the Imperial Council, unlike Giton's mother. But there would have to be certain alterations to the title of emperor. A new extension to the palace would have to be added—a southron-style harem for Antonio's personal and exclusive enjoyment. He would stock the Imperial Palace with wines. The court would learn how to enjoy life, and Antonio would be the instructor.

Later that afternoon, Antonio received word that legate Arsinio's legion had, indeed, left its camp outside Nichaea and marched along the Path of Tidus—north toward Dubaquis. For an hour he argued the logistics of feeding them, with the irate messenger proclaiming several times that "You act as if they do not need to eat!" But Antonio eventually got over his reluctance to starve the populace (and more pressingly, the Imperial court) and agreed to provide the proper food. Exhausted from the argument, he realized that sitting on the White Throne as emperor was more work than play; and perhaps that Giton's irresponsibility was the cause of his assassination.

He had hardly ended the conversation when another bombardment of messengers arrived, asking for decisions: the Ninth Paladian Legion sought permission to winter in Bregantium—yes, Antonio told him, and thought it an unwelcome reminder of those dark, rainy, quickly-approaching days; the High Priest in Sanctum wants to resolve a theological issue—no thank you, Antonio told him; the runners of Haroon Spice are growing more aggressive, and oh, whatever shall we do?—make routine searches of every ship, and imprison any crew members indefinitely, Antonio said.

At last the series of decisions seemed to come to an end, and then another messenger entered. This one did not come from the outer double doors, but from a side door. "Signore," he said. "Julia Seánus wishes to have an audience with you."

At last, an issue about someone who knew… although, Antonio noted, someone who had recently become much less important to him.

As Antonio expected, Julia sat in the room, a sobbing mess. Her makeup was smeared with tears and indeed she looked pitiful. Antonio almost felt sorrow for her, but sorrow was an emotion he could never quite conjure up even if he tried. She could no longer do much more for him, now that he—and not her son—sat on the throne. He walked up to the couch where she sat and looked down, then said—with a brusqueness borne of impatience—"What is it, Julia?"

"My son is dead!" Julia cried. "What do you think is the matter?"

"I am not a miracle worker, Julia. Do you expect me to raise him back from the dead?" Antonio sighed.

"What am I to do now? No one seems concerned about finding the killer."

"They have made me emperor," Antonio said. "It is a temporary position."

Julia stood up, eyes flaring. "What do you *mean*, they made you emperor?"

"I mean, *they made me emperor.* What is hard to understand about that? For six months, I am emperor and have full powers of martial law."

"You didn't set this up, did you?" Julia's tone cemented it as an accusation rather than a true question.

Nothing angered Antonio more than people accusing him of things, especially things he didn't do. "No, *lupa*," he growled. "And I don't appreciate you saying that at all."

"I can say what I want to say." She stood up, bared her teeth. "I am the Empress mother."

"You *were* the empress mother," Antonio corrected her.

She grabbed a fistful of Antonio's cloak in both hands. "I still have allies. I could send someone to kill you."

Antonio furrowed his brows. "I won't forget that comment. You've just threatened the emperor."

Julia spat in his face. Antonio wiped the unwelcome moisture from his cheek and then, grabbing the shoulder of her dress to restrain her, smeared it on her face.

"The Empire is under martial law. I am sending you back to Algabal where you belong." Antonio tightened his grip on her.

Julia's face flushed red. "I will tell the emperor that you forged the will."

"And I will tell them that you paid me to do it, and that your son's reign was illegitimate," Antonio said. "The truth paints a bad light on *both* of us. That's if the people of the Empire believe the truth. Pack your things, Julia Seánus. Your role on the world stage has come to an end. I'm sure the people of Algabal will welcome you with open arms."

"I refuse," Julia hissed.

"Then tomorrow, at first light, I will bind you in chains and *force* you onto a ship," Antonio said. "And if that doesn't work, I will kill you."

Julia's eyes bulged with infinite wrath. Antonio released her with perhaps more force than necessary, and she fell back onto the couch. As he left she said, "You will regret this."

At dinner, the cooks served roast quail smeared in hot Haroon sauce; bowls of salty, toasted walnuts; crispy sliced bread and dishes filled with olive oil or fish sauce; a basket of green olives and a basket of black olives; pork-stuffed dormice and generous helpings of wine. It was a several-hour long ordeal and several times the other diners— Bruesio, Speaker of the Council, and his wife Flora; two other councilors whose name escaped him; and a few of his fellow Imperial Guards—asked him why he did not touch his wine or eat the food.

"I have no appetite," Antonio answered, but in truth he wanted to make sure everyone ate a bit of the food before he tried it, and the wine was off-limits. In the nascent days of his reign, he knew some might want to poison him.

At the end of the feast, when everyone was stuffed, a few slaves came out of the kitchen to clean up. One girl in particular— from Gad, judging by her blonde hair and blue eyes—asked, "Domino, won't you drink your wine?"

I was right to be cautious. Antonio congratulated himself, then said in a firm tone, "Sit down." He motioned the other slaves to leave.

The girl went white as she took a seat next to Antonio.

"I want you to drink it," Antonio said. "The whole thing."

"But domino, it's fine Korthian stuff. I—I can't." The girl's hand was shaking.

Antonio had no pity for her. "Tell me, girl," he said, "who sent you to poison my glass. Tell me, or drink."

"But domino, it isn't poisoned," the girl said.

"Then drink."

"It was Lady Julia."

The confession surprised Antonio, but it very much made sense. "Gordo? Marcos? Secondo?" he said to the other Imperial Guard members at the table. "Flog this slave. I will go take care of Julia." He grabbed the wineglass and headed down the winding halls of the palace toward the women's apartments.

When Antonio kicked down the door, Julia's face indicated she knew why he was there, even though her words indicated otherwise. "What did I do?" she said. "What is it? What are you doing? Stop—"

But Antonio crossed the distance between them fast, hopping over the couch while spilling only a little of the wine. He forced her mouth open, and her attempts to bite him proved in vain. He shoved the wineglass into her mouth and forced the deadly concoction down her throat. Then he slammed the wineglass onto the floor.

"Thus ends the life of Julia Seánus," Antonio said with the aplomb of an actor. "Traitor to the end."

He held Julia down as her eyes shut, as her body convulsed, as she sank into unconsciousness and then into death.

"Julio, Julia, and Giton all are dead," Antonio mused. "The Line of Seáni is no more."

CHAPTER FIFTEEN: THE RED HAND

Anthea Abantes

Anthea couldn't forget the man she met at the grand reception, after she crept into the Imperial Palace and poisoned the emperor's wineglass. What was his name? Ah, yes. Claudio. How noble he seemed, how intelligent, how kind.

The very antithesis of every client of hers at Lady Ciutta's Den. The slobs with their unshorn hair and unwashed bodies, living on a steady diet of free bread. The adulterous old men, risking all for a night in the sack with Anthea. The criminals who made regular use of the Den; the murderers, the diseased, the ugly, the addicts, the creeps. Anthea couldn't stand any of them.

In her small private chamber, Anthea worked her light brown hair into a braid as she gazed in the mirror. She and Lady Ciutta were "going for a stroll," as they liked to say. Lady Ciutta—the middle-aged Imperial madam—hid secrets behind her short black dress and her white-powdered face, her red lips and plaited hair. Lady Ciutta told everything to Anthea, who was second-in-charge when it came to the brothel and vested with absolute trust.

A scent of perfume wafted into the room, and Anthea knew Lady Ciutta was behind her. Seeing her braid was done, she cast it over the front of her chest and turned to the brothel madam.

"Ready?" Lady Ciutta said.

Anthea nodded.

They strolled through the dangerous streets of the west side without a worry. The women of Lady Ciutta's Den were protected by the criminal "lords of the streets" and their assorted thugs. They headed to the notorious Paradise Park, a haven of muggers and thieves, and she and Ciutta went at night, no less. There they would discuss business, the first meeting since someone—who knows who?—had murdered the Emperor, and unexpectedly did Anthea's deed for her.

The Fraternal Order of the Red Hand sought, above all else, to kill whoever sat upon White Throne. If they only accomplished this task, the city's "underbelly"—the brothel madams, the spice runners, the thieves and the crooks—would find their emancipation. The Red Lord would herald in the end of all things. The tables would turn against the self-righteous. Anthea found the theology convoluted, hard to grasp, and often contradictory, but these criminals—her employer included—had zealously devoted themselves to this cult.

Emperor Julio Seánus, now dead, had ruled with unfortunate wisdom, and proven himself impossible to kill. The latest emperor, Giton, ruled with much less care. Anthea had gotten so close to killing him, and satisfying Lady Ciutta. But before she could kill Giton for the sake of the Red Hand, someone else did.

At last, they reached Paradise Park. The name could not be less fitting, Anthea mused. Within the shade of the cypress trees, the low-lives of the west side consumed packet after packet of Haroon Spice, chewing the heady mixture as it took their emotions to euphoric heights even as it turned their minds to jelly, their flesh to bones, and their eyes to eerie crimson.

Lady Ciutta led the way and within moments they reached the small clearing in the cedars. A few men gathered there: rough-looking, all, with scars on their faces and arms. Perhaps they gained them from street battles, or perhaps from a brothel-borne disease. Anthea knew which explanation "Lord" Tomo—the leader—would claim.

"Ciutta. Anthea," Lord Tomo said. "Now that we're all here… the emperor's been killed, gods damn it all. This new one is shaping up to be the worst… fitting for the Red Lord, but he's tough. He's a fighter, a warrior, and it'll be damned tough."

"And what shall we do?" Ciutta said with her typical cool composure. "Send Anthea up again?"

"We'll try something different," said Lord Tomo. "This emperor, people say, has a weakness for women. He's a devout worshipper of Brecko, people say." He chuckled.

Anthea smiled. Her clients often spoke well of the god of pleasure and wine.

"You will wait for an opportunity, Lady Ciutta," Lord Tomo said. "And then we will send Anthea. She'd better do her job this time."

"She will," Lady Ciutta said, and regarded Anthea with a fiery gaze.

Anthea shriveled under the lady's visage. "Of course." She could never say no to those black eyes of abyss.

Lady Ciutta turned back to Lord Tomo. "And your ears in the Imperial Court will tell us when an opening arises, will they not?"

Lord Tomo nodded. The scars on his face looked black in the moonlight. "It will be done."

Back in her small, drab concrete room, Anthea slumped onto her mattress. She thought again about the young man at the emperor's reception. Claudio. An upper class noble who, despite Anthea's admittance of her true profession, had treated her well and not alarmed the other partygoers. She had been slightly drunk when she confessed. She prayed to Issa, goddess of brothels, that they would meet again.

But then she remembered that this Claudio was a man of honor. She tried to remember which god represented honor. She remembered the province of Paladium, and the High Priest's sermons on justice and duty and honor. She prayed to Hieronus that they would meet again.

"Please, Hieronus, let Claudio and I meet again," Anthea said, then blew out the candles for her night's rest.

CHAPTER SIXTEEN:
THE BATTLE OF SAGE VALLEY

Claudio-Valens Adamantus, Grand Legate

The fleet had traveled swiftly.

Lorenus, God of the Sea, did not curse them with choppy waters or violent storms; instead, he blessed them with smooth waters and good sailing. Thus, they passed by the Isles of Marion and, after ten days at sea, came within sight of the shore of Eloesus.

Claudio—aboard the flagship *Vanguard*, largest of the war-galleys—led the fleet, heading southeast into what was known as the Thartan Inlet. At the end was the city of Imperiopoli. The two decks of oarsmen on the Vanguard began at once, propelling the great ship swiftly into calmer, more insulated waters. The inlet was deep enough for the ships to pass through.

By midafternoon, they came in sight of the long stone walls protecting the port and leading a half-mile inland to the city proper. Soldiers stood on the docks, but these were not Imperials. They wore caps of hardened leather, and carried shields of light wood or wickerwork. The mature among them had thick dark beards. On the walls, a different flag flapped on the turrets: not the war-eagle of the Empire, but the four-pointed star of the Fharese.

At the sight of the Imperial navy they fled, perhaps leaving to tell their superior officers. Claudio immediately ordered the ships to begin landing. Claudio cursed his misstep; he had thought that surely, the Fharese had not gotten this far. The walls of Imperiopoli were strongly built.

Dressed in the scale armor of the Imperial Knights, Claudio

formed his army within the port walls. Over a period of several hours, the Fharese did not return through the gate. When the sun was just a glimmer in the sky, Claudio took the lead and marched into the city proper, seeing the iron portcullis was open and the path to the city was clear. Claudio, marching in the front, was among the first to see the destruction.

The city was a blackened ruin. The brightly-painted statues of the gods were bashed, their marble heads decapitated from the body. The bloodied bodies of Imperial soldiers and citizens lay in the streets as he led the march through them.

Yet perhaps as an omen, the shrine to Imperium—the war-eagle of white marble in the center of the city—lay dented but undestroyed in the City Square. Even after concerted effort to destroy it, this monument—built hundreds of years ago after the Great Rebellion led by the "god-king" Heidathra—lay here still.

"The craft of our forebears have held it strong," a voice said from behind.

Claudio turned his head to regard the woman. She was an augur, wearing a winged leather cap and bearing a quarterstaff. The powers of wind and speed were at her fingertips; but also knowledge and cunning. "Do you know what happened here?" Claudio asked, motioning to the blackened buildings and piles of ash and debris.

"Obviously, it was burned," the augur said and put her fingers to her cap. "The Fharese have killed those who resisted, and sold the rest into slavery. The people we saw at the docks, I guess, were peasant-soldiers keeping watch—the least of our concerns. The Fharese army proper has moved on; they have *cataphracts,* knights covered head-to-toe in mail, and—I would guess—war-elephants brought from the south."

At the word "elephant," Claudio suppressed a shiver. The largest of beasts, so huge that towers were built on their backs. Behind him, to the side of the knights, were several more augurs. "And your name?" Claudio said.

"You may call me Maestra Fiora," the augur said.

"Go," Claudio said. "Find out where they march; be quiet, and tell me."

The augur nodded, then motioned for the others. Staves in hand, they ran out of the city faster than any other mortal feet could carry them. The augurs were swift, but not highly effective in battle; poorly-armed, but the best scouts and spies in all Varda.

The army pitched tents at the foot of the coastal mountains, spreading out among the downward-sloping fields of purple heather and hiding among stands of broad holm oaks. A few clouds drifted through the sky, threatening rain. Claudio knew winter approached, and the Middle Sea would grow treacherous to navigate.

Over the crest of a distant hill, Claudio caught sight of the augurs running toward camp, moving at the back of the winds they conjured up. Within a half-minute's time, they reached him.

The dozen augurs stopped their run. Fiora was at their head, breathing heavily. "We've found them rounding the mountains, almost to Korthos, destroying as they go."

"So their strategy is to destroy everything valuable, sell everyone into slavery, and retreat."

"That is what it seems," Fiora answered. They are rounding the mountains but there is a pass—"

"The Pass of Twin Horns. Call for Signor Cosimo. I will want to speak to him."

How sluggish Cosimo seemed, trudging up the heather-fields, compared to the amazing swiftness of the augurs. But eventually the middle-aged knight, veteran of a half-dozen wars, reached Claudio at the Grand Legate's tent, a lone figure stumbling up the hill.

"Signore," Cosimo grunted.

"The augurs say the enemy is rounding the peaks. I want you to take all the Imperial Knights in my command, and meet them from the north. I will engage them from the south, and when it is time for you to charge I will blow my horn."

Cosimo nodded. "It will be done."

"Leave right now. If we are in luck, some of them will be sleeping."

On his horse, Claudio rode at the vanguard of the army, urging them to go faster and faster. As they rounded the first peak, the figure of Signor Cosimo and the other three-hundred knights vanished.

"Faster!" Claudio growled, and the soldiers' marching picked up pace.

They entered the valley between the two small rocky ranges. Here, sage and myrtles grew in abundance. Under a red sky the legion advanced, never as quickly as Claudio liked. But after a long march, when the sun dipped low over the mountains, the enemy camp came into view. They were ready.

Indeed, the men they had seen before with their wickerwork shields and cheap weaponry were the least of their concerns. The army was lined up, facing south toward Claudio. At their vanguard were the cataphracts Fiora had warned about: men, covered head-to-toe in chainmail, riding horses in full steel barding. Interspersed between them were great tigers—orange-and-black striped—held by chains, which were, in turn, held by women in coarse black hides. In the front, the hulking forms of elephants were clearly visible, looming above the soldiers and outfitted with towers full of archers.

One of the cataphracts clopped forward on his armored horse. "Claudio-Valens, general," he said in a thick accent. "Do you surrender?"

"No," Claudio said simply. "Do you? This is your last chance to leave the Empire."

The cataphract laughed. "You are hopelessly outmatched. We have brought war-elephants from Sur, and the tiger-tamers of Saidoon."

Claudio glanced again at the tiger-tamers and—underneath their hoods—saw their faces painted white in swirling, abstract patterns.

"Your nation is young, infantile," said the cataphract. "Ours is more ancient, more wealthy, more wise…"

"I take it, then, that you refuse my offer to leave?" Claudio said.

"Absolutely, in—what do you northerners say?—no uncertain terms," answered the cataphract.

"You will be shown no mercy, then," Claudio said, then roared, "*Javelins, Launch!*" He ducked his head. The tigers bolted forward. The cataphracts raised lances. The first of the javelins went flying through the air, hundreds of them, and then others following in quick sequence. Many struck home, impaling soldiers in back rows and running clean through one cataphract.

As the ensuing rain of javelins fell, one struck a tiger, biting into its orange-and-black fur and sinking an inch into its ribs. The beast roared and tore into the ranks in a fury. As Claudio charged, raising his sword, a dozen spears thrust out and impaled the tiger before it could do more damage.

Claudio met a cataphract head-on, casting aside a spear as he charged. Drawing back his sword, he stabbed hard, biting deep into the chainmail protection and knocking him off his horse as he bled profusely. "Onward!" Claudio cried. He scanned the surrounding hills for any signs of the knights, but did not see any of their gleaming steel armor. He eyed the horn at his side.

As the dead tiger lay there, its tamer threw off her hood, revealing the bright painted face, then shrieked—whether in agony or in anger or both, Claudio couldn't tell—and drew two daggers. As if driven mad by her pet's death, she charged into the fray and, before she could even get close, an Imperial legionary's spear punctured her throat.

The elephants charged, carving a path through the Fharese

army and crushing some peasant-soldiers as they did. The mahouts, drivers of the elephants, commanded the archers to loose their arrows. They opened up a barrage. One arrow bit into Claudio's shoulder-plate, and he could feel a foul ichor enter him, a poison. Grabbing it by the shaft, he ripped it out forcefully and shuddered in pain.

The elephants—Claudio counted five of them—had by now stampeded into Imperial lines. The mahouts on their towers shouted orders.

"Cut their legs, and get out of the way!" Claudio screamed. "Strafe right! Follow me!"

Claudio wheeled the army around so as to envelop the Fharese in a classic pincer formation, and also to get out of the elephants' way. They would go mad when injured, and Claudio would prefer them to go mad in the Fharese army. He looked to the stony peaks in front of him and still saw no sign of the knights, no glints of metal in the quickly-dying sunlight. Had they met a horrid fate on the Pass of Twin Horns?

Above the army, it became clear to Claudio that a royal litter was being carried aloft: the Padisha Emperor rising above them all to watch the battle. Protected from arrows by a wall of alchemical glass, his form was clearly visible. As Claudio hacked ceaselessly at the army, he took note of the southern King of Kings. A golden brace stretched his neck to a great length; two golden rings pierced his nostrils, and one silver ring pierced his lower lip. Unlike most of his soldiers, his face was clean-shaven. Over his head he wore a turban of ornately-woven cloth layered with orange silk and gleaming with jewels.

With a forceful thrust, Claudio pierced through the wickerwork shield and into the chest of one of the Fharese peasant-soldiers. He yanked his sword out and blood sprayed onto his armor. The arrow-wound ached unimaginably in his shoulder. Around him, the noise of the battle raged in his ears; the shouting, clanging of metal, and the trumpeting of elephants.

Claudio looked back and saw one of elephant had run off; his mahout, strapped to the tower, dangled as it sprinted away from battle. The four others still remained, but Claudio's men steadily picked off the archers on the towers, hopefully not aggravating the poor beasts.

In all, as the sun set, Claudio got the sense that this battle was not going as he hoped. Indeed, a withdrawal might be necessary if the Imperial Knights did not arrive soon. Yet even then, the Padisha Emperor would pursue them to the last. The dark-hearted king had shown no mercy to the people of Imperiopoli. But if Claudio died, he would die for the Empire just as he had lived for it.

"Charge!" Claudio screamed in attempt to rile his troops. "Press the savage wolves!" He pulled his horn from his belt. He could no longer tell who was where, in this poor visibility, so he might as well blow it and hope the knights come.

He blew the horn so hard that his temples felt like bursting. Then he blew it again, even harder. He blew it a third time and shoved it back on his belt, panting. An elephant trumpeted, doubtlessly going mad; but Claudio could no longer see.

They fought in total darkness for the next two hours. No longer did Claudio hear the trumpeting of elephants, which he took as a good sign. Despite their service to the enemy, they were innocent and he hoped the beasts escaped with their lives.

Bit by bit the Imperial army withdrew, despite the constant urging of Claudio to advance. Though they defeated the tiger-tamers and perhaps the elephants too, the cataphracts remained. Claudio suspected the Padisha Emperor had a death-blow ready; and by the end of those two long hours his guess was confirmed.

The enemy army parted to make way for a thousand marching feet. These were the so-called Invincibles, dressed in heavy iron caps and long knee-length hauberks, and bearing spears and iron-rimmed wooden shields. On the flanks were magi in their white turbans and long purple robes, who at once conjured up orbs of flame and hurled them at the army. Over all else, a deafening, magically-strengthened voice called out, "Up until now we have only played games with you! Now we will truly go to war."

"Charge!" Claudio cried and for once the army listened, advancing several yards and pushing them back even as men were burned alive by the magi's searing flame. There were perhaps ten magi, but this was not an insignificant number; like few could be augurs, few men had the innate ability to become magi. "Charge!" Claudio repeated. He pulled out his horn again, blew into it until his temples near burst, and then blew again with even more force. And then, as if in answer to the desperate peals, Claudio caught sight of three hundred figures—spread out in a single, widely-encapsulating line—charging down the mountains with lances. But there were more with them; dark figures, perhaps several hundred more, that Claudio could not distinguish the shape of.

When the line of Imperial Knights met with the Fharese army, it was like a tidal wave washing in from the sea and crushing all in its path. Their charge drove in several lines deep, and the Imperial Knights killed perhaps twice their number in the span of a minute. The Fharese were totally and utterly surprised.

Claudio yanked his reins, and wheeled around the army to join the charge. "Onward!" he called out to the soldiers, noticing how very many had died and how the living trampled the dead. He reached Signor Cosimo, who had dropped his lance and now hacked furiously with his sword.

The Fharese army's mobility greatly weakened, now that the knights and the others—whoever they were—now attacked their rearguard and left flank. At some point in the heat of the battle, Claudio took notice that the litter of the Padisha Emperor was no longer visible, perhaps dropped; and that, as the other, shadowy force reached them, a group of magi, cataphracts, and others rode away swiftly, vanishing into the darkness.

Surrounded, overwhelmed, and terror-stricken, those Fharese

who did not make an early escape were quickly cut down. Loud, booming noises echoed through the air; and it became clear that hierophants—the famous thunder-wielders of Eloesus—had joined the fight.

Slowly, it became clear to Claudio that a native Eloesian force had come too. The tan warriors wore less armor than their Imperial comrades: simple chain shirts, at most; long spears and round wooden shields.

Finally Cosimo had a chance to speak after the furious fighting. "Prince Basil of Harkeon offered his troops," he panted. "That is the reason for our delay."

Within the hour, surrounded and—by now—outnumbered, the combined Eloesian and Imperial force slew the remainder of the Invincibles and the magi.

It was now the middle of the night, and the moon shone bright white above them. Claudio, badly wounded and panting hard, rode up to Prince Basil. The burly, broad-shouldered man wore a large steel breastplate emblazoned with the laurel-wreath symbol of Eloesus.

"My lord," Basil said, and bowed. "You have fought valiantly, and are the equal of your father."

"You've heard of my father?" Claudio said without thinking.

"Most have," Basil said. "I will always remember this battle in the Valley of Sage; the name 'Adamantus' will be honored among my family forever. If you ever need shelter in Harkeon Keep, let me know. It is just a few miles north along the valley, near the sea."

"It is my duty to serve the Empire," Claudio panted.

Basil smiled. "And long live it."

The next morning, Claudio took a walk through the battlefield. Bodies of men, elephants, tigers, and other strange beasts were strewn all along what the locals called the Valley of Sage. Two augurs died, but Fiora and nine others survived.

After a thorough search of the bodies, no one found any man with a gold-braced neck. The litter lay abandoned with its gold-threaded purple cushions. As he suspected, the King of Kings—and perhaps several others—had escaped.

The army was defeated. But—once he mended the poison wound—there would be no escaping the punishment Claudio would wreak onto the south. He would not exchange an eye for an eye, as is the way of the desert. For this eye that the Padisha Emperor took, Claudio would shake the very foundations of Khazidea. They would all answer to the Empire, and they would have no defense against the coming storm.

Onward, Claudio resolved, *and no mercy.*

CHAPTER SEVENTEEN:
TARSO

Marcus Silverus

They traveled several miles through the barren heathland on foot. It was high noon when—nestled between a group of hills—low wooden walls appeared. They were not the well-constructed palisade walls of frontier forts, but boarded-up timbers designed with no apparent concern for defense. However, the space they enclosed was large, providing ample room for a city; and the unpainted wood blended in well with the bleak scrubby countryside around it.

The pirates cheered. Marcus shifted uncomfortably and squeezed Tivera's hand a little tighter.

"At last, boys!" Perga shouted. "These two will fetch a high price! From there, it'll be wine, women, and song!"

The ramshackle gate opened to reveal Tarso in all its seedy glory. The ground was dirt, unlike the surrounding heathland. The buildings—never exceeding the height of the wall—comprised both spacious houses and shops, and tiny huts. Regardless of size, a layer of soot blackened the walls.

It was the people, however, that—more than anything else—served to make Marcus uneasy. Men with missing arms and feet—perhaps lobbed off in a fight with the Imperial navy—and beggars on the side of the garbage-strewn streets whom no one seemed to care about.

Near the gate, a harlot in a form-fitting dress called out to the pirates: "One silver penny for the night of your life." Her eyes were large and brown, her lips luscious and well-formed. Her hair, a dark blonde, hung to her hips. Perhaps once, she had been beautiful; but now venereal scars—red, irregular, and raw—marred her face and hands. It was no wonder she charged so little; who, in their right mind, would want to catch a disease and become like her?

Marcus squeezed Tivera's hand tighter. The poor girl was whimpering now. "It will be all right," he whispered.

At last they came to a large building: painted a garish green, a sign above the door indicated its purpose. The words TARSO TEMPLE were painted in the same color of the walls. Outside the door, a one-armed musician sang a bawdy song—his words were slurred, perhaps due to some sort of speech impediment, but Marcus made out several mentions of the female anatomy. The man had a small brass dish set at his feet for tips, but it was empty.

Within the vestibule, a fireplace lay untouched, bereft of flame. A group of harlots sat on wooden benches—some with clients and some without—and none of them bore any obvious scars or signs of social disease. Yet such diseases took time to ravage the body, and who knew whether—in a few years' time—these women would look just like the wretch outside?

Perga and the pirates led Marcus and Tivera through the door, past the vestibule, into the shrine. A stone altar sat across the room, caked with dried blood, and the bones of some marine animal lay upon it. Across the ceiling, shark teeth dangled from a black cord. Heraldic shields painted with sharks hung from hooks around the room. On the wall facing Marcus, blood-red letters greeted him: "BE THOU MY FRIEND, O DWELLER IN THE DEEPS."

Marcus had never heard of such a god. Obviously it was a marine deity; yet the symbol of Lorenus, god of the seas, was an albatross and not a shark.

A man stepped out of the shadows. He wore a black robe embroidered with sharks. His face was pale and bald. His eyes, an ice blue, had a predatory look about them, yet Marcus could not put a finger on why. "Greetings." His voice was shrill. "Perga... you have brought me spoils of war, I presume. You are such a pious man..."

Marcus did not see Perga's smile, but he imagined a wide grin. "If Orkus blesses me with riches and easy escapes," the pirate captain said, "then I may as well do what I can to please him."

The priest smiled.

"Orkus?" Marcus said, not knowing why he had said the word aloud.

Silence ensued, broken momentarily from Tivera's mumbling: "Save me from the bad man..."

The priest's blue eyes widened. "You do not know of Orkus. I am not surprised. The priests of Imperial City scorn his name, hiding his worship from the populace... did you know that Lorenus, patron god of the Empire, has a *brother*? That while Lorenus rides the sea-foam on his chariot, his brother Orkus—unknown to common Imperials—lives in the black depths where wrecked ships find their ultimate rest? He is Orkus the Great, lord of sharks and poison jellies, stronger than his brother Lorenus and yet utterly unknown to the Imperials." With each word, the priest's eyes seemed to grow wider, as if heathen zeal were filling him. "Orkus sits in the darkness of the sea's deepest chasm. He greets the sailors who sink to the deeps. He sides with the pirates, because the so-called 'good' men of the Empire... they worship his brother, Lorenus, whom he hates."

Marcus gulped. "And now you will sacrifice me to him?"

The priest smiled; it was a wide, sharkish grin. "Your body will rest in the deepest chasm... you will rest in the pitch darkness as an offering to the Lord of the Deeps. May his name be ever praised!"

Revulsion filled Marcus. To kill him with a dagger was one thing—a quick blow to the heart, a flow of blood, and it was all over. But to be shackled—presumably—with iron chains and cast to the sea bottom... he could not imagine a worse fate.

They should have stayed in Imperial City.

"Moreover," the priest continued, "though you will spend an eternity in darkest darkness, Orkus demands that his captives be kept in darkness even while they wait your fate. A special prison has been designed for you—black-walled and black-windowed—where the light of the sun will never touch your eyes."

The priest of Orkus dragged them through several corridors. At last they reached a door, painted black. The priest threw it open, and—together with the pirates—forced them in.

And there they were, entering a room small and pitch-black. In the claustrophobic darkness, they could not see each other. Yet they could feel each other; they were pressed tight together. Marcus realized to his shame that he was attracted to Tivera; though he would not let it happen.

She was not sane. She could not make rational decisions, and acting on his feelings would mean taking advantage of her. No; theirs was a relationship of protector and protected. He could never let this pure, innocent girl come to harm.

"I love you..." Yet Marcus knew it was more of her mad mumblings. "Mira the Trifold Mother... she has told me you are a good man... she has told me that you will save me from mother. She says you are safe."

"You will always be safe with me," Marcus said.

"Mira lights my path... Her husband is Luos. Are you Luos?"

"N—" Marcus started, but she cut him off.

"Mira is my mother. That's what she tells me... she says my flesh-and-blood mother isn't my real mother, because a real mother is a mother of the heart... Mira lights my path! She is the goddess of never giving up and loving your enemies and never striving and never envying. She is my goddess... do you believe in her? What is your name? I forgot!"

"My name is Marcus, and I do believe in Mira. Just calm down... I need to think of a way to get out of here. It won't be easy."

Tivera's breathing sped up, and soon she blurted out more words. "It's so dark in here... Mira tells me there is evil all around us... bad people, and ill will... she wants me to shine my light."

"Don't shine your light..." The words were slow to come out of Marcus's mouth. Seeing light would warm his soul; yet it was unwise. Tivera had a gift, and who knows what these men would do if they found out about it? Marcus did not understand these pirates or their crazed priest.

"Mira tells me you are a good man," Tivera said. "She tells me the way I feel about you is okay. She tells me to cling to you like a rock, because you can be trusted. You can be trusted, even though Mira says most people can't be!"

"Calm yourself." Her words touched him. "It will all be okay. Just relax… shut your eyes, and calm down."

"Mira tells me to shine… shine… *shine*…"

The familiar spark lit up the room, at first a small white flicker. Then it grew until it was a brilliant orb of radiant light, illuminating the room like daylight. To his own surprise, Marcus did not tell her to extinguish it. He reveled in the brightness, let the warmth of it fill him, and thought that perhaps it was not light at all, that it was something much greater. Somehow it seemed to reflect innocence and mercy, driving away the shadows of Marcus's soul. He stood there, grasping Tivera, realizing how very close they were, and reveled in the divine radiance.

In time her brilliant light died down, and once again they stood in darkness. They stood in darkness until—woken out of their sleep—they saw the priest of Orkus with shackles in his hands, and a sharkish grin crossing his lips. Their doom had come.

CHAPTER EIGHTEEN:
THE WAR HAWK

Bruesio Lornodoris, August

Bruesio did not approve of the murder of Julia Seánus, although the justification was clear. Unless that slave-girl lied, Julia drank her own poison. Now, as flocks of seagulls flew overhead, Bruesio stood in the docks of the city.

A stern procession was underway. A group of Imperial soldiers in full dress—horsehair-crested helmets and steel breastplates—carried a coffin toward a southbound ship. They would bury her with her husband, Urunam, in the town of Algabal and have the true funeral there. Professional mourners—a strange southron custom—wept and tore the hair of their black wigs as the soldiers loaded it onto the ship.

Julia was likable and intelligent enough in the few interactions Bruesio had with her. Her son's rule, however, had been a catastrophic failure. Along with the other emperors—in traditional Imperial custom—Giton's body had been cremated, the ashes put in a limestone jar and sealed in the Temple of Imperium. There he would rest with the other emperors, although he was but a shadow of them.

With the coffin loaded on the ship, the oarsmen prepared to leave the harbor. The Seáni were no more; and perhaps that was for the best.

After the morning funeral, the day began in earnest. The Imperial Council convened for further decisions. There was news: a message from the young Grand Legate, Claudio. Bruesio stood before the council as Speaker and, after a nervous hesitation, read from the scroll.

"Dear Councilors," he said, "I have good news." Bruesio's

muscles relaxed. "We have routed the foreign army, and they no longer form a threat to our nation, or to Eloesus. The good Prince Basil of Harkeon sent troops as aid and helped win the battle. Archamenes, however, has fled from battle. I have lost half my men and require an additional six thousand troops; the northern borderlands have not seen much battle, and a Bregantine legion will do well if you can land them in Haroon before the winter storms. –Your Servant, Claudio-Valens Adamantus."

There was silence for a few moments.

Then Councilor Fabiano began shouting. "That boy's ego has grown far too big for his own age! Probably incapable of growing a beard, and he wants to invade Khazidea. He blockaded Haroon—a sign of great pride, certainly—but winning new land for the Empire would turn this egomaniacal boy into a danger to everyone! His ego would be the size of the Empire itself!"

"We have worked tirelessly to build good relations with Fharas," sneered Councilor Kerius. "We sent them food during famine, repeatedly sent ambassadors to Seshán…"

"And look what just happened," Bruesio said, more to offer up a contradicting argument than to express his views.

But Kerius reddened and his voice turned to a shout. "And how would invading his territory in return, capturing Haroon and subjugating the people, make it any better? 'An eye for an eye' is the law of the desert, but it is not—as far as I remember—enshrined in our code. We have embarrassed Archamenes and driven him away. That is all that is necessary. We can forgive him—"

"Forgiveness has no place in the command of nations!" Councilor Geta shouted in return. The thin but fit councilor came from a small village in southern Gad and won his seat from the more militarist electorate in Imperial City, Bruesio noted. "Forgiveness may be a virtue in one's personal affairs," Geta continued, "but doing so on the national stage—especially against a brazen, arrogant warlord like Archamenes—is a sign of cowardice and weakness. Look at what you're saying, Councilor Kerius! What nation in history would harbor a man like you, especially in the government? Only *we* are fools enough to suffer your presence! I am in full support of dealing Fharas a crippling blow, and I think it is every man's duty here to agree with me!"

"Let us be careful with our accusations," Bruesio said. "None of us here are traitors." Geta's words reminded him of the historical Emperor Eratis, who executed several councilors for insulting the Empire. "We all wish to do what is best for the people, and for ourselves."

"Eliminate 'the people' from that sentence," Geta said, "and you will be closer to the truth. It is ineffable to me that anyone would refuse the Adamantus boy's request. And though I would not label you a traitor, Kerius, because you have not murdered anyone, you are something close."

Kerius' face did the impossible: grow redder than it was before. "Do not make such accusations! You come from a backwater village in *Gad* of all places! What place do you have in Imperial City? A city that harbors all manner of people and many Fharese too, I might add! Its greatness is in its variety, and you wish to squelch that. You wish for war! To invade a sovereign nation!"

"That invaded us?" Geta hissed.

Worried they may come to blows, Bruesio shouted, "Enough! We must debate like gentlemen, though I know it is difficult with such opposing views. You have both argued, and argued well. But let me be clear—there are other reasons not to send a Bregantine legion to Haroon. A rebellion in the north of Anthania…"

"Are we truly worried about a bunch of poorly-armed rebels?" Geta laughed.

"Rumor has it that they possess dark powers," Bruesio said. "Yet our choice is grim. The winter storms will soon be here, and it will grow far more difficult to transport them if we do not decide soon. We must take a vote."

In the seats, both Geta's and Kerius' eyes burned with wrath.

"All against?"

Bruesio counted the raised hands: seventeen.

"All for?" Bruesio said, and raised his own hand, though even with the twelve other votes his will could not be done. "Very well. The Bregantine legions—and others—will remain where they're currently stationed. I will present our decision to Antonio."

As they went on to the next topic, Bruesio couldn't help but notice Geta's seething expression and Kerius' smug glow.

CHAPTER NINETEEN:
RECALL

Regent Antonio Laureana

"Regent, I present to you a letter from the bel of Algabal," the dark-haired Khazidee said, his accent thick.

Antonio, sitting on the White Throne and feeling particularly commanding, shouted, "Read it, then, slave!"

The messenger broke the seal and read from the yellow paper: "Utnam Bel says this to Regent Antonio: You have killed my brother's wife. You have disgraced my family with your murderous hand. You will pay. By our law, I demand moneys of one-thousand marks, paid in gold and silver coin. If I do not receive it, I will take a white bull and sacrifice it to our god Sagar; and a curse of war will be upon you."

Antonio laughed. "Not worthy of a response, really. Crumple the letter. Tell him I fear his white bull and his strange god less than I fear my own shadow."

The messenger knew better than to sneer or glare. With impressive restraint, he silently walked away. As he left through the double-doors, Antonio called out to the Imperial Guard at the door, "You sure let the riffraff into the White Chamber, don't you?"

Bruesio entered through a side-door. "Not only riffraff," the elderly Imperial joked.

"What is it, Signor Bruesio?" Antonio asked.

"I come for your approval of our recent resolution… denying the Grand Legate's request for more men. Claudio wishes to invade Khazidea and perhaps Fharas."

What ambition, Antonio thought to himself, *and a victory like that would make him very popular*. Yet Khazidea was rich: glutted with ancient gold, and made wealthy by the productive farmland the Empire depended on. "So you mean to say," Antonio began, "that he has defeated Archamenes."

"Yes," Bruesio said.

"Soundly?"

"It appears so."

"Good." Antonio's voice couldn't hide his disappointment. He clenched his teeth. He could not let this Claudio invade Khazidea. Such a conquest would give Claudio incredible wealth, undue popularity, and increase the boy's ambitions. Such a conquest would turn the Middle Sea into the Imperial Sea and it would all be due to Claudio.

No, Antonio could not allow this. "I affirm your resolution," he said. "In your letter, tell him to immediately return to Imperial City with all of his soldiers. Tell him we need him for the rebellion in the north."

"It will be done," Bruesio said.

CHAPTER TWENTY: THE HAREM

Anthea Abantes

With this new emperor, the Order of the Red Hand struck gold; people close to the Imperial court told Lady Ciutta—and she, Anthea—that the new emperor built a southern-style harem and searched for women to fill the positions. Despite the distinct southernness of it all, the rumor circulated that Antonio, the regent, preferred blondes. And so, that was why Anthea stood in the storage room of Lady Ciutta's brothel, her hair soaking in a vat full of dye. Instead of the dark-haired Eloesian girl everyone knew, Anthea would transform into a blonde-haired, brown-eyed warrior queen from Gad.

She had no choice; Lady Ciutta told her what to do, and she was helpless before those abyssal black eyes. But she could think of worse jobs than working as the chief harlot of the west side's best brothel. Complaining did no good.

Next, with her hair now a bright, flowing gold, she applied generous amounts of perfume and headed east toward Imperial Square in broad daylight. The new regent held his auditions in the newly-remodeled wing of the palace. For what seemed like an hour she pushed through the sweaty, roiling heat of the crowd. The noise of the shouting street vendors, the irate cries of imperial officials guiding the flow of traffic all formed an overwhelming cacophony as she struggled under the shadow of towering apartment blocks, through the thick miasma of a thousand different animals and a hundred different foods.

But at last she reached where she wanted to go. A man—an Imperial Guard, judging by his steel, war eagle-emblazoned breastplate, and his red half-cape—stood there. "What do you want?" he said.

"I come to audition," Anthea said, not wanting to be more specific within earshot of the roaring crowd; but the Imperial Guard's mouth twisted into a grin.

"Ah, yes. You'll do nicely," he said, and pushed her through behind him. She tripped, stumbling through an open door through darkness and into the other side.

Before her was a glittering southron harem. The glare of flaming torches, their light cast through veils of red and green, illuminated a floor piled with satin-lined pillows. Golden idols of strange gods lay strewn about the room; strange zoomorphic creatures with bulging eyes and long, protruding tongues. At the fore of it all was a golden throne with armrests formed into the shape of dragons, and upon it sat the regent.

Unlike the room, his attire was not especially southern: he did not wear a gem-encrusted, flame orange turban, nor did he wear colorful robes of silk. He did not even wear the Imperial Circlet on his head. He was clad only in a white tunic and long white breeches like a common Imperial.

"Hello," Anthea said. "I come to join the harem as one of your women."

"Hush," the regent said. "Your hair is blonde, but your eyes are brown and your skin is olive like the Eloesians… I like it. The two features complement each other. And you have a great shape. You are, by far, doable…"

Anthea snorted at his choice of words. Gently she pulled at her shirt, but now—with her nerves flaring up—removing it seemed a difficult task. She struggled embarrassingly for several seconds, before she received some welcome help.

The regent himself pulled off the shirt. His muscular arms did the job much better than she ever could. Her face flushed. The regent's dark eyes had the shallow, animal look of lust. He wanted to claim her.

He grabbed hold of her with his strong arms and she fell onto the pillows. He began his deed. It struck Anthea that the ruler of the whole Empire was her mate; she and the most powerful man in the world would be one, and she grew faint.

Not long after it began, it was over: the regent, a pleased man grinning ear-to-ear; and Anthea, still caught in throes of bliss. This regent, this Antonio Laureana, made her forget all the years at the brothel. As she looked at him, she realized she could not kill him. She wanted to tell him everything, all about the Order of the Red Hand and its goals, and all about those who wished to kill him. She bit her trembling lip to quiet herself. But she knew she could not tell him.

Anthea would never underestimate Lady Ciutta. If she rebelled, Ciutta would have her head mounted on her wall. The sadistic madam had done worse things to lesser offenders.

"Yes, you will do nicely," Antonio said.

Anthea looked into his dark eyes with a half-smile, knowing she had to kill him, but wondering if she could.

CHAPTER TWENTY-ONE:
BAD FAITH

Claudio-Valens Adamantus, Grand Legate

For two days, Claudio and his army marched down the Imperial road, over the high hills covered in holm oaks and the windblown purple heather. Food was in fair supply, thanks to the numerous towns and villages along the way. Eventually the road took a sudden turn, and—beyond the mountains—Claudio and his legion found themselves in a desert.

The cloudless blue sky gave no hope of moisture. The sun beat down on this barren waste unforgivingly; the dry, cracked dirt indicated how infrequently rain fell. This mostly-flat land—the monotony of its sunbaked black rocks and windblown dust only rarely broken by dry brown shrubs—stretched into the horizon. The paved stone of the Imperial road pierced through it in a straight line.

Despite the road and its evenly-placed food stockpiles and cisterns, the journey seemed to sap everyone's strength. For ten long days, they traveled the hellish waste underneath a scorching sun. They had gone many miles without the relief of water when—in the distance—a green horizon appeared, and a few of the parched legionaries cheered.

Cautious it could be a mirage, Claudio signaled the legions to wait and keep calm. He had little doubt the region of Ten Cities lay close-by, but running through this scorched wasteland—which the geographers termed the Little Desert—would only worsen their thirst.

They continued down the road as it pierced through the sand and rock. Eventually, the green haze took shape: thick grass, pink-flowered bushes, and an occasional cypress tree. The singing of birds and the gushing of a nearby river greeted them. If Claudio's memory held correctly, a river indeed ran through here, allowing for irrigation and providing a source of water and wild game for Ten Cities. Those ten settlements—according to reports—lay under the thrall of the Padisha Emperor, Archamenes; but without his army, he had no power except threats.

At the sound of water and the sight of verdant greenery, the legion broke rank and stampeded down the road toward the distant river. Claudio smiled and laughed quietly, knowing he could not stop them. Once the legionaries had their fill of water, they would continue on to Megaris, the queen of Ten Cities and the home of the prefect.

After leaping into and gulping the fresh, clear waters of the river—full of egrets and herons and all manner of birds—they returned to the Imperial road. The last leg of the journey awaited them. Now, with water, food, and people nearby, they could travel with ease.

On the nine-day journey north, the legion passed near three of the Ten Cities—Kythera, Galea, and Biblis—before reaching the open gates of Megaris, capital of the region. Through a maze of tall houses, shops, and limestone temples, the blue waters of the Middle Sea were visible.

The legion entered without a struggle.

Apelles, an Eloesian nobleman of some kind, had apparently taken control after the murder of the Imperial prefect Felix. As the army waited outside, Claudio took his personal bodyguard and entered Felix's former home, the House of the Divines. There, in a spacious room with four marble columns and ten tall, gilded statues of the local 'gods,' Claudio looked Apelles in the eye and said, "Where are the Fharese?"

"They have left, following the news of your approaching force," Apelles explained. "They fled back to Haroon."

"And the cities have renewed their allegiance to the Empire?"

Claudio meant it more as a command than a question.

"Despite the stifling taxes," Apelles began, "we are still with the Empire, for the most part."

Claudio clenched his teeth. "You just let them into your gates, didn't you? Archamenes promised sweetmeats: stacks of desert gold, perhaps? A promise of no taxes, maybe? If it weren't so dark during the battle, perhaps I would have seen some Ten Cities men fighting in Fharese dress."

Apelles' silence cemented his guilt. Claudio grabbed the man's shoulders, fingers digging in hard.

"Your actions will not go unpunished." Claudio glared at him. "At the harbor we will wait for more men. Then, my friend, we will see what is to be done with you."

Apelles' nostrils flared and his eyes bulged. Then he spoke. "You are mistaken," he said. "Urbanus?"

An attendant brought a scroll. The remnants of an Imperial seal clung to it.

"Read," Apelles ordered.

"Words from Regent Antonio Laureana: Claudio-Valens, I demand you return to Imperial City at once with your troops. I forbid you from attacking Haroon without my consent and I do not give it."

By the time the letter-reading was finished, a smug smile had crawled over Apelles' lips.

This will not stop me, Claudio thought. He snatched the paper from the servant's hands. "Do you know what this is?" Claudio said. He shredded it in two. "This is a slip of paper. Worthless. The new 'regent' may be a spineless sea jelly, but I am not."

Apelles' smile disappeared. "Disobeying Imperial order is a crime. You would be well-advised—"

"What do you know of the Empire?" Claudio sneered. "You let Archamenes into your own gates. You are as spineless as Antonio."

Apelles bristled at the accusation. An insult hovered under the tip of his tongue, but— perhaps eyeing the steel-armored, sword-bearing bodyguards around Claudio—he refrained.

When Claudio entered the stone-walled harbor district of Megaris, dotted with palms, he saw—as he expected—that his fleet awaited them. The square sails of the galleys shone bright white in the heat of the day.

After an arduous boarding process, the soldiers entered them. By nightfall, Claudio rode on the deck of the *Vanguard*. It had been a troubling few days. The regent had shown his true self: whether a coward or an envier, he did not know. The soldiers did not know of Antonio's orders, but when they arrived at Haroon perhaps Claudio would tell them, and every man that did not wish to serve the Empire would be ferried back to the ill-minded man who sat on the White Throne.

They sailed into the night, and the oarsmen did not stop rowing until darkness fell. The whole time, Claudio stood above deck in the cool night air, thinking of what would unfold. For too long, Haroon had sat in the Khazan River Delta, growing rich from both the north and the south. Now Claudio had his chance. The Empire had its chance. With Archamenes' army soundly defeated and the King of Kings in quick retreat, Claudio would disobey the emperor and do the impossible. Politics, cowardice, and the unspoken threat of the Padisha Emperor had prevented almost everyone from attempting such an invasion; but the time was now.

Eventually sleep overtook him.

He awoke at the sun's first rays. A few clouds hung in the sky. To the south, the new morning light illuminated reddish mountains. A screech rang out and Claudio looked up. Before him, a figure danced in the blue sky. It was reptilian, similar—in some ways—to a crocodile, but with bright red scales, luminous blue eyes, and huge bat-like wings.

"Is it a dragon?" Claudio mumbled, more to himself than anyone else; and yet the Vanguard's captain, Prospero, answered.

"No. The dragons are long-gone. These are Sand Drakes; fierce, but they do not eat humans except when they are starving. They are territorial, though; the Khazidees stay away from them and for good reason. They rarely come this far out to sea. You're lucky to see one. It will not harm us."

The day faded to afternoon; the afternoon into night, and still they sailed through the Middle Sea, hugging the shore. Claudio drifted to sleep once more. When he awoke in the mid-morning, the sea had grown busy with ships: huge grain-freights bound for various cities, passenger-ships heading in all directions, and sleek trade-ships sailing to their ports of call. By mid-afternoon, Haroon lay before them: a red city of sandstone.

The buildings were clustered around the insulated bay. Onion domes topped the temples that overlooked the wave-splashed embankments. Thin towers rose high above the skyline. On the turrets of the walled-in bay, Fharese flags rattled in the wind: a four-pointed star on a purple field. Further in, the streets of its harbor swarmed with people. As Claudio waited on the deck of the Vanguard, he caught a scent of curry and cinnamon and spice; yet whether it was just his imagination or not, he didn't know.

Most pertinently, the blockade had ended. The Imperial fleet Claudio expected was nowhere in sight. That regent—gods damn him—had lifted the blockade, making Fharese trade-ships, and perhaps war-ships, free to travel the seas without harrying.

A small dhow was sailing out of the bay. The lateen sail bore the four-pointed star of Fharas. Claudio had a feeling it was a government ship; and in time, his feeling proved true. A man in a long, gem-encrusted purple robe and a flame-orange turban stood there on the deck of the dhow, surrounded by soldiers.

"My lord!" the man shouted as the two ships creaked in the wind. "I am Faridún, satrap of Haroon, in service of Archamenes the God-King! But I also serve Queen Astarthe of Haroon, and she wishes to inquire of your reasons for coming to our hallowed city!"

"I do not come with peaceful intent!" Claudio hollered over the deck. "If you do not surrender to the Empire, I will show no mercy!"

"Your ruler just lifted the blockade!" Faridún shouted back. "He said the Empire's squabbles with Archamenes had nothing to do with Haroon!"

"Tell your queen that she will either surrender, or her city will fall to the legion!" Claudio roared.

Faridún's eyes lighted with trepidation. "Do you want a tribute? I can deliver you ten-thousand marks, paid in gold!"

Ten thousand marks would make Claudio the richest man in Imperial City, but riches were not what he sought. Claudio had one thing in mind: to punish the Empire's enemies, to defeat the traitors and put a worthy man on the White Throne. "I have no interest in money."

"Then Astarthe herself wishes to speak with you," answered Faridún.

The dhow sailed back to harbor.

A riverboat arrived from the harbor. The slender vessel had five pairs of oars and a high prow. In front of the oarsmen, the queen of Haroon lay lengthwise across the deck, completely nude. Her body was tan, her hair dark. By her posture and her feathered headdress she imagined herself beautiful, a goddess; but her features were masculine, her nose bulbous and strangely-formed. Her arms were long and gangly. Lotus flowers lay strewn all about her.

"I come to offer myself to you, mighty Imperial!" shouted Astarthe. "I, a widow; a vessel of Issa, almighty goddess. By her fertility—by her presence in the sky, the moon—I offer her potency to you, mighty Imperial. I am a widow; my brother-husband Anakh has passed on. I am Astarthe, embodied moon, and you will take the place of Anakh, embodied sun. You will reign as King Anakh, and you shall be lord of Haroon, the City of Issa."

The religious gibberish made no sense to Claudio. Despite the distinct plainness of Astarthe, he had not been with a woman in a long time and felt a budding attraction to her naked form. "I do not understand your foreign ways," Claudio began, "but let me understand this: you claim to be a descendant of the goddess Issa." He grew hot and his voice trembled. "You are some sort of divinity—"

"Take me, Imperial," Astarthe cried out. "You shall reign as King Anakh; you will forgo your barbaric northern gods. You will embody Atman, the great god of fertility who rides the sun, and reign with me—Issa, the moon—over her great city. You will be reborn."

The riverboat drew closer.

"No!" Claudio roared with a strength he didn't know he had. "I will not worship the strange gods of Khazidea. I, Claudio, serve the god Imperium; and you will revere him, and him alone."

The prow of her riverboat struck the starboard side of the Vanguard. "So be it!" Astarthe groaned. "The Empire shall first force himself upon me, and then rape the City of Issa for all its gold."

"That's right I will!" Overcome with lust, Claudio leapt off the deck of the Vanguard and struck the riverboat, which wobbled.

He undid his belt and forced himself upon her as she said, forcing himself into her like an animal until she stopped moving and both were left breathless and satisfied.

"It is done," Astarthe panted, covered in sweat. "What has long been prophesied by the Godlings of Qabash has finally come into fruition. *Shall I fear the east wind? / Nay! Their time is fading fast / Shall I fear the south or west? / Nay! When th' North Wind comes at last / Then will come an iron age, ignoble and unjust.*"

No longer bound by her spell, completely released of his lust,

Claudio clenched his teeth and stopped himself from striking the queen. "We are *not* unjust," he shouted. "We are called by the gods to rule over the nations. Now let the prophecy be true, Astarthe. Do not get in the way of it. The north wind has come." He tied his belt again.

"So let it be!" Astarthe called out. "Who is to argue with the godlings? Who is to argue with the prophecy? Who is to argue with *you*? You are greater than the godlings; for even the godlings answer to me, the queen. But you... you answer to no one."

"Now take me to the royal palace," Claudio said. "I will ride in my own ship, and the army will dock in your port."

In small groups, the Imperial soldiers filtered in to the so-called City of Issa. Perhaps a hundred Fharese soldiers remained within the walls, keeping order. Claudio ordered them all put to death. A few managed to escape, but the city was his. In time, the green river delta that stretched east, west, and south for many miles would all be the property of the Empire.

Queen Astarthe led Claudio personally into the Royal Palace. An airy walkway of red pointed arches led into a garden: blossoming pink myrtles, purple saffron crocus, fig trees and date palms combining into an intoxicating aroma. By now Claudio's lust returned, and they made love again, like two animals, in the midst of the greenery. Truly she was some sort of witch; for though she was plain and strangely-featured, she had cast her spell over him.

In the middle of the lovemaking Claudio shouted, "Witch, will you call Imperium your god?"

"I will call *you* my god!" Astarthe cried.

At last the deed was done. Claudio stood up, filled with shame, and saw a few gardeners staring at them. At *him*. A wholesome Imperial knight from Gad, fornicating with this desert queen in public view. What had happened to him since he departed from the family ranch? What was he turning into? "What have I become?" he said aloud.

"Anakh!" Astarthe cried. "You have become the last of the

proud line of brother-kings, joined to me, your sister-queen."

"Stop the gibberish!" Claudio roared. "That's a command. Now where's my crown?"

"We have no crown," Astarthe answered. "The lord of Haroon wears a blue turban with a diamond aigrette, in the manner of Fharas."

"Useless woman!" Claudio didn't know what else to say, but the shame was building inside him. His face flushed red. He tied the belt tighter. "I am now lord of Haroon. But you will lift your spell from me, Astarthe! Your city is under Imperial control; the Empire is not under the control of your seductive wiles. Now restrain yourself!"

"Restrain *my* self?" Astarthe said. "You are the one who is so drawn to me, the Goddess of Haroon, embodied moon, Vicar of Issa."

"I said stop the gibberish!" Claudio demanded. "Now take me to the crown."

In the middle of a spacious red chamber, the throne of Haroon beckoned. There, Claudio took a seat.

When the High Priest of Atman entered to perform the coronation, Claudio thought—due to the high voice, the garish face-paint and the women's robes—that it was a female. The closer the priest drew, however, the clearer his faint masculine features became until Claudio knew beyond a doubt that a male eunuch stood before him, dressed in feminine garb according to foreign custom.

The androgynous priest knelt before him. "My lord, crowning you and naming you brother-king will take seven days." The high, boyish voice seemed so odd to Claudio; he had never met a eunuch. "The people of Haroon will fast, and at the end of the week you will receive your turban. At that point a great feast will begin, and you will be named brother-king Anakh, great king."

"Give me the crown, now," Claudio snapped. "That is the command of the Empire." He jabbed his sword threateningly.

The High Priest hesitated, but after glancing into Claudio's eyes his resolve seemed to soften. He scurried away to obey the command.

An hour later, the "crown"—a cyan turban with a diamond aigrette—lay on head of Claudio-Valens Adamantus, the Bel of Haroon.

CHAPTER TWENTY-TWO:
INTO THE DEPTHS

Marcus Silverus

The priest of Orkus and several armed guards escorted Marcus and Tivera through the chaparral. Perga, the pirate-captain who had brought them to accursed Tarso, had long gone with his crew. Surely now—as Marcus awaited his plunge into murky doom—Perga sailed through good winds and warm skies, stealing and murdering, and yet escaping the wrath of the gods… if the gods even existed. Yet Tivera's faith in Mira, the Trifold Mother, seemed stronger than that of many priests Marcus knew. Into the slimy depths she would go, but her faith would sustain her… and there, in the darkness, Marcus would thrash and scream, desperate for air, no consolation, nothing to cling to. His end would be abyssal misery.

Thinking about that did nothing for the fluttering in his stomach, the constant shaking, the sickened feeling overcoming him. He didn't know why it had to come to this, he thought, as the priest's men forced them onto the ship—a small vessel with one sail, so unimposing that it was a wonder it was seaworthy. They could not be going out very far; but the waters around Anthania were deep even a short distance from shore.

They set out. The priest's men had to take out the oars. The wind—perhaps due to Tivera's prayerful mutterings—did not favor them. The oars creaked on their hinges; and with each stroke Marcus' shivering increased, his breath colder and shallower.

Yet in time—and, upon first glance, in sight of shore—the men stopped their rowing. The priest of Orkus' eyes widened. The wind had picked up from the west, and in that direction, steely gray clouds had gathered.

"You may not think we are far from shore," the priest of Orkus rasped. "You may, mistakenly, think you are safe. Yet here, beneath the deck of this vessel, is one of the deepest chasms of the ocean. A rift of incomprehensible depth; and some say, if you sink here, the world will end before you hit bottom." The familiar sharkish grin crept over mouth. "And now, Orkus, lord of sharks, friend of pirates… I commend these souls into your gaping jaws…"

"Tivera!" Marcus blurted in desperation. "Tivera! *Shine!*"

Tivera made a startled sound: half a gasp, half a whimper. At the command her eyes brightened; convulsions overtook her, like those of childbirth. She obviously wanted to shine, yet loosing this power from herself obviously caused her pain. She let out a whimper; her skin turned translucent, a light shining through a veil.

"Dump them!" the priest of Orkus hissed.

A pirate laid his meaty fingers around Tivera's shoulders.

She screamed. She was a lamp; light burst from her luminous skin, shining like a star. The priest of Orkus cowered before the blinding light. Marcus hid his eyes, but even through his flesh the light was blinding.

Tivera screamed, as if in pain. The priest of Orkus fell out of the boat and landed with a splash in the water. The priests' servants cried out.

Despite the blinding light, despite the pulsing, radiant energy illuminating from this girl—this insane and gifted lass, this freak, as some might call her—Marcus stood up, and squinted just enough to look at his environs.

In a second's lapse, the light ended. Tivera crumpled to the deck in tears. The men grasped about, fumbling this way and that. She had blinded them. But she—perhaps on purpose, or by her goddess's will—had not blinded Marcus.

Everything suddenly seemed dark. Still, Marcus finished what he intended when he had stood up. He yanked a sword out of one of the pirate's sheaths, cheap thing that it was, and—leaning precipitously out of the boat—thrust the steel blade at the priest of Orkus. The wicked man was, perhaps, three feet out into the choppy waters, but he was blind and offered no resistance. The blade bit through his thick cotton robe like it was air, sliced through ribs and striking the heart with a spurt of blood. The water turned red.

One by one, Marcus finished off the rest of the priest's men. They, too, were blind, and offered no resistance. Grasping air, eyes white and useless, they resembled—in Marcus's mind—what they truly were. Dark-hearted, blind to life and honor, ignorant of all goodness, grasping for the wind.

He stabbed them and tossed them into the water, one by one. The water, already grown red by the priest's blood, grew an even brighter shade of crimson. Then, spattered with blood, Marcus laid the sword down on the deck, and rested his bones. All thanks to Tivera, Marcus could live another day. It was a debt he could never repay.

She had collapsed to her knees, and the sleeves of her gown were already wet with tears. He stooped over her and put a firm hand around her shoulder. "You did a great thing, Tivera… you saved my life."

"I feel blood on your hands," she said.

The words surprised him. "It was necessary."

"It was not," Tivera said.

Marcus surveyed the seas around him. The gruesome spectacle—the bodies floating in the water—indeed looked like a spat of reckless carnage. But it was necessary. "If I had not done that, they would have killed us."

Tivera's eyes opened. They were red from weeping. "Mira, my goddess… she blinded them. They did not stand a chance to hurt us. You killed them. I'm sad for them. Mira's light touches all… Mira's light blinds evil… it does not kill evildoers. Killing is bad. Killing is always bad!"

Her trembling lips were apple red. Marcus looked at the skies. He could not operate this vessel. A wind was blowing from the west, and already the water had grown choppy. Though they were—distantly—in sight of land, it would still be a treacherous journey to swim there. In these waters, it would be very difficult.

"Do you swim?" Marcus asked.

"No!" she screamed. "I can't swim… I hate water… we need to get out! We need to get out!"

"It will be okay." Yet Marcus's words did nothing to ease the trembling that had overtaken her.

He tried to row, but the wind was strong; it was blowing them steadily east into the sea.

A ship appeared in the distance; a large galley with several sails and many dozens of oars. As the wind bore them across the seas, Marcus called out, "Shine! Shine again, Tivera!"

Tivera listened to him. Though the light was smaller than the burst of radiance before, it was bright enough to shine like the beacon of a lighthouse. So, too, was it shorter-lived; it was a burst of light, lasting perhaps five seconds, and then gone. Yet it was enough; for the ship began to sail toward them. Tivera collapsed in exhaustion, but she had saved them twice today—first in overcoming the priest of Orkus, and then in drawing in these sailors.

Silently Marcus prayed that these were good men, that they were not pirates or thieves or murderers. But—as he watched Tivera lay there, drawing in exhausted gasps—he knew he would find out very soon.

Soon the ship reached them. The men aboard did not look like pirates, at least from what Marcus could tell. They did not seem to be military men, though a few wore swords on their belts. One man leaned over the railing and called out, "Are you in danger?"

"Obviously!" The shouted reply was perhaps more brusque than Marcus intended. "We need help! If you are going anywhere, take us. We are in poor condition."

"I see that!" the man replied. "There is blood all over you."

"We ran into pirates! Their undoing was their own fault. I only sped up the gods' justice."

"We are bound for Zoar, but we are stopping in Peregoth as

our port-of-call… you may ride with us there, or to Zoar if you wish to go that far."

Marcus could think of a lot worse places to stay than Peregoth, ancient founding city of the Empire—though now her glory was faded like a flower in autumn, and the center of power had moved mainland, she still held a place in the hearts of men.

He glanced at Tivera. Without thinking beforehand, he asked her, "Can we trust them?"

"Yes!" she answered. "Yes! They will do as they say…"

Marcus led Tivera onboard and soon the ship was on its way.

The city of Peregoth, though its name was no longer revered like in the past, was still impressive to look upon. Layers of white concentric walls, going ever higher and higher until reaching their pinnacle, stretched high above the waters of the bay. The Colossus—famous around the world—greeted them, an emblem of the city's former glory.

The ship docked in its port of call. Marcus thanked them, though he had no money; it had all been confiscated, ripped from his hands by the pirates and their dark priest, and now he would wander the streets penniless.

Out of the harbor district, through the gate of the first wall, they entered the city of Peregoth. Townhomes—all built of stone—overlooked the paved streets. Within their rooms, old Imperial families went about their affairs. They had money, unlike Marcus.

The sun was dipping below the western ocean, beneath the endless waters never explored by man. In the fading twilight, he held Tivera tight; he huddled into an alley. And as he did, he realized a priestess was walking toward him. In her slender white hands, she held a shepherd's crook. Her head was completely bald. She was a priestess of Amara, the Good Mother, and removed her hair—the pride of womankind—to show her devotion.

"You look troubled." Her voice was soft. "Do you have a place to stay?"

"No…" Marcus frowned.

"The Temple of Amara houses the desperate. You are always welcome… you may follow me there, if you wish. It does not matter if you are sick, or crippled."

"Thank you," Marcus said. "Thank you." And he hugged her.

He could think of a much worse fate than staying in a hospice. Until he got back on his feet, he would spend Yule here, in this ancient city of man, and New Years, and perhaps more holidays after that. But for now, he and Tivera had a place to stay and meager fare to eat; and for that, he could not help but be thankful.

CHAPTER TWENTY-THREE:
DISOBEDIENCE

Bruesio Lornodoris, August

"The first order of business," Bruesio told the Council, "is some disconcerting news out of the south." He read from a scroll. "'Apelles of the Pharsis Family, of the City of Megaris, says this: Be advised that your young general, Claudio, has disobeyed your commands and set sail for Haroon. May he come to ruin! Whether he has met with ill fortune or completed his insolent goals does not matter. He is proud and dangerous."

"Good for Claudio!" shouted the—according to some, warmongering—councilor from Gad, Geta.

"Enough!" Bruesio roared. "And Kerius, do not rebuke him. We do not need any more petulant bickering from you two."

Kerius was glaring at Geta. Bruesio knew the two never agreed on anything. "Now," he continued. "That is not the last of it. A new missive from Haroon." He dropped the first on the floor, took another one and opened it. "It says this, councilors: 'Dear regent, the city of Haroon has been conquered and utterly subdued. Claudio's soldiers pilfer treasure from the holy temples, and the boy himself wears the turban of a great southron lord. Yet resentment is building; for Queen Astharte, a great temptress, has cast her intoxicating spell over him and rumor has it they have begun an affair. Signed: Edelio, Tribune.'" Bruesio looked over the twenty-nine faces that stared at him. Some were stricken with abject horror; others, with anger. Only Councilor Geta looked pleased.

"He has disobeyed Imperial order," said Councilor Kerius. "Therefore, Claudio must be brought back to Imperial City and executed."

Through gritted teeth, Geta growled his reply. "The only people you wish to execute are those who stand against the Empire's enemies."

"Enough!" Bruesio called out. "I will not tolerate another bickering match, as I said before."

"We should send the Nichaean Legion to fight him," suggested Councilor Fabiano. "He has grown arrogant. And with this victory over Haroon, he will become the most prideful man in the whole Empire! He will be a threat to us all!"

"That is complicated," Bruesio said. "The rebellion grows in the north."

"Who cares?" hissed Councilor Kerius. "This boy must be stopped! He obviously hates the Fharese! He invades a sovereign land, robs temples, and proclaims the Empire's virtues! The Empire has committed injustices too numerous to count. We invaded Eloesus long ago, a great center of learning, and now we want to add Fharas?"

"Do not forget Gad," said Councilor Geta. "I come from Gad; my family comes from Gad, and I am glad the Empire rules us."

Councilor Kerius sneered. "Oh, you brown-bread Gadites, blond and pasty—having no culture or science, always urging people to war, yet you are poor and the least of all peoples. It is no wonder you cling to your swords and your farming gods and farming festivals, because you are so destitute and wretched, and cannot possibly understand great intellect."

Geta went red.

"Stop!" Bruesio roared. "No more personal insults, Kerius, and no more hawkish statements from you, Geta."

Geta's face reddened even further.

"Solutions, councilors!" Bruesio demanded. "That is what we are called to do."

"I make a motion that we send the Nichaean Legion to face him," said Councilor Fabiano.

Bruesio shook his head. "The rebellion grows in the north."

"Are you really that worried about a bunch of runaway slaves?" Fabiano laughed.

Bruesio decided to play devil's advocate. "Winter nears."

"We still have time to transport the troops," said Councilor Arappo, a man from Bregantium who took an amateur interest in sailing. "We have one or two weeks before the storms begin in earnest."

"And where will the fleet winter?" asked Bruesio. It was an important question, one that needed to be answered.

"If they cannot return in time, they can winter in Megaris," Arappo said.

An easy solution, Bruesio reflected. "So we will send the Nichaean Legion to Haroon, capture Claudio and bring him back to answer for his crimes. That is what we propose?"

"I would add something," Councilor Kerius said. "Once Claudio is taken care of, we will send a delegation first to Haroon and then to Seshán. We make a formal apology to both the queen of Haroon and to Archamenes himself, and make it clear we do not agree with Claudio's conquest."

Geta was nearly purple.

"I would agree about apologizing to the queen," Bruesio said, "though I would venture to guess the damage is already done. However, apologizing to Archamenes seems inappropriate, as he just invaded one of our territories."

"Finally, some sense!" Geta cried.

"Shut it, Geta," Bruesio snapped. He looked at the other councilors. "So here is the proposition, good members of the Council: The legion disembarks from Nichaeus, arrives in Haroon several days later. We defeat Claudio's army, and bring the spoiled brat back in chains. We send a delegation to make formal apologies." Bruesio scanned the councilors in their seats. "All for?"

Twenty-eight hands went up.

"All against?"

One hand went up—Geta's.

"I will bring our decision for the regent's approval," Bruesio said.

CHAPTER TWENTY-FOUR:
INSOLENCE

Regent Antonio Laureana

The news was disconcerting indeed. "You mean to say," Antonio began, "that Claudio has successfully captured Haroon."

"It appears so," Bruesio answered. "But the Council has—with your permission—made a proposal."

"What of it?"

The proposition about the Nichaean Legion was in good judgment, as far as Antonio was concerned. "Let it be done," Antonio said. "We must punish Claudio. He has no idea what his place is."

Really—since the place was established—Antonio only cared about his harem. Thirty girls served within, and he often bedded more than one a day. Anthea, the blonde Eloesian girl, Portia, the redhead Anthanian, and Anica, the blonde and blue-eyed Gadite, were his favorites. Life had never been this exciting. Now any girl in the Empire with half a mind would be his.

Some prudes might call it an unhealthy obsession, but truthfully, it was every man's dream. Occasionally, he told himself there were things more important than the harem, but his animal side wouldn't listen.

As he sat on the White Throne, he was getting anxious to go back downstairs to the pleasure house. But it appeared Imperium, Divine Force of the Empire, had other plans. A messenger arrived bearing a letter. It had an Imperial seal, indicating official business: a man of some import had apparently written it.

"My lord emperor," the messenger said, "a letter from Grand Legate Claudio-Valens Adamantus."

Antonio repressed a shudder. "Read."

The messenger broke the seal and read it: "Lord Antonio, it has become clear to me that I am the only one in the government who cares about the Empire. Your request for me to return is denied. Neither you, Antonio—nor any of the members of the Imperial Council—fit the example of the founder of the Empire, Peregothius. Imperial City has become a den of vice and cowardice. Let it be known that the city of Haroon and the entire Khazan River Valley is completely mine, and all its riches now belong to me. I request you change your mind; else, I will have to change it for you. –Signed: Claudio-Valens, Grand Legate and new Lord of Haroon."

"I will not tolerate threats!" Antonio roared. "Tell me, messenger. Whom do you serve?"

"The Empire," the messenger answered.

"Do you serve me, your emperor, or do you serve the Empire like this spoiled boy?"

"I don't know," the messenger said. "Can't one serve both?"

"The emperor *is* the Empire," Antonio said. "I will spare your life. Leave me now before I change my mind."

The messenger hurried out the door.

"Fetch me Artavio," he told the Imperial Guards in their red halfcloaks who stood beside him.

In time, Artavio, chief clerk and a man of eastern learning, arrived in the throne room. "What can I do for you, lord regent?" As always, he had his wax tablet in hand, for writing and making writing public were his sole duties.

"Write this letter and send it to the governors of every province. Say this: 'Claudio, the son of the legate Lucento has—without the consent of either the Council or the sitting Regent—entered the city of Haroon. While there he has fallen under the spell of the lecherous Queen of Haroon. As a witch she has captured him, and as her willing slave, he wishes to conquer the whole of the Empire for her. If he has his way, he will let her rule as a despot in the style of Fharas, with neither the Council nor the governors to keep him in balance.' Send one to Bregantium, one to Sanctum, one to Thénai and another to Peregoth; and have the governors send heralds to every magistrate to announce his treason!"

"It shall be done, Your Worship," Artavio said.

Antonio dismissed him with a wave of his hand. One thing Antonio demanded of all people was respect. Now, with that snide missive the spoiled boy had sent him, he wouldn't play fair. He would turn all the people of the Empire that Claudio loved so dearly against him. He would send the full force of the legion, and he would personally lead it.

That night he lay awake in the harem, wrapped around Portia in a postcoital embrace, hands running gently through her tresses of red hair.

Man-for-man, he could overcome almost anyone. His skill at the sword outmatched anyone he knew. He had learned it from his life as an Imperial Guard. But leading an army required strategy.

An Imperial Guard pushed his way through the thin red curtains. "My lord Antonio," he whispered, "there is treachery in the palace!"

"What do you mean?" Antonio pushed away from Portia and stood to his feet; she mumbled something incoherent but kept sleeping. The guard's words dispelled any sleepiness Antonio felt.

"I found a vial of poison under one of your girls' pillow," the guard whispered.

"Whom?" Antonio boomed. Such behavior would not be tolerated.

"Anthea Abantes."

CHAPTER TWENTY-FIVE:
PUNISHMENT

Anthea Abantes

Anthea could see the coming storm; she could read it in Antonio's eyes. He grabbed her, face red, eyes wide. She melted before him onto the pillows of the false harem. Her missing poison vial should have warned her. Now she would have to face him, and Anthea didn't know if she could.

"Why?" he snarled.

Anthea's eyes watered. "I'm sorry."

"I've given you a good life." Antonio shoved her so hard it knocked the wind out of her. He picked her up and slammed her against the concrete wall. "Why?"

"The Order of the Red Hand," Anthea whimpered.

"What are you talking about?"

The other dozen harem girls in the room looked at them in confusion. "I serve the Red Lord," Anthea managed to say, "but I only serve him halfheartedly."

"What in blazes are you talking about?" Antonio gave her another shove.

"The Red Lord hates all the self-righteous… the Order of the Red Hand—its goal has always been to assassinate the emperor, but it's never worked. I was their best one. They thought I could do it."

Antonio shoved her hard, digging into her shoulders with his fingernails. "You are insane."

"The cult is insane," Anthea wheezed. Tears streaked her cheeks. "Lady Ciutta is insane. Lord Tomo is insane. But I'm not insane… they forced me into it…"

"Shut it, *lupa!*" Antonio hissed. "My men found out it's basilisk venom… expensive as hell, and imported from the Venom Flats south of the Red Mountains. Hard to find, hard to get. Not exactly tasteless, but a taste is all you need and you'll drop dead. Where did you get that venom?"

"I think Lord Tomo bought it," Anthea wept.

"Whom?"

"A criminal from the west side… he's a runner of Haroon spice."

Antonio bared his teeth. "I would kill you right now, but I have better plans. The Venom Flats are near Haroon. I will give you what *you* tried to give me. I will leave you out there, and a *real* basilisk will put its venom in you. We'll see how you like it. I'm bound for Khazidea anyway." With that, he slapped her hard against the face.

She slumped to the ground, weeping with heartbreak and shaking with fear. She convulsed as she lay on the pillows, as Antonio stalked away. She wept, and she thought of that young man from the party, and she told herself that not all the elite were like Antonio. Again she prayed to Hieronus, God of Honor, that she would meet Claudio again. "Let me meet Claudio again," she whispered under her breath, and collapsed in exhaustion.

CHAPTER TWENTY-SIX:
THROUGH THE DESERT

Claudio-Valens Adamantus, Grand Legate

Claudio never knew he could hate a woman and yet be so attracted to her at the same time. In his mind raged a constant, volatile battle between his incredible draw to Astarthe—this libertine southron queen—and an intense, passionate desire to destroy her. Throughout the few days after the conquest, he made it clear that—though he would sleep with her—he demanded total respect from her to him and, above all, to the Empire that now controlled her lands.

And then, in bouts of compassion, he felt for Astarthe: this strangely-featured queen, this humble and submissive woman, this descendant of multiple brother-sister marriages. She was strange, she was foreign; yet at heart she was human, and Claudio knew she was not wholly bad.

The city of Haroon was his, and yet Claudio would not be satisfied until he had Archamenes' head. To invade the ancient city of Seshán, capital of Fharas and seat of the King of Kings, was the ultimate unthinkable. No man in the north had attempted it since Tarchon the Mad, and even he had failed. But a fire had grown in Claudio's heart; a burning wrath against the King of Kings, and against his own countrymen who refused to take a stand.

Claudio was sitting on the throne, which he often did while in thought. He called for the satrap Faridún. In time the man entered the room in the long purple robe, and fell prostrate.

"Rise," Claudio demanded.

He obeyed. "What can I do for you, O godly king?"

"Tell me," Claudio said, "whom you serve. Do you serve me, or Archamenes?"

"You," Faridún said, "for you have overcome Archamenes, whose name is God Manifest; and the magi say your name is written in the stars. And if you have overcome a living god, then what does that make you?"

"The wealth of the city belongs to me. Now tell me, Lord Faridún: where are the best of the warriors? I, your king, must expand my numbers."

"The peasants of Khazidea are not warriors; we make sure it is so," Faridún answered. "The magi are powerful beyond any else, for they can conjure up flame and scorch the battlefield; but they are few in number, and they are sworn to serve the King of Kings. The cataphracts are even more deathly loyal to the padisha. The greatest warriors are the Asa… the nomads who wander the Red Mountains, following after the Sand Drakes and eating what's left behind of their prey. The Asa can ride horses while sleeping, and they drink horses' milk; and they are so skilled with bows that they can shoot a fly from a hundred yards away!"

Claudio frowned. "Doubtful. Send a delegation, offer them coin. Make an offer of a silver a month, and increase if necessary."

Faridún shook his head. "They would kill the delegation. They would only respect a king."

"And how would I get there?"

"East through the desert," Faridún said. "But there are many oases along the way… you cannot miss them."

Claudio looked intently into Faridún's eyes, and wondered if deceit hid behind them. "You must come with me, then."

"And who would govern the province in your absence?" Faridún asked. "Astarthe?"

"No," Claudio said. "I do not trust her, either."

"I am not welcome among the Asa," Faridún said. "The policies of Astarthe have been one of hatred toward them."

"I don't need you, anyway." Claudio frowned. "I will leave the city and the river-valley in the command of one of my tribunes. In my absence you will have no powers over either the people or the city."

Faridún's mouth contorted to a snarl.

"Perhaps one day you will earn my trust."

Claudio appointed Milo, a tribune and a trustworthy friend, to command the area in lieu of him. Then he took a small force of about fifty Imperial Knights, and loaded several donkeys' worth of water pouches. Then, before the sun reached noon, they headed east toward the desert.

For several hours of riding, the land remained green. Around him lay the wheat crop that Imperial City so depended on. Patches of watermelon, wiry pomegranate trees, and green rows of chickpeas grew in abundance.

But eventually the greenness faded away, and the desert took over: a parched, baking-hot land of cracked red earth. A few hills appeared as a haze in the horizon. Little bits of scrub brush occasionally appeared, but for the most part it was a desolate land.

And so it went for the first day, and the second, and the third. By the fourth day—when their water pouches ran dry, and the thirst began—Claudio realized there were no oases to be found. He had been a fool to listen to Faridún, and, if his words were proved untruthful, then if it was in his power, he would have the treacherous satrap burned alive.

He remembered the Sand Drakes he saw on the ship to Haroon, and that it had taken days past that to get to the city proper. Therefore, he guessed it would take many more days across the desert. Perhaps he was less than halfway; he had no idea. But the pouches had run out, and he had no recourse but to continue going. A scholar had taught Claudio that a man dies from thirst after three days.

As the sun set on that fourth day in the desert, and the cold settled in, he told the knights they would have to make haste, put all their effort into making it to the Red Mountains.

At the dawn of the fifth day, Claudio and his knights rode at a quicker pace than ever before. Even the horses needed water, and if they died the knights would have to travel on foot. Claudio guessed they rode ninety miles that day, and still there were no Red Mountains in sight. Claudio went to bed thirsty, parched out of his mind; and the horses were worse off.

He realized it was quite possible he would die in the desert. More than his life to be saved, he wanted Archamenes to answer to the Empire.

On the sixth day, the horses would not ride as fast as they had on the fifth. Throughout the day, twelve died along the trail, and the rest slowed to a lethargic stumble. Claudio went crazy with thirst. A headache overtook him and many of the men. Without the horses they were slow. Perhaps Faridún would gain his wish. The sun set; the sixth day ended. The coldness of the desert night settled in. Claudio was sure they would die.

The sun rose on the seventh day. Mad with thirst, Claudio left the tent and scanned the horizon. Even in this state, he knew nothing he saw could be trusted; he learned from his tutor about desert mirages. Wanderers in these barren lands thought they saw an oasis in the distance; they followed after it, but were invariably disappointed, and then they died of thirst.

Died of thirst. The thought filled Claudio with anguish. As he began the slow walk, his mouth dry and his skin drier, he wondered if there was any worse way to die.

Hours passed through the desert. Winds began late in the day, blowing up sand. One by one, the rest of the horses collapsed. The men weren't much better off.

Claudio had grown lightheaded. The splitting headache had

worsened. He wondered if there was any moisture in the scrub-brush spread throughout the desert, but whenever he touched one of the rigid blue plants he could not help but notice they were dry as his hands, if not drier.

By noon their pace had slowed to a stumble. A few knights collapsed. Still Claudio staggered through the sand-blown desert, but the men were losing the will to continue on. Black shapes appeared, but Claudio did not think much of them; they circled around them and a thunderous beating of the dirt echoed through the air. He could not make sense of it, but he didn't need to.

The sun was high in the sky, baking everything around them. At some point, Claudio realized he had reached a flat white area. A salt pan, he realized on further thought. But, spread throughout the white sheet, were pools of water; yet they looked green and fouled, and perhaps weren't water at all. The area swarmed with giant lizard-like things. He tripped over one, fell down and did not get up.

A sharp, excruciating pain jolted Claudio out of his delirium. One of the giant lizards had bitten him. It was a huge beast, black-scaled but with yellow patterns along its back; and orange eyes with such an intense glare he would never forget them.

Water splashed Claudio awake. No longer was he in the salt pan filled with terrible lizards. A face hovered above him: a dark complexion and with long, unshorn black hair.

"Where am I? Who are you?" Claudio said. His throat was very dry.

The man yapped something in a foreign language, and then forced some more water down his throat. He left. Claudio realized he was in a tent of some kind.

A few minutes passed. The man from before returned with a

woman of similar dark complexion. With a thick accent, she spoke the Eloesian tongue, in the Ten Cities dialect. Claudio could understand most of it: "I am translator," she said. "I am of two worlds."

"Who are you people?" Claudio said in the Eloesian tongue. In his still-delirious state he could not be more graceful.

"We are Asa," she said. "Chieftain Nued believes you are a god. Yellowback Basilisk did not put venom into you. If basilisk respects a man, he is a god. Basilisk respects no one except living gods."

"Water," Claudio said.

"Even gods need to drink," the woman said.

The man left the tent, and returned with another water-pouch. Claudio took it and gulped it down. His mouth still was dry, but he decided to speak. "If I am a god," he said in the Eloesian tongue, "then will you serve under me?"

"If basilisk respects a man, then we Asa respect him," the woman answered. "I am wife of Nued, chieftain. I will serve under you."

"Do you know the way across the desert, to Haroon?"

The woman nodded. "We know you came from place of unmoving tents. I think it is strange that a living god chose such a foolish route. Where were you trying to go?"

"To the Red Mountains," Claudio said, "to the Asa… to win your respect."

"We are many leagues from mountains. They are still out of sight." Her eyes grew thoughtful. "The men that were with you are dead. Tell me, living god, why do you want us Asa?"

"A mortal has slighted me," Claudio said, deciding to use the supposed godhood to his advantage. "The city of Seshán… it must be destroyed."

"That city is many miles away," she said. "I only know it because I am woman of learning."

"What is your name?" Claudio asked.

"Those who dwell in unmoving tents, they name their women.

But my name is only wife-of-Nued; and before my marriage my name was daughter-of-Calim."

Strange people with strange customs, Claudio thought, but they are respectful. "Where is Nued?"

She motioned to the man next to her. She turned to him and yapped in her foreign tongue. He said something back.

Wife-of-Nued turned back to Claudio and spoke once more in Eloesian: "He will ride with you; and so will all five thousand of our tribe. And he will give you Borak, best of our horses."

"We must go to Haroon." Claudio realized they might not know it by that name. "The river. The unmoving tents—"

"We know what place you mean," Wife-of-Nued said.

Borak was a white stallion. Unlike the bulky chargers that Claudio bred at his family ranch, the horses of the Asa were thin and sleek. The Asa themselves wore thin white shirts and tight breeches, and had short bows. Even the women had bows, with wife-of-Nued no exception.

Outside the tent, the five-thousand Asa on their horses looked more fearsome than Archamenes' army ever had. They had gathered around a large waterhole and some were filling their pouches. Around them the desert stretched, the dry scrub-brush and sand-blown fields. It was morning and the heat of the day had already arrived.

Claudio didn't know why the basilisk had not injected the venom. For a second he wondered if it was true—if the Asa were correct in saying he was a living god—but he wouldn't let it get to his head.

CHAPTER TWENTY-SEVEN:
A Dead Hawk

Bruesio Lornodoris, August

In the early morning, before the daily meeting, messengers informed Bruesio that Geta—the warmongering councilor from Gad—had died last night while dining with his wife. The coroners said that, judging from Geta's symptoms, someone had likely poisoned him.

Bruesio didn't particularly care about the news. Of course, he would make a big fuss and try to seem sad, just for appearances' sake. But Geta's hawkish words were not well received by any in the Council, and indeed he had been a thorn in the side of intellectual discussion. He had sided with Claudio-Valens, that disobedient young man with the huge ego. As he sat there before the mirror in his bedroom, plucking untidy eyebrows, Bruesio realized that no, he didn't care about Geta's death at all.

In the Council House, Bruesio began with the obvious first matter of discussion. "Yesterday we had thirty councilors. Now we have twenty-nine. We must announce the news to the public and hold another election…" Doing so would be tiresome.

"Well," Councilor Kerius began, "if the people elected a troublesome councilor like Geta, who knows if they would not do it again?"

"An election must be held regardless," Bruesio said, though he did so with regret. "The people often err in judgment, but they elected *you*, Kerius."

Kerius looked bitter. "They elected me in a different season of our culture, when they tired of war and bloodshed and wanted to make peace with the nations. Now they have grown restless and prideful, arrogantly believing they are as intelligent as the Augusts. This disease of mind has spread from warlike Gad even to the streets of Imperial City; and they will shame us by choosing another warmonger. They are unable to decide rationally for themselves. We saw this when the crowds rioted against Emperor Giton—may he rest forever in Highest Heaven! The boy was our last best hope."

"An election will be held, as it is written in the tablets of law," Bruesio said. "We of the Council must adhere to the law of our fathers, even if it is an ill-conceived tradition."

"It is not ill conceived," said Councilor Galvano. "I disliked Council Geta, but he is not the true problem. That arrogant child Claudio must be stopped!"

"Thank you, Galvano, for bringing us to our next issue." Bruesio frowned. "The Nichaean Legion has agreed to face Claudio. We have sent the fleet to transport them, but we are truly cutting it close. The winter storms are nigh upon us. Let us pray they make it before a northeaster blows them into the wide ocean."

"My lord councilors," Kerius said, and Bruesio suddenly got the impression he had planned a speech, "I have a proposition. Since Geta's death I have thought this over. I wish to take a delegation—completely unarmed—and head to the holy city of Seshán. I want to have a serious discussion with Lord Archamenes and give him the respect he deserves. I believe the reason he invaded Ten Cities was because of our profound disrespect for him and his culture; and I want to ensure him that it will never happen again."

"A bold proposition in wartime," Bruesio said. "Perhaps we should let the matter of Claudio settle before we take such actions."

"What if he is so bold as to attack Seshán, and he corners you?" Galvano suggested.

Kerius laughed. "I don't think even Claudio is that stupid! The southrons have won many victories over us for endless centuries; they are a stronger race, and an older race. No one in their right mind would attack Seshán. It's suicide to face the Fharese on their own turf."

"And what if the Fharese attack *you*?" said the usually-silent councilor Marsilio.

Kerius laughed again. "The Fharese are not intrinsically warlike, as the common brown-bread folk of the Empire are. The Fharese are cultured, and respect those who respect them."

"I don't think any of us will stop you," Bruesio said, "and I will get you a swift ship and a crew to steer her if that is what you wish to do. You must hurry, though, because of the winter storms."

"I know what winter storms are, Bruesio," Kerius sneered. "And I will accept your offer on the ship. I will also need a guide who knows the way to Seshán."

Bruesio nodded. "There are many resident Fharese in the city. I will fetch one of those as well."

"Then I will go, and pay the Padisha Emperor the respect he deserves." Kerius frowned. "If the brown-bread electorate chooses another war hawk in my absence, then they will get what is coming to them. As for us—the Council—we will make the respect we have for Archamenes very clear."

CHAPTER TWENTY-EIGHT: DARK CLOUDS

Regent Antonio Laureana

Antonio had been gone from the harem only three days and already he had gone crazy in its absence. He missed the thirty girls in his possession, and his whole body ached now that he left them. Once exposed to what common men could only dream of, suddenly ripping yourself away from it hurt.

He began to question his decision to personally lead the charge as he boarded the flagship *Victory*. But he needed to correct that arrogant cur, Claudio, and just thinking about the letter Claudio sent him infuriated him to no end.

Clouds were gathering when they left the harbor of Nichaeus, sending the garden-snake of unease wriggling through his gut. Winter lurked in the horizon and the air cooled every day. Soon it would rain, and the sun would hide its face from the people of the Empire.

A steady wind began from the south. The sailors assured Antonio that it was nothing to worry about. He had brought Anthea with him. Before he fed her to the basilisks, he would have his fun.

CHAPTER TWENTY-NINE:
COMING DOOM

Anthea Abantes

Bound in steel chains, Anthea lay immobile below the deck of the flagship *Victory*. She shut her eyes and tried to soothe herself.

Better women could find consolation in the gods, and in Heaven; but Anthea had not led a perfect life. Perhaps, the gods would understand the circumstances that made her turn to prostitution. But Anthea had done worse than sell her body to the night. Under pressure from the terrifying Lady Ciutta, she beat the lesser brothel-girls when they refused to take on an ugly or frightening client. Under pressure from Ciutta, she dropped poison into the wineglasses of innocents. Despite the pressure from her madam, Anthea could have stopped it. She could have refused. She could have run away. She could have fled to Sanctum and become a vestal.

Simply put, she was bound for Hell.

At the thought a shiver ran up her spine, and she convulsed. *I was born a poor Eloesian girl*, Anthea prayed silently. *No one ever gave me a chance. I fell through the cracks… I lost my way. I am a victim as much as anyone else.* Hot tears ran down her cheeks. She wiped her eyes with her sleeves.

Antonio towered above her. Despite her sobs, there was no empathy in his eyes, only anger. When she first saw him, she never guessed what a monster he was. She showed the intent of poisoning him; that was enough for a death sentence. But to drag it on for days and weeks… to force himself upon her and beat her until welts covered every part of her body! All this with the threat of the basilisks.

At the sight of him, her bruises ached as if in expectation.

"Well, well, Anthea." Antonio smiled. "Do you know there is a certain species of spider… I'm not sure what it's called, but the name doesn't matter. Once the dominant finds its mate, and has its way with her, he eats her, little by little. That's the way of nature, I guess. You are passive, Anthea. And I am your lord, your domino… your god. And—like that spider—I was I'll do whatever I like to you. And you don't have any choice."

She spat in his face. "You aren't a man!"

Antonio's face flared to a cherry red. He fell upon her and beat her with his fists. Softer than the branch he used last night, Anthea mused. But the welts flared up with each punch and soon she was sobbing quietly, "I'm sorry… I'm so sorry… forgive me my lord, my domino…"

She hated him more than ever; but fear is stronger than hate. She crumpled before him as his blows continued. She let him have his way with her; she let him enter her, and she prayed again that the one from before—that Claudio—would save her… the only good man in the world.

CHAPTER THIRTY:
SESHÁN MUST BURN!

Claudio-Valens Adamantus, Grand Legate

Claudio rode Borak through the wilderness. The Asa—on their quick, sleek horses—meandered from one watering-hole to the next, knowing every detail of the dry, sandy desert. At night, they picked the few plants that grew throughout the bleak landscape and made a special brew. When Claudio first tried it, he spat it out and thought it was the most foul-tasting concoction he'd ever put to his lips. But as the nights progressed, it tasted better to him; and soon he liked it better than water. The Asa called it *akil,* and said that boiling the plant cleaned the water and gave the drinker vigor.

Day by day, watering-hole by watering-hole, the Asa made their way across the desert. Soon the green took over: irrigation ditches flowing from the Khazan River, its wheat-crop nearly ripe for the cutting. Date-palms, patches of watermelon, and barley grew also; but the Asa did not bother with such luxuries. As Nued, and Wife-of-Nued, told him, they followed the demigod Claudio's command; and he wished to return to Haroon—what the Asa called the Place of Unmoving Tents.

At last it was before them; Haroon, red city of sandstone. Jewel of the Desert, some called it. But as Claudio approached at the Asa's vanguard, he could see—on the turrets—the flag of Fharas, the Four-Pointed Star. The gates were open. The satrap Faridún did not expect Claudio to return alive.

"*Ehu!*" Charge. As soon as Claudio gave the order, the Asa understood. They plunged through the gates, galloping and throwing a cloud of dust into the air. Under a clear blue sky they thundered through the city. Women screamed. Men ran out of the way, bolting into alleys to avoid the horses' trampling hooves.

None could stand before the Asa's might. Soldiers in full armor shrieked and fled before them. Claudio led them through streets and up hills to the Royal Palace of Haroon. Soon the red wonder stood before him. The iron portcullis was shut, and a group of five guards—black-bearded, in Fharese dress—stood watch. Their hands trembled but they had nowhere to go.

As it should be. Claudio smiled. "*Il bahar,*" he said. Kill them.

In a moment's span, the bows went up and the arrows flew, piercing the guards like pincushions. They drew in their last gasps and sank to the floor one-by-one, unable to talk. The Asa's reputation for marksmanship was well-deserved.

How will we get in? Claudio wondered. The Asa were fierce fighters, but Haroon's royal palace was of stone and steel. Flaming arrows could not draw the Queen of Haroon and the scheming satrap out. So what could?

For several minutes, they stood in the shadow of the gate. Claudio wondered what had happened to the Imperial army he left; had the Queen of Haroon slaughtered them all? The army outnumbered the queen's and outmatched her men in skill, so that seemed so very unlikely.

Claudio felt the queen approach before he saw her. She walked up to the portcullis, wearing a beaded headdress and a red midriff. For an instant, Claudio saw her bulbous nose and masculine features, and wondered how on earth he had lusted for her so badly. Then he looked into her eyes and her spell once again fell over him; this time, he realized it was a spell, and diverted his glance.

"Foul queen," Claudio said, not looking at her. "What have you done with my soldiers?"

"Claudio," Astarthe said, "truly you are born of heaven. Under an evil moon you traveled the desert; but you have returned with the fearsome Asa."

"Shut your mouth, *lupa*!" Claudio snapped. To call a queen that name was an insult bordering on sacrilege, but she deserved the title. "You swore to honor Imperium, Spirit of the Empire. You betrayed my trust." Claudio kept eyeing the ground. "Open the portcullis or I'll have the Asa kill you where you stand."

"Look at me!" Astarthe shrieked.

Her words proved to Claudio that she was a wise-woman of some kind; a weaver of emotions, a shaper of wills. Some eldritch power was in her eyes, and despite her strange features she had great power over men.

"Open the portcullis! You have five seconds. Five... four... three..."

From Astarthe's mouth came a loud, ear-piercing caterwaul. But it ended as soon as it began; she screamed, "Open it!" and the steel barrier lifted.

The Asa bound her in rope made of twisted desert brush. Claudio ordered her blindfolded. He told the Asa horsemen to stay behind and block the exit, and then—with Chieftain Nued, Wife-of-Nued, and a handful of dismounted warriors—entered the Royal Palace. The sandstone corridors brought back memories of the queen's bewitchment. Now she was helpless, at *his* mercy.

As it should be.

In time they reached the throne room. Faridún stood near the throne itself. When he saw Claudio, his eyes widened, and he screamed. He turned and ran but the Asa warriors were quicker; their muscular legs carried them like the wind, and they cut him off at the door. Nued and his wife remained by Claudio's side.

Claudio grinned. He would make an example of this satrap.

The Asa grabbed Faridún, restraining him with their strong dark hands.

"Achar," Claudio ordered. Still. He looked into Faridún's wide

eyes, and saw wormlike terror in them. "What shall I do with you? The man who led me into the desert, thinking I would die? The Asa revere me as a god. And now what shall I do with you? I know one thing: I will flog you senseless first. But after that… do you have any suggestions? Shall I feed you to the basilisks? Shall I roast you on a pyre?"

Faridún was mumbling incoherently. Astarthe, blindfolded, let out a shriek.

"You are a worm, Faridún," Claudio sneered. "Admit you are a worm. Say it. Say 'I am a worm.'"

"Imperial dogs!" Faridún hissed. He looked up at Claudio, eyes suddenly lighting with anger, and spat.

"Beat him until he stops moving!" Claudio growled. "Then we will roast him. And this one…" He eyed Astarthe. "What to do with her? Perhaps I will grant the *lupa* mercy if she tells me where my soldiers are."

The Asa warriors near Faridún grabbed candelabras. The treacherous satrap cried out as the first blows landed.

"My lord," Astarthe mumbled. "You know I have sworn fealty to you."

"Where are my soldiers, *lupa*? I will not ask again!" Claudio tightened his grip on her.

"They are many leagues from here. I convinced them that they should serve Archamenes; a lord of Sur is taking them to the King of Kings. They are probably in the desert, or already to Gor Ilán and the Satrapy of Seshán."

"Your words make sense." Claudio threw her to the ground. "But in all my time with you I have never known you to be honest, Astarthe. I would threaten you with death, but that hasn't worked. I have made you swear fealty to me, to the god Imperium."

"To the god Claudio," Astarthe corrected him.

"Shut your mouth, *lupa*. I am not a god." Claudio glared at the blindfolded queen. "Killing a woman is something I hoped I would never have to do. It is the lowest of all lows. It is against what my father taught me. But I've realized, now, that it is necessary. You, Astarthe, I cannot leave alive."

"So ends the thousand-year reign of holy Anakh and Astarthe; brother and sister, man and wife, purebloods to the last generation. Alas for me!"

Claudio pitched back his sword. "Alas for you, indeed!"

Astarthe turned and ripped off her blindfold. She looked up at him; her eyes were like black marbles, soulless and mad. "Do not kill me!" she boomed. Claudio nearly obeyed the command, but the blow was already coming. The blade sliced through her neck and severed the queen's head. Her body hit the ground with a thump, and a pool of blood collected where it lay.

The conquest of Haroon was complete.

Claudio received reports that the enslaved soldiers were not far-off. Astarthe's bewitchment apparently occurred the night before, and they were still in the Khazan River Valley. Men of Sur held them against their will.

With the Asa, Claudio galloped out of the gates of Haroon. The last dying screams of Faridún—roasting on a pyre—soon vanished from Claudio's ears.

The Empire never left a soldier behind, let alone six thousand. In the middle of the night, they reached the camp—a gathering of tents in a rare break in the wheat-fields. The Imperial soldiers had turned against the men of Sur; perhaps the spell had broken with the sorceress's death.

But one man of Sur remained alive. He was a lord of Sur, and perhaps they thought he would fetch a high ransom.

"Do not kill him!" Claudio shouted. They would need a guide.

Astride Borak, Claudio gazed at his troops, one after the other.

"Seshán must burn!" he roared. "The King of Kings must answer to the Empire! Southward! We must go southward into the plains of Gor Ilán. Seshán must burn!"

"Seshán must burn!" the soldiers roared in return.

Astride Borak, Claudio turned and headed south. Behind him rode five-thousand Asa and the Imperial soldiers—a force that now numbered eleven-thousand.

The words repeated in his mind: *Archamenes must answer to the Empire. Seshán must burn! Onward!*

CHAPTER THIRTY-ONE:
An Empire In Decline

Lucello Seldano Kerius, August

Kerius' journey had begun a week ago. They sailed from Imperial City to Zoar and—with a small group of Imperial soldiers and a band of desert-men guides—navigated the treacherous desert beyond Kheroe and reached Gor Ilán ("High Plains" in the Fharese tongue). He handed the desert-men several pouches of silver as promised, and bade them goodbye. They rode off on their camels.

Over the days he had noticed how polite and respectful they were. They were so unlike the insolent individualists of the Empire: the ungrateful, unintelligent and worthless citizens Kerius presided over.

Before him was a vast, rolling plain of knee-high yellow grass and an occasional juniper. The sun beat down with unbearable strength, and even hidden in the light white robes of the desert-men, sweat covered every inch of Kerius's body. Down a winding dirt road, Kerius—accompanied by his soldiers and his translator—began the southward journey toward Seshán.

An ancient city. The Queen of Cities, as some called it. A jewel that hardly any man in the north had ever glimpsed.

For two days, they traveled down the road. The villages they passed were shabby, composed of unadorned mudbrick houses and unkempt streets. The men wore long brown robes of uncolored wool. The women did not wear veils—the red and green lace veils of Khazidees seemed to be noblewomen's attire. They were poor, but they respected authority. They respected Archamenes, unlike the arrogant Imperial citizens who despised their rulers.

The Empire's ceaseless robbery caused these people's

poverty. They were disadvantaged because of the Empire's aggression, because of the Empire's domination of trade in the markets of Haroon. The imbalance needed righting, but with such an insolent, greedy populace, the Imperial Council would have to work very hard to correct this great wrong.

On the afternoon of the second day, a group of Fharese warriors rode in on horses. All but one wore simple mail shirts and wielded curved steel scimitars. Their leader was covered head-to-toe in mixed plate and mail armor—as was his horse—and he gripped a spear in his right hand. The extensive armor proved his identity as a cataphract, the strongest of Fharese warriors and the superior of any Imperial soldier.

In unison the Fharese drew their scimitars. The cataphract barked foreign words at Kerius.

The translator spoke. "He says, 'Northerners, by the look of you. And of such little number! Have you lost your minds?'"

Kerius laughed and smiled warmly. "Tell him, 'I come to bring a message to your lord Archamenes. A message of great hope! Our empire has been aggressive in its dealings with you, and I want to express our sorrow to the King of Kings, God Manifest.'"

For a while, the cataphract said nothing; his face was unreadable through his steel visor. Finally he answered, speaking again in his tongue.

The translator explained. "He says, 'I don't understand.'"

"I wish to make an official apology on behalf of the Imperial Council," Kerius said. "I wish to express to the King of Kings, God Manifest—glory upon him!—that we act as one. That we are equals."

When the translator finished, the cataphract shouted something in return. He sounded angry, and Kerius got a sinking feeling.

"He says, 'You are not equal to the King of Kings. You are

dirt, and he is a living god.'"

"Tell him, I should not speak so rashly." Kerius improvised his response. "We are not equals. But our nations... we wish to make changes in our strategy. We wish the Empire to respect Fharas." He fumbled over his words. "We wish for the Empire and Fharas to act as one, to be allies, and—"

The cataphract said something else, and the translator explained. "He says, 'It is not for Fharas to be anyone's ally. It is the natural order for Fharas to dominate. One day, everyone under sun and moon will call the King of Kings his lord.'"

"I agree, it should be so," Kerius said. "I despise my own countrymen. They are arrogant and violent. They are eager to war and greedy. They have no respect for authority. *They...*"

The cataphract cut him off, saying something else.

"He says that he agrees with you on all those things," the translator explained. "He says 'Your people are dogs. But I still do not understand why you have come. You are one of those people; one of those dogs.'"

"I am not," Kerius replied. "I am above my people. I hate my people. I think they are a force for ill in the world; I think the Empire has acted pridefully. All the people who died during Archamenes' invasion... they deserved it."

The cataphract shouted something, and before the translator could speak, the Fharese warriors galloped forth and fell upon the Imperial soldiers with their scimitars. Kerius shut his eyes and crumpled to the floor. Screams, whinnying, and the sounds of slicing flesh echoed through the air.

When Kerius opened his eyes again, he noticed—in addition to himself—the translator was left alive. The Imperial soldiers and their hacked-off limbs lay strewn about the grass in bloody pools.

The scimitars' curved blades dripped with blood. Kerius felt cold, yet he realized the cataphract had left him alive. The Imperial soldiers were symbols of oppression. Perhaps this noble warrior understood. Yes, he understood.

The cataphract spoke again.

"He says, 'Did they deserve that?'"

Kerius answered, "Yes!" He could sense bloodlust in the cataphract. Fharas' hatred for the Imperial citizens was well deserved. "I hate the Empire!" Kerius continued. "Long live the King of Kings! May all our cities fall, and may our people die from his spears! Archamenes is rightly called God Manifest!"

The translator's own voice trembled as he relayed the message in Fharese.

The cataphract gave a loud belly laugh. He shouted something else.

"He says, 'You have proven to me what Fharas already knew. The Empire is weak. It is crumbling. You have proven to me the Imperials are the lowest of dogs, and you the lowest of the low. The Empire is in decline, and its people are cowards and not men.'"

Kerius gasped and stumbled backward to catch his breath.

The cataphract galloped forward and arrowed his spear through the translator's chest. Hot blood spattered Kerius' face. In a thick, barely-understandable Fharese accent, the cataphract spoke in the Imperial tongue: "Did he deserve that?"

"Yes!" Kerius shouted, overcome. "Yes! He deserved it too!"

The cataphract raised his visor. A wide grin was on his dark bearded face. He hopped off his horse. He stepped forward and kicked Kerius to the grass with a steel sabaton.

Kerius screamed. This was impossible. "The Empire deserves it, but I do not!" he shrieked. "I hate my countrymen. I hate my people! Don't you understand—?"

The cataphract thrust his spear into Kerius' chest; the steel head went through him like soft butter. Again and again, the Fharese warrior slammed the spear into his chest.

Kerius tried to scream but only gargled blood. *If hating my own people will not endear me to the Fharese, then what in the world can?*

As he took in his last blood-drowned gasps, the cataphract

spat on him, then mounted his horse and rode away. Like a piece of garbage he lay there, food for vultures.

CHAPTER THIRTY-TWO:
A BAD WIND

Regent Antonio Laureana

The fleet passed within sight of the island of Acronesis. Its steep cypress-covered mountains projected far above the gray sea. Antonio knew that to its southwest was Peregoth, birthplace of the Sea Kings and the Empire. Far away, many miles to the direct south, lay the city of Zoar and the surrounding client kingdom of Kheroe.

Around him, the winds had grown stronger, and—as he patrolled the deck—Antonio detected unease in the sailors' eyes. The sun had not shown its face all day, and the waves swelled bigger and bigger with each passing hour. The air grew chill, and a constant misty rain made everything colder.

Antonio gulped. He could no longer deny it. The regent—emperor in all but name—was afraid. He hurried across the deck of the war-galley and approached the captain, Florens.

"Signor Florens." Antonio tried to look tough. "I think we should perhaps winter in Tiverium." The main settlement of Acronesis was small compared to most cities of the Empire, but it had a good harbor and could probably provide for the men.

"Yes, yes, my lord," Florens answered. "A storm is coming." He raised his voice. "Head for Tiverium at once!" He gave the signal, and the other fleets turned south. Tiverium faced the Middle Sea, but it would be long before they could reach the safe harbor.

It seemed they had drawn no closer to the slopes of Acronesis when a wind of hurricane force ripped across the sea. The rain picked up. The ship lurched southeastward.

"We must ride it out!" Florens shouted over the howling wind. "We will let Lorenus take us where he will. Take shelter, Antonio. It will be a rough ride."

Below deck, Antonio's prize lay bound in lengths of chain. The ship careened and Antonio stumbled. She rolled, revealing her bare, welt-covered arms.

Such a beautiful face, he thought. Those dark eyes and the curves of her body would make her the desire of any man. Yet Antonio wasn't any man. He was a bad man. Like the widow spider, he liked to hurt his prey.

He stalked over to her. She cried out. The ship careened again, this time to the other side. Antonio stumbled and hit the wall.

The hurricane winds howled from above. *I will not survive this storm.*

CHAPTER THIRTY-THREE:
WRECK

Anthea Abantes

Antonio slammed his fists onto her shoulders, onto her arms, creating new welts, new bruises, new wellsprings of pain. "Filthy whore!" Antonio cussed. "Filthy as Issa's loins! That's what you get for poisoning the emperor."

You aren't the emperor. You aren't even a man. Anthea almost said it, but she had to act wisely. She curled up, ignoring the pain. She raised her head skyward as Antonio had his way with her. She prayed again to Hieronus, god of honor: *Let Claudio save me.*

It was no use. *If Antonio doesn't kill me, the storm will.*

The next morning, the pain paralyzed her. She tried to raise her finger but pain shot up through her arm, through her near-broken bones. She retched.

Standing up would kill her. The winds wailed all around her. She wondered whether it was morning or noon, or the middle of the night. She shut her eyes and drifted to sleep.

For three hellish days the winds continued. Three days of lying in the cold; three nights of Antonio's torture. Anthea decided on the second day that she wanted to die. She could not move. She could barely breathe without pain. Her only human contact was Antonio, whose only goal was her misery. He had succeeded.

Some time on the fourth day, a deafening crack rocked the ship. Anthea skidded across the wooden floor and struck her already-aching shoulder. She yelped. Then all was still; the waves beat the ship this way and that. They had run aground.

For an hour she lay there. The winds steadily died down, but the damage to the ship was done.

Eventually, Antonio appeared before her. She greeted him with neither a groan nor a whimper. She shut her eyes, and didn't cry out until he grabbed her and hauled her into his grip.

He carried her up the steps, and, for the first time in many days, the light of the sky reached her. The rain had died to a drizzle; the skies were somber and gray. But light! Light, at last! Despite the chill of the air, she was gone from the dank darkness below-deck and into the fresh air, into the bright, life-giving light.

Outside, beyond the split ship, lay a wilderness: rocks and tall, newly-green grass. Though the ground was still slick with rainwater, the storm clouds had begun to retreat.

The rush of the waves, for the moment, put Anthea at ease.

"Gods be damned!" Antonio's eyes widened; his face went red. "Where are we, Florens?"

The captain, a thin waif of a man, answered. "The wind has blown us many miles off course… southeastwards. Looks like we're somewhere in Kheroe, probably the east. But I do not know exactly where. I am not a Kheroan, after all."

The once sixty-strong crew had dwindled; apparently a few had fallen out of the ship in the midst of the storm. In the damp chill, Anthea surveyed the greenery and took in the wondrous scent of lavender and pines. She had never been to Kheroe. She had never been outside of Imperial City since she arrived there. Anthea's birthplace was Imperiopoli; her mother, a sacred concubine at the Temple of Issa, was unable to take care of her, neither financially or emotionally. At age seven, Anthea had gone with a troupe of Imperial officials; they had delivered her directly into the hands of the dark madam Lady Ciutta.

And now, here she was: soon to be food for the basilisks. Covered in welts, doomed to death and to hellfire soon after. As Antonio and the sailors left to find the other ships, Anthea prayed again: *Lord Hieronus, let Claudio save me.*

CHAPTER THIRTY-FOUR:
THE THRONE OF THE GOD

Claudio-Valens Adamantus, Grand Legate

Claudio thanked the gods that his men had left the lord of Sur alive. He could not speak the Imperial tongue, but he could speak the tongue of Fharas. One of Claudio's soldiers—the tribune Milo—had learned the language of the southrons, and Claudio spoke through him.

He said the lord of Sur was named Shen, and that Shen did not like the emperor Archamenes any more than Claudio did. Shen said that he had no choice but to serve the Fharese, and, in doing so, serve the treacherous satrap Faridún.

Claudio didn't believe a single one of Shen's words. But he ordered Shen to lead them via the best possible route to Seshán, and that—if Shen took them to the ancient city without quarreling—he would earn a share of the plunder.

Shen agreed.

For twenty days, they followed the River Khazan and the flourishing farmland that sprouted from either bank. There was a sizeable village every square mile. The temples were composed of columns and domes, built of red sandstone like the other public buildings. On the walls of these great temples, masons had carved faces with strange, primitive features and flaring tongues; or humans with the heads of animals.

It struck Claudio how well fortune had smiled on these people. In time beyond remembrance, they had settled into one of the richest farmlands in the world. And it struck Claudio, too, that the further south they went, the more out-of-place he felt. The Khazidees were not like the Imperials; their gods were strange to Claudio, and the people stared at the soldiers with dark, painted eyes.

Yet it was more than just the physical aspect. A feeling came over Claudio that he was truly marching to the edge of the world, to a land beyond northern knowledge. And indeed, he was. Only Tarchon the Mad had attempted to conquer Seshán; and he had failed.

Yet the flame in Claudio's heart would not extinguish until he had utterly subdued the King of Kings and brought his realm under Imperial rule.

At dusk of the nineteenth day, the river took a sudden turn east, where, if they followed it, they might someday reach its impossibly distant source. Once again Milo translated for the lord of Sur: "In another six leagues, past the land of the Rock Forts, are the fields of Gor Ilán."

"We will commence tomorrow," Claudio said. He needed to rest his bones, anyway. Imperium, Spirit of the Empire, had set a difficult task before him.

At dawn, they left the security of the river and went directly south. The Asa, on their multitude of horses, obviously tired of traveling so slowly. But Claudio would not leave his soldiers behind.

They marched through a yellowish land of natural rock pinnacles and wide canyons. With the advice of the man of Sur, they took the least-traveled road. Claudio had no doubt the main thoroughfare was heavily trafficked, and he wanted to minimize the risk of alerting Archamenes. Still, Claudio could not avoid the Fharese merchants that traveled along the road he chose, nor could he avoid the forts, carved from rock, which peered over the countryside; but he had no other option.

At dusk, the rocky land ended and—below a five-foot cliff face, a rolling yellow plain stretched into the horizon.

Thus they began their journey through the fields of Gor Ilán. On the night of the twenty-first day, the lord of Sur spoke to Claudio within the Grand Legate's tent.

"Great lord of the north." Milo translated for him. "Seshán lies just sixty miles to the south. There, on his throne, the King of Kings sits proudly. A crowd of worshipers live there, existing only to venerate him. But if you expect a city like the wonders of the north, you are mistaken. The city exists only to serve the Padisha Emperor, worshiping his name. I warn you… the magi have long predicted that if an unworthy man comes in sight of the King of Kings' throne, he will melt."

"Tell him that his superstitions mean nothing to me." Claudio looked into the lord of Sur's narrow eyes. "Tell him that I do not fear the King of Kings, and do not consider him a god."

When Milo explained Claudio's words to the lord of Sur, he paled. Perhaps none in the southern kingdoms had ever dared utter such words.

For three more days they passed through the open plains. Only impoverished mudbrick villages and small cattle-ranches broke the monotony. They had avoided the more populous parts of Gor Ilán—or more accurately, the lord of Sur avoided it at sword-point.

Thus it was late morning of the twenty-fourth day when they finally neared Seshán. At last they could no longer avoid the roads, nor could they avoid the merchant caravans and the small clusters of population that surrounded the city proper. Already Archamenes was doubtlessly alerted to their presence but despite the unease building in Claudio's heart, he would come upon the King of Kings with the fury of a storm.

A red colonnade lined the southbound road. Colossal statues of past kings towered above the soldiers as they passed by. Yellow grass sprung up in the few places that brick and stone did not cover.

Seshán seemed a collection of monuments rather than a real city, but people did pass through the roads: brown-garbed worshipers laying votive offerings before the statues of emperors; and magi in their purple silk robes. They all fled before Claudio.

It seemed a mountain appeared before them. But quickly Claudio realized it was not a natural formation; it was a series of steps, a ziggurat, leading up to an immense stone chair. The figure of Archamenes was barely distinguishable from his titanic throne.

At the sight of him, the lord of Sur whimpered.

Claudio drew his sword. "He is undefended. It seems strange for someone called God Manifest."

Milo, standing behind him, grunted agreement. "Perhaps they do not believe any man would dare to touch him. The people of Fharas are enslaved by the fear of him; they are fed his lies from birth through adulthood. To speak against their god is sacrilege."

"I will face this 'god' myself," Claudio said, and began climbing the steps.

The throne was a half-pyramid, with small steps leading up to a great height and then abruptly dropping off. On the stone chair was Archamenes himself. His long gold neck-brace might give him the appearance of might and godliness in his own culture, but anywhere else would make him look strange. Jeweled bracelets covered his arms; gold anklets ran the length of his legs. Dark blue eye-shadow and bright red lips might indicate his status in Fharas, but it only made him look womanly in Claudio's view.

"You are not a god," Claudio said. He looked deep into Archamenes' brown eyes and saw, behind the façade, a mortal who knew the statement was true.

"*Adiwan!*" Blasphemy. The shouting of the word could not mask Archamenes' trembling voice. In a heavy accent he spoke the Imperial tongue. "I am Archamenes Well-Born, Beloved-Of-My-Father. My father was also God Manifest but he has now ascended to heaven; and yet I will be greater than him. On the day of my birth, the magi saw a brilliant star and foretold my destiny: to destroy the arrogant Northern Empire. Do not insult the God Manifest, barbarian."

Claudio struck him across the jaw. Archamenes cried out; such an act was unthinkable among his own people. Touching him, even ascending the throne steps, was so incomprehensible that Archamenes did not employ a bodyguard.

"*Adiwan! Adiwan!*" Archamenes cried again. He sobbed in pain and slumped further into his stone chair. "I hold your life in my hands. If I clench my fist, I can snuff out your life… I can control the storms and summon cyclones, and bring on the night."

Claudio spat on him.

"*Adiwan!*" Archamenes' eyes lighted with anger. He tried to stand up but Claudio forced him back into his seat.

"Don't move again," Claudio growled, "or I will kill you."

"You cannot kill me." Archamenes bared his teeth. "I am the God Manifest, Beloved-of-My-Father, Well-Born, the Good…"

Claudio struck him, and kneed him in the groin.

Archamenes' voice turned to a low sob. "*Adiwan…*"

Claudio grabbed Archamenes and hurled him from the throne. "So ends the reign of the God Manifest!" he shouted as Archamenes fell down the stone steps. "I will parade you through the streets of Imperial City. Your people will know forevermore what happens to my enemies."

"*Adiwan.*" Archamenes choked on his words. He had curled up in pain, lying upon the stone steps. "*Adiwan!*" he cried again.

When Claudio forced Archamenes into the ranks of the Imperial army, the soldiers jeered.

"That's what you get!" snarled one.

"If I'm not mistaken, Claudio just captured a bloody *god*," laughed another.

Milo pushed through the ranks of soldiers and smiled. "Looks like you got the big catch."

Claudio pushed Archamenes down. The "God Manifest" tripped over the bricks and fell on his face.

"And, though he claims to be a god, he will be treated worse than any of my soldiers." Claudio smiled. "He calls himself a god, but he is the lowest of worms." Claudio looked to the north. "Bind him. We need to start our journey quickly. The plains of Gor Ilán await us, and it is a long way to Haroon."

CHAPTER THIRTY-FIVE:
DRUMS OF WAR

Regent Antonio Laureana

After combing through the surrounding coastline, they found several of the ships and many legionaries on shore. The rough landing would not deter Antonio. They would march to Haroon, bring Claudio back to Imperial City in chains, and feed Anthea to the basilisks on the way there. Yet even Antonio, not a cartographer by any stretch of the imagination, knew that the green land of Kheroe was separated from Haroon and the Khazan River Valley by a wide desert. He would ask the locals what to do. Though the desert was inhospitable, men lived within the dry expanse: men with dark pasts, hiding from the law; the wild desert nomads; and religious fanatics enduring unnecessary suffering for the sake of their god.

First, of course, he had to find out where in damnation they were. Kheroe was a very large swath of land—at least a hundred miles from west to east, if not more.

The legate Nicator—a broad-shouldered hulk of a man—approached Antonio. "Commander! We left with a force of fifteen thousand; I fear many have perished in the storm, or wrecked elsewhere. The coast of Kheroe is treacherous…"

"How many do we have?" Antonio ground his teeth together to avoid striking Nicator. "Or more pertinently, how many have you lost?"

"I would guess we have eight thousand with us." Nicator frowned. "Perhaps we should turn back."

Pressure built in Antonio's chest. He grabbed Nicator by the shoulders. "*No,*" he snarled. "That little cur, Claudio, must be taught a lesson. And by the gods, if you do not come with me, Nicator, I will have you drawn and quartered."

"I live to serve my commander," Nicator said. "I will do as you say."

"That's right you will." Antonio shoved him back, and he almost fell over. "Now we must find out where in Hell we are, and march for Haroon."

A few hours later, a high-ranking tribune named Adelfo returned from a journey of reconnaissance. "My lord," he said, "We are near a small city called Hadash… it's about five miles to the east. The bel of Hadash says he welcomes you and is honored to have the Commander of the Empire in his territory—"

"Cut it," Antonio snarled. "I do not care about these petty low-lives. Kings of mudbrick palaces! Small fish in small ponds! I don't even know where the hell Hadash is."

"It is about forty miles from the desert," Adelfo explained. "From the border, it will take about ten days—"

"Quiet." Antonio glared at him. "Go tell this pathetic 'bel' I do not care if I am welcome. Tell him I require guides across the desert, and if he does not provide them, I will raze Hadash to the ground."

Adelfo nodded. "I will do so, commander."

Antonio sneered as he walked into the distance. Kheroe was what the Empire called a "client kingdom," meaning "a province in all but name." Magon of the Rabah clan—supposed king of Kheroe— was nothing more than a pawn in the Empire's hands. There was talk among the Imperial Council of restoring power to Magon, of gradually easing away the Empire's control of their lands. This angered some members of the populace, but Antonio didn't care one way or the other. He just wanted this Claudio tortured and butchered. No one disrespected Antonio and lived to tell about it. No one.

It was dusk when the tribune Adelfo returned. "Commander,

the bel of Hadash says he will gladly provide guides, and that he will have them to you by dawn tomorrow."

"As expected." Antonio glared at Adelfo. "Everyone with a lick of wisdom will obey me."

"He says he has offered a white bull in your name, and he has prayed that Sagar, god of war, will lead you to victory."

"Flattery doesn't work on me. Hell, I wish I could burn Hadash, and take them all as slaves. But even *I* wouldn't get away with that."

Sure enough, at dawn, a group of a hundred men on camels arrived. Some of the beasts of burden were heavy-laden with packs of food and water. Antonio's stomach turned at the thought of what these Kheroans ate.

"My lord emperor," said a man riding at the front, dressed in loose white clothing, "we will show you across the desert. It is a divine honor to help the commander of a great nation."

A nation that controls your lands. Antonio managed not to voice the thought. "Carry on then. We must hurry to Haroon."

Winter had come, and the army marched through darkness, rain and wind. They traveled past many villages; the fields of wheat and barley, the rows of millet, went on without end. Within the villages, the Kheroans had erected statues: stone effigies of animal-headed deities; gods with primitive faces and long, forked tongues; and grotesque mother-goddesses with multiple breasts—surprisingly to Antonio, something he did not want to see.

The greenness faded gradually; the trees spread out, then gave way to tiny shrubs. By the third day since Hadash, the grass vanished and turned to cracked yellow earth. The winter rains stopped, and at last the sky was clear and blue.

They traveled from watering-hole to watering-hole for twelve days. A coalition of regional officials had provided them with dry road-bread and salted pork—no lizards or cuttlefish, as Antonio made abundantly clear.

The meager fare they did have was not fit for a king's halls, or a regent's. Hunger was omnipresent through the difficult journey; but he had to ration out the food carefully, or they would starve, miles from nowhere. No Imperial road ran from Kheroe to Khazidea; in winter, a hellish trek was the only option.

But finally, the wheat and crops of Khazidea appeared, growing in lush fields along the heavily-irrigated earth. Lifeblood of the Empire, and now under the control of that insolent cur Claudio.

It was noon when they reached a village. The uneducated, illiterate farmers did not know a word of Imperial. But there were Khazidees serving in the legion, and they translated the gibbering words.

From the farmers he learned that Claudio had gone south into Fharas. Claudio intended to conquer the holy city of Seshán. The Imperial Council would go mad at the news. He could hear them now: "What a breach of etiquette!" "What a betrayal of our trust!" "Who does he think he is?"

At the same time, Antonio couldn't help a stab of envy. Taking on such an impossible task—a goal that only some crazy Eloesian king in ancient history had attempted! That took manliness, and a confidence that Antonio did not have.

It was also good news. Claudio had certainly died. Yet even that good news had its bad side. Antonio wanted honors for killing Claudio. He wanted more than anything to wring that Claudio boy's neck and beat him with a rock until every bone in his body was broken.

He now had time to think. He wasn't sure he would free Haroon. Now the Khazan River Valley was a conquered kingdom, and Antonio could claim the victory as his own. He could become Antonio the Conqueror, beloved of the people, and march through the streets of Imperial City in a grand triumph. And if anyone ever claimed that Claudio had done it—the truth—then that person would be imprisoned, or worse.

Antonio then caught sight of his captive, Anthea Abantes—bound, now, in chains—and remembered his plans. He would feed the Eloesian slave to the basilisks, and he would watch the whole ordeal with a smile on his face.

CHAPTER THIRTY-SIX:
A PRAYER

Anthea Abantes

"Please, Lord Hieronus," she whispered, "let your servant Claudio save me."

CHAPTER THIRTY-SEVEN:
SACRILEGE

Claudio-Valens Adamantus, Grand Legate

The eleven thousand-strong force hurried through the plains of Gor Ilán. The Asa were eager for war. Chieftain Nued grumbled at the lack of bloodshed, at the slow pace of the footmen compared to his horses. But slowly, in his scouts' reports, it became clear that the Lords of Fharas were preparing to strike.

The capture of Archamenes no doubt sent waves of anger through the land; anger, yes, and perhaps a bit of fear. Their god and king—whom the magi declared invincible—had been proved mortal.

Still, the scouts' reports showed that lords throughout Fharas were calling upon their vassals, gathering armies of cataphracts, and that the magi of the Fire Temple were joining the effort. Apparently, the satrap of some city called "Taifun" also summoned a force.

They were only fifteen miles from the land of the Rock Forts when news arrived. An army of three-thousand cataphracts and twenty-five magi were at their heels. The magi—according to the scouts—were veterans, the best of the best, who wielded fire like extensions of their bodies.

The sun began to set. A horn pealed.

Nued looked at Claudio, his eyes gleaming with war-lust; he gibbered something, and Wife-of-Nued translated, speaking in the Eloesian tongue: "War-Chief of Asa came for *war!* We came to serve Claudio, god of war, and to plunder. We have heard… enemy is near. We must *fight!*"

Claudio nodded and jerked Borak completely around. He swept his sword out of its sheath. He could not turn back now; he commanded a host of incredible size. He could not be a coward, like so many of his countrymen. He ordered the legions to turn around.

He sallied forth, riding up and down the vanguard. The soldiers waited there tensely, at full alert. The ten surviving augurs stood in the center.

"Tonight we fight Fharas!" Claudio shouted in the loudest voice he could manage. "We have deposed the haughty King of Kings and removed him from his prideful throne! Now his servile flatterers come to claim him. They are at our heels! They will not prevail. Tonight, we fight for liberty, for empire, for the god Imperium and for our homeland! Let the southrons fear our country's name forever!"

The army's deafening cheers reminded Claudio of the Imperial Arena back home.

They waited, and within an hour, their enemy revealed itself. Despite the obvious inferior number, the sight of the three-thousand cataphracts—completely covered in steel plates and mail, and bearing scimitars—sent a shiver through Claudio. Riding on white horses were magi: black-bearded men in decorative purple robes and holding shepherd's crooks. Little was known about the magi in the Empire, but Claudio heard that—in addition to wielding magical power—they served the fire-god Athra and kept his sacred knowledge in their mountain enclave.

One magus—perhaps the chief among them—extended a hand, and in his palm flame began to grow, at first just a flicker but growing fast.

"*Ehu!*" Claudio called out in the Asa tongue. Charge. The nomad horsemen thundered forward, white clothing gleaming in the fading sunlight. In a series of volleys, they shot their bows. A hail of arrows struck the Fharese host. One pierced a magus in the chest. The rain of death stuck the cataphracts like pincushions, but the heavy armor was difficult to pierce.

"Javelins!" Claudio cried in the Imperial tongue.

In unison, the legionaries readied them. The cataphracts charged the Asa, and a magus scorched a legionary with white fire-lance.

"Launch!" Claudio's voice trailed off, but his soldiers obeyed the command immediately.

Two javelins struck home, sinking easily through the magi's purple robes. More fire-bolts, sent like darts from the magi's hands, exploded in the front lines, killing dozens.

"Charge!" Claudio roared, and on Borak he resolved to fight like a hero, like the ancient King Peregothius, who had led all his charges. He plunged forth at the head of the lines as fire consumed his men left and right. Huge balls of flame exploded, scorching the grass, devouring men and leaving blackened skeletons. Some of the magi immolated their enemies, turning soldiers into pillars of fire. But they could not match the fire within Claudio that burned against them.

Borak galloped swiftly. Claudio reached a magus and slashed in a hard cross-cut as he rode by, lopping off the fire-wielder's head. As the legion ran for them, the magi worked their powers of fire with even greater fervor. It was like the gates of Hell had opened up: great columns of fire scorching the earth, balls of flame melting soldiers' armor and consuming their flesh; but the Asa had drawn out the cataphracts, and without their protection, the magi's fire-storm ended as the legionaries cut them down one-by-one.

When at last the roar of the flame stopped, a new thundering sound took its place. The cataphracts—exhausted from chasing the swift Asa—had turned around, and now barreled toward the weary Imperial legion.

How many had died from the magi's fire? Claudio could only guess. The augurs had done their best to divert the flame with their powers of wind.

The Fharese charge reached them before Claudio could ponder the mystery. The legionaries, already thinned from the magi's fire, faltered and fell back. The cataphracts had drawn their lances, and drove deep into the front lines. After the throttling impact, they dropped the bulky weapons and swept out scimitars, hacking down with the curved blades as their horses reared up. Eyes wide with heathen zeal, they slashed open many men.

As Claudio prepared to charge, a loud shouting echoed across the battlefield. Even in the dim illumination, he could see Archamenes' flailing form. He was calling for help.

The Asa came thundering back, and unleashed a volley of arrows. Several Fharese fell from their horses. Claudio galloped ahead. "Charge! Charge! Kill them all!"

The Fharese were now surrounded. One of them drew a horn to his lips and blew. A peal echoed across the battlefield. He blew it again. He was calling for help.

"Press them hard!" Claudio roared. "Kill their horses!"

They set upon their task. Horse and man alike fell before the Imperials' spears and the Asa's ceaseless volley.

The Imperial military considered killing horses dishonorable. Even in rebellions and skirmishes with the barbarians beyond the Wall, legates rarely employed it. But these men, and the horses they rode, were different creatures altogether than the people of the north; they worshipped strange gods, oppressed their own people, and throughout the Empire's history had killed many hundreds of thousands of citizens, all for the sake of their King of Kings.

Within the hour, the Fharese fell to the spears and swords of the soldiers. Not a single man of the three thousand was left alive.

"No mercy to those who give none!" Claudio shouted, and—astride Borak—surveyed the thousands of Fharese and their horses piled on one another.

Some men, still in their death-throes, lay there shaking and spitting blood. Others with hewn limbs lay there with glazed eyes, groaning in agony.

"Finish them off," Claudio said. It was more for the dying's sake than his. But the soldiers had no chance to obey his command before they were interrupted.

Lights had appeared at the peak of one of Gor Ilán's gently-sloping hills. Torches, illuminating men with bows and arrows. Men of Sur, judging by their amber complexions and the dragon embroidery on their leather gear. More tellingly, a few had whips clipped to their belts, but these were not spiked whips meant for war. They were meant for punishing slaves.

Claudio had no idea how numerous these reinforcements were. But as both sides stood there, waiting, one of the slavers shouted something in the tongue of Sur; the force wheeled their horses around and galloped away.

"*Ehu!*" Claudio barked at the Asa. He rode with them.

Borak carried him swiftly across the plains of Gor Ilán; and the thundering of hooves against grass echoed for over an hour. Surprisingly, the horses of the Sur-men—lacking the bulky steel armor of the cataphracts—held up against the Asa's relentless pursuit.

It was late when the Sur-men slowed. They reached a gathering of tents, and there—massed between them, bound in iron shackles—were thousands and thousands of slaves.

The Asa unleashed a volley of arrows. Claudio turned to Wife-of-Nued and shouted, "Tell them not to kill the slaves!"

She barked the words to her husband. Nued growled and glared at her, as if disappointed, and then he shouted the orders at the top of his voice.

One by one, Sur-man by Sur-man, the opposing force dwindled to nothing, falling off their horses and dropping torches onto the yellow grass. Eventually all was silent, except for the groans of the dying and the trembling voices of the slaves.

"Who are you?" one shouted in the Eloesian tongue.

These slaves were from Eloesus. "Claudio-Valens, Grand Legate," he answered. "Where are you from?"

"Imperiopoli!" a woman shouted in reply.

Claudio nodded grimly. After Archamenes' sack of the city, this group had been sold as slaves. Who knows where the men of Sur would have taken them? To slave markets in the South Seas? To some sweltering jungle? "You are free," he said. "Come with me."

From the slavers' coffers Claudio confiscated several chests worth of gold, a few silver dragon idols and a handful of ruby amulets. If the slavers meant to take the Imperiopolans to Sur, it would be another several weeks of journeying. The southlands were vast, and Seshán—far though it was from the Empire—was only the northernmost tip.

The journey that took an hour on horses took much longer on foot, thanks to the Imperiopolans' slow walk. The sun's rays were just beginning to spread over the plains when they reached the Imperial soldiers—and there, in the light of new day—Claudio comprehended the carnage.

The bodies of the three-thousand Fharese had been gathered in many piles and now charred on an open flame. Imperial citizens traditionally bury their dead—with the exception of the emperors—but in Fharas, fire was sacred. If the soldiers intended to disrespect the corpses, they made a cultural error. If, in fact, they meant to accord them honor in the Fharese way, they succeeded; and good for them.

The carnage was not limited to the Fharese—not by any means. The charred corpses of soldiers, devoured by the magi's flames, lay there in greater number than the enemy. Thousands upon thousands of soldiers had perished, their armor melted from the searing flames. Claudio would have to do a count of his soldiers, but he had underestimated the power of the fire-storm; he guessed half of his men had gone to see the gods.

The Asa had fared better. Only a few of their number had passed on.

Claudio looked back at the bodies of his troops. A weight fell over him; a weight for the wives and children of these brave soldiers, of their lives suddenly taken from them. They had succeeded; Claudio had succeeded. Archamenes, King of Kings, the self-proclaimed God Manifest, was now bound in chains and en route to Imperial City. The lord, now without title, no longer sat on his mountainous throne. The Empire had been avenged; and Archamenes had answered to Imperium. But was it worth all these lives? For a second, Claudio wondered.

He rode up to his troops on Borak. "We will bury these men!" he shouted. "It is a shame their resting-places are in a foreign land. But perhaps they will be a testament to our mission, lying underneath the Plain of Gor Ilán."

They set to work at once, digging vast holes where they could bury the brave soldiers. Together, they said a prayer. Then, in mid-morning, they departed and began the journey north.

They crossed the yellowish land of the Rock Forts, this time riding openly down the main road. It was wide, and crammed with Fharese merchants. Claudio would not restrain their trade, although he could see Chieftain Nued eyeing the rolls of silk and canisters of spice. Several times, Archamenes cried out for help; each time, his attendant beat him, and eventually, even the proud King of Kings learned his lesson.

Now, in the full light of the sun, Claudio could tell only three thousand of his troops survived the magi. He was at half-strength, not counting the Asa; and who knew if they, with their strange customs and beliefs, could be trusted? Gods knew, there were cowards and traitors among his own countrymen that would take advantage of his weakness, exchange his gains for treachery and capitulation. He had disobeyed the orders of the Imperial Council. He had gone against the wisdom of the elite for the sake of his people, for the sake of his homeland. There would never be any shortage of traitors in the

Empire.

But as the sun faded, they came within sight of the River Khazan, snaking across the desert and bringing life and greenery wherever it flowed. Before darkness fell, they reached the land of Khazidea, the queer home of a strange people.

Along the river, through the fertile fields, wound a hard-packed dirt road. It was dark, and the night chill had settled in, when a young Khazidee came running for them, flailing his arms. *"Bel 'ai, bel 'ai!"* he cried. *Milord, milord!*

Claudio, riding at the vanguard, called out in a loud voice: "What is it?"

A Khazidee within Claudio's ranks translated the boy's reply: "An Imperial lord has left his army by itself, intending to sacrifice a girl to the basilisks. In his absence, the army has looted and killed and raped. They defiled the Temple of Great Sagar and stole the Holy Candlestick. Some of them even raped the sacred concubines of the goddess Issa—they must choose the ones they take in holy union. The soldiers have committed a great sacrilege. Please help us, *bel 'ai*."

Claudio shouted his reply. "I will help you! The Empire has always ruled its subjects with respect."

Once Claudio words were translated, the Khazidee smiled. He bowed low, then fell prostrate.

Claudio got the uncomfortable feeling that it was an act of worship. "Stand up, signore," he demanded. "I will do what I can."

But there were more pressing matters, first.

CHAPTER THIRTY-EIGHT: VENOM FLATS

Anthea Abantes

There they were, larger than any lizards she had ever seen. Larger than the crocodiles of the Khazan River. Skin so smooth that it was difficult to notice the scales. Dark green skin—such a dark green it looked black—with bright yellow patterns that indicated to Anthea its incredibly potent venom. Basilisks, clustered around bright green pools… denizens of a salt flat.

Perhaps she deserved this; she had killed many men. Women, too. But even in the face of this, all she could think about was her dry throat, how she would give anything for water, to gulp it down and bathe herself in its moisture. Water, lifeblood of mankind.

A basilisk looked up and hissed; its forked tongue shot from its snout and retreated. The beast's eyes were yellow, like a crocodile's except brighter; there was no soul in them, no compassion or warmth. Anthea would say she saw cold, animalistic hunger in those eyes, but that was untrue; beyond coldness, the basilisk's eyes reflected malevolence—a desire to kill even beyond necessity.

But all she could think about was thirst; as the basilisk took cautious steps toward them—as Antonio restrained her—she dreamed of waterfalls and rivers, of verdant desert oases.

A low hissing sound emitted from the basilisk's snout. In the distance, other basilisks crept cautiously up to the new specimens. Antonio had come here himself, just to watch her die. His bodyguard and the packs of water—water, precious water, which she had not been allowed to drink—were beyond reach of the reptiles, beyond reach of these cold killers.

As the basilisk approached, looking imperious with its yellow crest, a whimper escaped Antonio. The weakness broke something loose in Anthea: pent-up feelings she had not dared express. Anger at her bruises, anger at the insults, anger at his horrible treatment. She let out a wild shriek and—for the first time—struggled against Antonio.

She underestimated the strength of his iron thews, grown strong from his many fights and his frequent conditioning. He was like a statue; but Anthea determined to fight harder. She had taken his abuse for so long, and now, if she died, she would die trying to kill him, to make him face even a small portion of what he had given her. The man had forced himself upon her, entered her without her consent, beaten her savagely, and now—now!—she would fight him with everything she had in her.

She underestimated Antonio, yes; he was strong beyond any man she knew. But she used her intellect against him, kicking a foot beyond his calf and launching her entire weight onto him. Even he, an athlete, could not prevent the fall.

With a grunt, Antonio hit the white salt of the pan. "*Lupa!*" he hissed.

He had called her worse.

He flipped her around, digging his hands into her shoulders, brown eyes blazing with incalculable rage. The basilisk was almost upon her. Then, a noise so faint it was hardly perceptible; a puncturing of flesh.

Antonio let out a hoarse gasp. Anthea savored the terror in his eyes, the subtle trembling of his lip as the poison coursed through his veins.

"Thank the gods for you, basilisk!" Anthea gasped. "Look at you, Antonio! You failed! You failed!"

But judging by his shut eyes and convulsing body, he was near dead.

She ran all the way back to the horses and the dozen bodyguards. Rough men, they were; soldiers of fortune, living only for their daily pay. Not as rough as Anthea's former clients—not as smelly, as deformed as them—but much tougher. She was utterly at their mercy. Anthea was an assassin, and a successful one; but her ways were subtle, and she wielded poison and a beautiful countenance as her weapons, not the sword.

She fell to her knees and clasped her hands. "Good soldiers of the Empire," she begged, "your lord has died. I am a wretch. Please have mercy on a poor, pitiful girl. I am a bad girl, in truth, but have mercy on me. Don't kill me, I beg of you."

Their faces were set in stone, unchanging; Anthea searched their eyes and found no pity in them. One scratched his bulbous nose. Another spat on the sparkling salt-pan.

"We got to kill her," said one, whose face was heavily scarred. "Legate's orders, even if he is dead."

Anthea backed away, wondered why in gods' names she had not run into the desert. After a life in the west side, why had she made the ultimate error—trusting in the goodness of mankind?

The soldier with the bulbous nose yanked a sharp steel dagger out of its sheath. "Such a pretty one. Too bad she's got to die."

"Wait." The shortest of the soldiers put a restraining hand on his comrade. "She *is* pretty. We got no commander anymore. She could go for a few thousand gold pieces. Gods know, those southrons are randy folk, and they like northern women the best of all."

"Good point," said Bulbous Nose. "We should sell her."

The other soldiers murmured agreement.

They had no honor. And now, it would be as they wished: she would serve as the mistress of some strange man of Sur, or worse— gods help her!—some tyrannical lord of Fharas who treats women as chattel. The thoughts sent waves of revulsion through her. To be a slave in the Empire was one thing; she would serve her years in the land she knew and loved. But to be sold into the impossibly-distant slave markets of the south, in a foreign nation where she could not speak the language, to a master with character yet undetermined. Escaping the basilisks had thrust her out of the cookpot and into the smoldering coals. She chafed at the thought, and fell sick.

CHAPTER THIRTY-NINE: MARAUDERS

Claudio-Valens Adamantus, Grand Legate

The sun dawned, and the rosy sky illuminated a pastoral scene: the river Khazan, swiftly gushing across the dry landscape; fields upon fields of wheat and chickpeas; cattle ranches; and, in the distance, a village. Yet despite the pastoral aspect, it was alien to Claudio: crocodiles coasted the waters, and the mudbrick houses were not as beautiful as the red-roofed houses and villas back home.

Home. The thought of it… the thought of the large northern horses chewing grass in the open pastures. The thought of his mother Catalina, kind-hearted and loving, probably missing him like never before. Here he was, thousands of miles away, and—for once—homesick.

Yet it was only a passing feeling. The army had pitched tents a hundred yards from the river. Like always he had awoken at dawn, but even at this early hour someone was approaching him: a soldier, judging by his standard-issue armor, sword, and spear. But Claudio did not recognize him.

"Signor Claudio." The soldier bowed slightly, then looked up at him to reveal a swarthy face and unruly black hair sticking out of his helmet. "I am honored to meet you."

"Speak your mind," Claudio told him.

"I come to bear news that Antonio is dead. He was once my commander. I hope you can forgive that misdeed."

"It is forgiven," Claudio said.

"I believe a soldier without a legate is like a beast without its head. I pledge myself to your service, if you will have me—"

"I will."

"—and there is something else."

"What is it?"

"I don't know if serving in Antonio's legion has poisoned their character, for Antonio is surely a bad man!" the soldier said. "But my comrades have broken into small groups… they've been robbing temples, raping the women, defiling the holy places!"

Only then did it dawn on Claudio that this man was a Khazidee. True, people from the south served in the legions. Sometimes, the Empire used auxiliaries: archers, light cavalry, and the prized Fingers of Barukh. But many—and likely, this man—were deserters from their own country. Khazidea, unlike the Empire, had an extremely rigid social structure that was all but impossible to climb.

At the top was the satrap—Faridún, before he died—and the brother-sister royalty. From what Claudio understood, the second tier included the minor lords (*bels*) and the priests, each of whom owned a swath of land. If you were not a satrap, royalty, or a minor noble—and the vast majority were not—you were abjectly poor, and did not even own the wheat and cattle you farmed. The people owned no weapons, and therefore could not rise up against their oppressors. Besides, they lived in such fear that "rebellion" was never spoken of.

Yet obviously this Khazidean legionary still had respect for his old gods, and was sufficiently disturbed by the soldiers' desecration to defect to Claudio's side.

It was admirable.

"Do you know Khazidea well?" Claudio asked.

The legionary nodded. "Like the back of my hand."

"Then you will be my guide. We will go from city to city, and purge the province of these evildoers."

The legionary—Barca, by name, though he had taken on the name Juliano when he escaped to the Empire—led them to the first village. The most impressive edifice was a temple of sandstone pillars and pointed arches; this, Barca explained, was a temple of Issa. One could tell, he said, because of the frieze along the roof, which depicted her symbols: white tigers and golden crescent moons.

Without further ado, Claudio entered the vestibule. There, two dozen girls—some barely middle teens—stood there, covering themselves modestly with blankets. Nearby, a group of five Imperial soldiers were busy fixing their breeches; their tousled hair and discarded helmets proved what they had done.

"By the authority of Imperium," Claudio boomed, and the soldiers turned in fear, "I sentence you to die. The Empire conquers, but it governs with respect, affording each subject people the right to practice their religion and culture. We are first among equals, and you five have abandoned this principle."

"C-Claudio?" one of the soldiers stammered. "I am a *citizen*… I have rights! You c-can't just kill us. That's illegal…"

"Unfortunately, he is correct." Claudio frowned. "You will stand trial in whichever province you reside. Until then, lay down your arms; you are my captives."

The soldiers removed their swords from their belts and threw their spears on the ground. Claudio's men bound them with rope and led them away.

Barca approached the temple concubines. "Oh, you poor girls… they did not understand, they did not care, that you alone can choose to enter holy union. They forced themselves upon you, defiled Issa's chosen daughters…"

"What is one of our own people doing in Imperial dress?" one of the girls ventured to say, speaking through the lens of a heavy Khazidean accent.

Barca looked down; perhaps he had no answer. "Purify yourselves, girls… then again embark on the task the goddess has given you."

Claudio said nothing. The idea of this supposedly Heaven-ordained prostitution sickened him, and the thought of the diseases these pitiful girls might be exposed to racked him with chills; but it was not the Empire's way to change the customs of a newly-annexed province. These poor girls—pious, perhaps, but enslaved to this sickening tradition—would go on doing as they wished. It was none of Claudio's business how they earned their daily bread.

From village to village, Barca led Claudio and his army. The Imperial soldiers, being citizens, could not be killed indiscriminately and required a fair trial. Claudio disarmed them all.

One night, halfway through the northward journey, they camped beside the river. Wife-of-Nued approached Claudio in his grand tent. "My lord," she said, and bowed deeply.

"What is it?" Claudio said.

"My husband says you are still a god… but he has changed his mind on one thing. You are not god of war, like we thought. You do not kill your enemies. You are womanly and take them captive. He says you are god of women and feminine mysteries, and of cycles of life. We will serve you no longer. We leave tonight. Horsemen are already gathered. Goodbye."

Claudio flew to his feet and reached for his sword; he grasped air, for he was dressed for bed and his sheath was halfway across the tent. Through clenched teeth, he growled in the Eloesian tongue: "You and your people will face the full extent of my wrath when I am crowned emperor."

Only then, after the words were spoken, did he realize his goal all along: not just to restore the Empire's glory, but also to sit upon the White Throne.

He continued with the thought. "Your taxes will be onerous. You will serve as full soldiers, but I will treat you as less than citizens. I will evict you from your homeland…"

"You lie," Wife-of-Nued said. "No one can defeat us… Conquering Asa answer to no one except gods of war." And she departed.

Blood boiling, Claudio thought of harming her, but he held back. Starting a skirmish with these powerful warriors might spell the end of his already thinned-out legion. Instead, he struck the tent and growled to himself, cursing these proud nomads. "I'm keeping Borak!" he shouted after her.

And indeed they left Borak to him. Riding on the swift horse, they continued through Khazidea for a matter of weeks, securing control over the various villages and towns. It was more difficult without the fierce Asa, and with Wife-of-Nued's caustic insults hanging over his head. But at last, by the middle of Candlebright—the first true month of winter—the sandstone walls of Haroon lay before them. Justice had been done; the people of Khazidea were free to practice their customs as they wished, and the once-proud King of Kings lay bound in chains, treated like the lowest of slaves. Antonio's soldiers were in captivity, their weapons discarded.

Haroon drew nigh.

The gatekeepers had no choice but to let them in. Here, they would spend the solstice: Yule, a cheery festival in the otherwise gloomy season of winter; but Claudio did not know whether the Khazideans observed it. One thing he did know: with the month of Freezedeep approaching, New Years was on the horizon, and this year marked the millennial celebration of the Empire's founding. Every town and city across the provinces would celebrate; it was the thousandth Year of the Empire. Raucous celebration would fill the streets from Imperial City to Thénai, from Ten Cities to far-flung Brilium. Priests would ask the gods for another thousand years of prosperity and benevolent rule. The Pontifex would speak on the honor and justness of the Empire from his seat in Sanctum. It would be a New Years to remember.

But for now, he had more pressing things to worry about. The mid-afternoon sun beat warmly upon them as they entered the city of Haroon. Its red sandstone edifices dominated their vision. As they passed through the gates, the dry, burning heat of the sun continued; the light that guided the day was not kind to Khazidea, and even in winter, it scorched the populace. The moderating effects of the Imperial Sea seemed absent to Claudio; the capital did not feel any cooler than further inland.

Yet the sight of civilization—as foreign as it was, as unknown and unwholesome—filled Claudio with relief. Inward they marched, through the packed-dirt main thoroughfare. If Claudio had any say in matters, the Empire would pave its streets as a gift to the new provincials.

Forming a massive line, with Claudio at the vanguard—riding on Borak—the soldiers marched past temples to Issa, patron goddess of the Khazidees, and those of her lover Atman; Athra, god of fire favored by the magi; Sagar, god of war; and countless shrines to other divinities that Claudio did not recognize.

At last they came to the city square, one of the few paved parts of Haroon. The Royal Palace loomed over it. As the soldiers marched in, the people in the square scattered.

Strange, Claudio thought; but soon he realized that a slave auction of some kind had been underway, and that Imperial soldiers, not Khazidees, were the ones running away.

A man of Sur was the lone straggler; perhaps he had made a bid. Yet on the platform next to him, the "commodity" lay untouched: a young woman in her late teens or early twenties stood there, bound in iron shackles. The bruises that covered her, the weak gaze of her eyes and the trembling of her arms, failed to mask her incredible beauty. Long, dark brown hair, and chestnut eyes; a perfectly-curved body, and a kind face that seemed a fit model for any artist.

For once, in the many weeks since Astarthe's dark spell, Claudio—conqueror of Fharas, friend of the Asa nomads, capturer of the King of Kings—felt utterly undone by this slave, unworthy of her presence.

Nervous.

In battle he had led the charge against the magi; he had penetrated deep into enemy territory without turning back. Now, he lacked the courage to even meet the slave's glance. Yet he did find the courage to shout, "Free her!"

And a group of soldiers, perhaps less intimidated by this woman's beauty, hurried up to the platform and—not without a struggle—undid her chains. As Claudio watched, she half-ran, half-stumbled over to him; with each step his gut clenched.

And when she finally reached him, looming above her on Borak, she fell face-first before him—prostrate—and shouted, "I commend myself utterly into your service! It will be my honor to become your slave."

"Up! Stand up!" Claudio's voice cracked. "I am not a southern despot. I am not the King of Kings. Stand up… if you must bow, bow only slightly. If you must show respect, show only a little."

She stood up, and her slowness in completing the deed indicated reluctance. "You are Claudio… I met you in the Imperial Palace. I will die happy if you take me as your slave. You, alone, out of all the men in the Empire, are good and kind."

It all came flashing back to Claudio: the beautiful girl in southron costume, the—in her own words—whore from the west side. She was a prostitute, a *lupa*, yet Claudio would not hold it against her. "You will not be my slave!" he said. "But you may stay in my entourage. I will house you for the winter here, and you may stay with me as long as you wish."

"Thank you, thank you." She repeated the gibbering words many times, as if supplicating some foreign god. Judging by the desperation of her tone and the state of her body, she had been under severe duress. "You truly are different. You truly are set above…"

Claudio's soldiers took up residence throughout the city, and Claudio—with his personal bodyguard, and joined with this new girl (whose name, he soon learned, was Anthea)—took up residence in the

Royal Palace. Archamenes, under the constant supervision of soldiers, was kept in the grimmest Haroon prison Claudio could find.

And thus, Claudio and Anthea spent the first evening in the palace living quarters. Wrapped up in blankets to ward off the chill of the desert night, they talked quietly. In time Claudio learned of the true character of Antonio, of how he beat Anthea and forced himself upon her; of how he attempted to feed her to the basilisks. The fast-acting poison was a much quicker death than he deserved, but surely his final resting place was Hell, home of the dishonorable and evil-hearted. Tortured by demons, prodded with spears and burned in the fire-pits, perhaps he would get his justice.

And as they talked, Claudio couldn't deny his growing desire for Anthea. At the same time, he knew it could never be: Claudio was a knight, and—according to the laws of the Empire—could not marry prostitutes.

His time spent pondering was short, however. In the light of the morning, the sun illuminated an incoming ship. On its sail was the war-eagle of the Empire; a message from the Imperial government was on its way.

And, as Claudio sat in the throne room—seat of the Khazidean kings—the messenger broke the seal of a letter, and read from it.

"On behalf of the Imperial Council, a message for Claudio-Valens, Grand Legate of the Imperial Army: We condemn your actions in the strongest possible terms. You have disobeyed the orders of both the sitting ruler and the Imperial Council. With utter disregard for both the Council's demands and the moral compass that guides you, you have annexed the sovereign land of Khazidea, and—as we have just learned—captured Archamenes, King of Kings, a sovereign ruler. Your unlearned, insolent actions can only end poorly for the Imperial people. You are hereby summoned to Imperial City to stand trial for treason: the punishment is death. However, we are merciful, and if you release Archamenes, the King of Kings and sovereign ruler of Fharas, we will reduce your punishment to imprisonment."

Claudio laughed. Incredulous, he was, but not surprised. "I will go to Imperial City, but it will not be me standing trial. Messenger, you are hereafter my captive. The seas are impossible to navigate in winter. I will march through the rain and cold, and I will have every sitting member of the Council stand trial, with *me* as the judge. I am not a traitor; they are."

CHAPTER FORTY:
THE LONG MARCH

Claudio-Valens Adamantus, Grand Legate

Honor could prevent Claudio from pursuing his goals. His mother could prevent him from pursuing his goals. But wind, rain, and cold; a march of many hundreds and thousands of miles; the disapproval of the wormlike, treasonous villains who sat on the Imperial Council… none of those could stop Claudio, or quell his wrath. There were things in life more important than safety. To serve the country that he loved, and to punish those who did not love it… that was more important to Claudio than anything else.

And so, the very next day, Claudio gathered his troops and announced the news: they would march all the way to the compact streets of Imperial City, into the Council House, and drag each villainous worm from his den for the Empire's justice.

As he informed them, shouting from a high lectern in Haroon's city square, the soldiers cheered; for unlike the vermin who sat in the Council House, they still loved the Empire and ignored its flaws. Like Claudio, they pretended no flaws existed. And that was how it should be.

Claudio pronounced Lucello, a centurion, the governor of Khazidea, and thus they set out. It took a week over barren land and through a high mountain pass before they reached Ten Cities. The treachery of those metropolises would be forgiven, if they issued an apology; but it would never be forgotten. Claudio could no longer trust the people of Ten Cities, living in such proximity to the King of Kings and his domain that they—despite his oppression—began to empathize with him, and call him their padisha.

From Ten Cities they went on through the Little Desert and,

after an arduous journey, reached Imperiopoli. How good it was to see the grass, the sage and the holm-oaks after so long in barren desert lands. The air had grown cold; the sky, a constant mournful gray. But the denizens of the city—rescued from slavery—returned to their homes, and seeing their joy warmed Claudio like nothing else. Thus it was the fifteenth day when the departed Imperiopoli. Korthos was just two days' march away.

Under a constant veil of cold rain, a constant shivering overtook Archamenes. Claudio continued on, ignoring the King of Kings' plight just like he had ignored the struggles of Fharese country peasants. For five more days they traveled along the paved Imperial road—which, thanks to engineering, remained solid in winter.

Five more days down the roads, through cities small and large, and they reached the gates of Korthos; yet Claudio ordered his soldiers not to enter. They passed it by, and went on for the long march toward Kersepoli.

Several times during the northward journey, Claudio pondered how the councilors, and perhaps the citizens, would think him mad for marching across the Empire's breadth in winter. Yet he marched with a purpose in mind, stern and unyielding against the coldness and rain; and he would not stop until the Imperial Council answered for their treason.

Ten days later, they reached the gates of Kersepoli; but Claudio would not stop there, either. They continued past the great walls down the road toward Thénai, capital of Eloesus and seat of many an ancient king.

The next day, a soldier alerted him that Archamenes had collapsed. The King of Kings had fallen face-first into the mud and stopped breathing, succumbing to the cold. The soldier led Claudio to the corpse. Astride Borak, he ordered, "Throw him off-road, in a ditch. It is a pity he did not receive justice. Nonetheless, we will not allow him to receive a proper burial, or a funeral of any kind. He will be food for the vultures."

A group of soldiers did Claudio's bidding; and then they continued on. Archamenes had died from the cold, and in truth, more than a few of his soldiers suffered as well. Claudio ordered them to add layers to their clothing, then bade them carry on.

The road to Sanctum, capital of Paladium, was fraught with suffering. For fifteen days they traveled through the freezing rain. Many took ill and collapsed. So, too, were there deserters; but Claudio did not consider it treason, because he could understand the soldiers' wretched state. In truth, he thought more than once about stopping in some flyspeck town and wintering there, waiting until the dry summer sun and the wondrous but far-off days of blue skies and heat. But he remembered he went with a purpose; to show weakness and relent on this journey was to stoop to the same wormlike cowardice that the councilors exhibited every day. He owed it to the people of the Empire, and to the Empire itself. At all points, at all times, he imagined Peregothius, founder of the Empire, staring over his shoulder; and questioning whether he deserved to fly the war-eagle flag.

They reached Sanctum. The high-walled city, overlooking the sea, was not as large as the metropolises of Eloesus or Anthania; its power and glory was over the hearts of the faithful. Sanctum was the home of the Magisterium and the Pontifex, high priest of Hieronus. But again, Claudio ordered that they go on; it was a long journey to Bregantium, and they had to start at once.

In time they reached Bregantium. The idyllic town at the mouth of the River Gad was the northernmost province's crown jewel. If Claudio traveled for many days up the gushing waters, he would reach a land of stalwart oaks and maples; a land where snow lay on the ground in winter. To the north lay the lumbering town of Brilium, which in their tongue was "Brill." But though Claudio had great respect for the fair-haired, blue-eyed denizens of the Empire's northernmost province, he would not tarry. Onward he went down the road, through a land well-farmed and thoroughly tame.

When at last the Goldenhorns appeared in view, Claudio realized it was a short journey to the family ranch. Here he was, on the border of Anthania, and yet he would continue on; he would march down the road, south to Imperial City, and his mother would not know.

As they traveled the Path of Tidus, cutting through the central valley, Claudio couldn't help but notice the darkness of the clouds. Though the skies were always cloudy in winter, these seemed ominous, even evil. Rumors reached his ears of a rebellion of some kind. But if there would rebels, he would face them without mercy.

PART THREE

CHAPTER FORTY-ONE:
ARMIES OF THE UNDERWORLD

Bruesio Lornodoris, August

"Dark times," Bruesio said, and a thunderbolt answered. The winter rains pattered against the dome of the Council House. Inside the air was cold and drafty, and the councilors wore cloaks over their traditional robes.

Despite the chill and the rain, Bruesio knew very well that the rebels stood outside in the midst of the elements, surrounding the city. What they desired, no one knew, though the Council had offered them the world. They would not elaborate; and Bruesio wasn't sure if he wanted to know.

Councilor Fabiano frowned. "Alas, the times will get darker... if the rebels are appeased, the boy Claudio remains alive..."

Bruesio nodded. The arrogant young man was last seen in Bregantium, marching through the cold rain and the damp. A defector reported that Archamenes, King of Kings, had died; Claudio discarded him like a piece of refuse somewhere off the road near Thénai.

"You speak truth, Fabiano." Bruesio frowned. "The boy has gotten us into a world of trouble. The Lords of Fharas will not cease fighting until we are punished. All the gold and bribes in the world will not stop their wrath. To enter Fharas is enough; to pluck the King of Kings from his throne, let him die of cold on a muddy road..." He shuddered.

A horn pealed, breaking the monotony of the rain. Bruesio looked around at his fellow councilmen. He could be wrong, but he guessed it was the rebels.

His suspicions soon proved correct. A rebel—with Bruesio's consent—climbed the stairs of the Council House and presented herself. At the sight of her black clothing and the red band tied around her wrist, several councilors visibly paled.

Beautiful chestnut eyes met theirs. Her white, bony face twisted into a smile. "I am Kyra. I have no last name. I am not August. I am not a Knight, or even an Imperial. My mother was a slave, and her mother before her. I think my father was our master Donato. He never treated me like his child. He fed my brother to his fish. He enjoyed other people's pain; he loved nothing more than torturing his slaves. He forced himself upon me… I wonder if he knew I might be his child, if he liked it better because of that…"

Bruesio's stomach clenched, grown light as feathers. "My dear Kyra, what can we do for you? Anything you rebels ask for, we will give."

"What do we want?" Kyra laughed. "A better question is, 'What do we not want?' Lord Yblis wants the bodies and souls of everyone in Imperial City. In time, a sinkhole will open up and the depths will swallow all the buildings and people. The Empire will be unmade: the nation of slavery, of injustice, will all crumble."

"What do you want?" Bruesio's voice trailed off.

"What we want is simple… everything of value. Once the pit is opened, the city will fall into the earth, into the subterranean world beneath our feet. We want an order from the Imperial Council that all gold, all silver, be stolen from the people's homes and delivered to us."

"Very well…"

Kyra half turned.

"But why? Why would you not simply come to the city and take it all yourself?"

"The sinkhole could open at any moment. We 'rebels,' as you call us, will not risk that. It is the rich and the powerful that Yblis wants to punish, not us."

Kyra walked away. As soon as she got out of earshot, the Council House erupted with frantic talk.

"Silence!" Bruesio demanded. "I know what we must do. The talk of the rebels must be true. Therefore we have one reasonable path;

we must risk the winter storms… flee the city, go to Tiverium or Peregoth or some closer island."

"Do you truly believe that superstition?" Councilor Galvano hissed. "There will be no sinkhole. These rebels are mad, simply-put. I am staying in Imperial City, though the times are grim…"

"I will go with you, Bruesio," Councilor Fabiano. "Sinkholes and underworld gods? Stranger things have come to pass."

"I will, too," Councilor Karo said.

"Me also," added Councilor Juliano.

"I will arrange a ship." Bruesio had gone cold and undoubtedly bloodless. "Though we may flounder in the waves or find ourselves miles out to sea… I fear the rebels more. If we stay in Imperial City, we will certainly die."

CHAPTER FORTY-TWO:
IMMORTAL FOE

Claudio-Valens Adamantus, Grand Legate

The Path of Tidus stretched before him, perfectly straight as it pierced the countryside. Despite the rain, the water filtered from the paving stones, and thanks to the brilliance of engineers it remained as it always had.

As it always had, that is, except for its silence and loneliness. Where merchants, farmers, and assorted travelers once packed the road, emptiness now reigned. Still, Claudio's army—about eight thousand strong, having swelled from Antonio's forces—marched on. Many had taken sick in the constant damp chill. Claudio had caught a cold, and a septic dribble refused to relent.

The citizens along the Path of Tidus gladly fed Claudio and his army. The people of Gad especially had offered what they could: bread, meat, and preserves. The former regent Antonio—whom posterity would despise—had tried to feed lies to the provincials in Gad and elsewhere. But even in their lies, bits of the truth had reached them: Claudio arrogantly, or insolently, or brazenly—whatever descriptors they added—had conquered Khazidea and slain the Fharese emperor. Despite all other falsehoods, they took to Claudio and many joined the army. He had started a new rebellion, not against the Empire but against the Council: against the cowards and the traitors, against the worms in their midst.

Three days after they crossed the Anthanian border, they neared Aurelea. A small city built along the Path, it had no walls. Like many cities of the interior, the people of Aurelea did not fear war.

But when they finally reached what should have been the city, they saw only a hole in the earth, a gaping maw. The immense sinkhole had swallowed the entire city; a funnel of dirt ended in a black chasm of inestimable depth.

Crows called out. A few soldiers called out in fear. This had to be the work of the mysterious northern rebels. In the midst of this dark, rainy day, Claudio hopped off Borak and knelt before the fallen city. He said a prayer in the midst of the falling rain, asking for strength; strength, that he might decimate the rebellion and its dark powers, and that he might destroy the cowardly worms who allowed it to happen.

It was not long before the loneliness was broken. A man—poor, judging by his torn gray clothes—circumvented the giant funnel.

"Signore! Are you Claudio?" he shouted. "I have heard so much about you!"

Claudio tried to smile, but he could not. *All those lives, snatched into the belly of the earth.* "Hello, signore…" he managed to say.

"Aurelea was once my hometown. I had gone on a pilgrimage to Sanctum… and I saw this happen. The rebels serve the underworld god. They claim there is a whole civilization, a whole *world* beneath our feet! Legions have broken on them like water. They are invincible. I think it is the end of everything… the Last Days are upon us!"

The man looked gaunt, the skin of his face stretched tight across his bones. Doubtlessly he had gone hungry for days.

"Come, have something to eat," Claudio said.

"Thank you! Thank you, signore!"

The more he heard about these rebels, the more Claudio was convinced that the man spoke truth. If he faced them man-for-man, on a field of battle, Claudio would fail. He would die like his father—gods rest his soul—and most importantly, he would fail the Empire.

"So what?" Claudio presented the problem to Milo, tribune and friend.

His dark eyes at once filled with thought. "A rebellion of immortal power cannot be defeated by mortal means."

"A wise observation." Claudio frowned. "Wise, but not entirely useful. How can we defeat them? Could we order the Pontifex to offer up bulls in the gods' name?"

"That old man can't solve a theological problem with an army of priests! Could he really solve one of such magnitude?"

Claudio laughed faintly. Indeed, the question of whether ratlings had souls had taken ten years to decide, and when the answer—Yes!—had finally been chosen, a few high-ranking priests had called for further deliberation. The question remained unresolved. Claudio wondered exactly what constituted a soul, and why—if ratlings had emotions, and could speak to humans—the question was even asked.

Claudio looked into the dirt. He pondered a while, until at last all the racing thoughts formed into spoken words: "The oracle…"

Milo looked surprised. "The Pontifex wouldn't like that."

"The Pontifex doesn't like anything."

Milo grinned. "Yes, I suppose that's right. The Pontifex is all rules, regulation, and debate… the oracle is wild, inspired, and maybe crazy."

"It is worth a try, no?" Claudio said. "The Empire is at a crisis. Anything and everything must be tried. The Pontifex would have offered a solution if he had one. And if he had one, I would have heard of it by now, though I am a rebel."

"He has been silent, as far as I know." Milo's grin widened. "He only runs his mouth when it's not wanted. As soon as we need him, he shuts up."

"I'm not sure, though… Mount Hylea is far away. It could be a lot of effort for naught. When has the oracle really helped anyone, or anything?"

"Emperor Varius… Emperor Secundus…"

Claudio pursed his lips and nodded slowly. Emperor Varius had saved his life thanks to the oracle's mad mutterings; she had identified every conspirator in his midst. She had given invaluable advice to the Emperor Secundus in his wars with the northern barbarians.

Long ago the oracle had done her work in Eloesus, in the wild land of Themuria where she prophesied with the wild satyrs. But after the conquest of her homeland, the emperor had moved the oracle and her spiritual descendants to southern Anthania. He had changed the name Mount Metellus to Mount Hylea to make her feel at home, and provided her with whatever she asked. A long shot, but what options were there?

"You're right," Claudio said. "It's out of the way, but what else can we do?"

~

Down the road they marched, braving the constant cold and rain. Several days later, midway through Anthania, a path diverged. It would take them to the southwest, and eventually to Mount Hylea. But the dark clouds above, and the strangely ghostlike wind, filled Claudio with unease. He remembered what he heard of the oracle, that she was mad, and gave a passing thought to long-dead Queen Astarthe. Then, he walked on.

CHAPTER FORTY-THREE: A STRANGE GODDESS

Anthea Abantes

He had seemed so interested in her at first. Now, he acted like she didn't exist. He deflected all attempts at conversation, not maliciously but with a look of determination in his eye. His goal of saving the Empire, of punishing its enemies, had consumed him. All well and good, but Anthea wanted him. Anthea, a whore from the west side, wanted Claudio-Valens: a Grand Legate, an Imperial Knight. If her mother still lived, she would laugh at her.

They were turning, now, off the famous Path of Tidus with its great width. Another road, thinner but just as straight and well paved, shot off to the southwest. A wooden sign illuminated the matter: To Isle of Serpents, Mount Hylea, Lornatium and the Ocean.

She had heard of such places in passing, but not in any detail. Isle of Serpents lay miles out to sea, a great volcano in its center; snakes of enormous size slithered through its beaches, as its name suggested. As for Mount Hylea… a mad woman lived on that mountain, claiming to receive messages from a strange goddess.

Memories rushed back to her: memories of a half-remembered dream. Images of a mad woman with white, blind eyes and her mother, a goddess who wished to change the world.

CHAPTER FORTY-FOUR:
LETTERS

Bruesio Lornodoris, August

It took the better part of a day to find a sailor brave, or stupid enough to sail the Middle Sea in winter. Eleven Imperial Councilors, their wives and children—a group of about fifty souls—packed tight into a galley.

Bruesio's wife Flora hated the idea, but after a serious talk and a few harsh rebukes she finally consented. She did not want to leave their spacious house, their hound Rufus, or their friends. Her brown and gray hair was uncharacteristically tousled and wild as she climbed onto the ship; she had no time to fix it. She loaded several boxes of jewelry and luggage onto the galley and Bruesio reflected on how much he loved her. Unlike most other councilors, they had stayed together through tough times; one marriage was enough for Bruesio. Two people, one marriage, one life.

He smiled, then hauled his feeble self onto the galley. The rain had briefly stopped. The waves were choppy and rough, and at the sight of them Bruesio's gut clenched. He wondered if this was a bad idea after all.

Ahead of him lay the isle of Dualmis and its many mansions. As the sailors prepared to leave the dock, he looked back at the city he had loved. It had been a great cause, a great ideal. But the Empire had failed; it had disrespected the noble King of Kings and invited his wrath. It had mistreated the slaves, sold the proud and intelligent Eloesians into bondage under rude Imperial masters. Perhaps—he thought as they pulled away into rough waters—the Empire deserved this.

He sat down on a wooden bench and laid his hand on Flora's shoulder. He reminded himself that—even if the Empire fell, and its cities burned against rebel and Fharese torches—he still had a life. He had money stored in temples and safe-houses across the former Empire. If he switched allegiance, whether to the Four-Pointed Star or the red swath of the rebels, he would go on with Flora as they always had.

It happened so quickly. The sailors did their best, but the current overpowered them. Before Bruesio had a good idea of what was happening, the prow of the galley had shattered on a rocky patch of Dualmis' shore. Bruesio went flying and hit the sand, breaking a tooth and perhaps a rib. People were screaming; he glimpsed Councilor Juliano flailing in the water as he was pulled out to sea.

Trapped in Dualmis. Bruesio could think of worse places to spend a winter. He did not like the proximity to the rebels. But he had had friends here: wealthy merchants, former governors... yes, they'd take him in.

His friend Silvio had a mansion on Dualmis. After the explanation, Silvio—as expected—took Bruesio and Flora in, and, moreover, invited them to dinner.

There, slaves brought out bowls of spicy lamprey stew, crispy loaves of sweetbread, and crystal goblets filled with red Korthian wine. Silvio, his wife Marcia, and their aloof son Jacopo shared the meal with the Lornodoris family. Bruesio made sure not to alarm them with the "sinkhole" threat, which now seemed a distant memory; but the talk of the island, and probably the whole Empire, was the rebels.

Flora retired early, and Silvio's family followed. In the spacious common room, Bruesio took a seat, feeling at peace with the world. What better time to reminisce about his long and fruitful life? He opened Flora's luggage.

There was the pendant he bought her, made from lapis lazuli

and silver; golden necklaces, ruby rings and her beloved emerald earrings. In another box lay her clothing: a Fharese-style woman's robe of silk, complete with the Four-Pointed Star; a purple dress with gold embroidery that he had bought her for their anniversary; and strangely, a small brass key.

Next, a smaller box he didn't recognize. He tried it, but it was locked. Bruesio raised a brow and grabbed the key; it fit perfectly. Inside, he found letters.

He picked one up, and the more he read, the colder the room grew. Soon, he was shaking:

To dearest Flora:

You say you will never forget the summer of 975... You say you will always hold it dear to your heart, like I held you. Neither will I forget it. You, in truth, are a beauty on the outside and also within. I will remember you always; but I am soon to be wed. I know this hurts you but I am marrying Catalina. Perhaps it is for the best... for though I held you in my arms, you are wed to old Bruesio. Though feeble he holds much power, even if undue. And though that night was beautiful, he has the influence to remove me from the legion. Just remember that I will remember you.

Flora and Bruesio had wed in 961. He was shaking, nearly convulsing, now. A legionary, or a legate, wed to a woman named Catalina. He grew nauseous.

The letter was signed:

L.V. A.

Lucento-Valens Adamantus married a woman named Catalina. No. *No.*

"No," he said aloud.

But it made sense. Around 975, Lucento had been stationed in Imperial City. He had dined with Bruesio… dined with the councilors. Dined with Flora.

"No," he said again, louder this time.

Their marriage had been a sham. Of all people, why Lucento? Of all people, why an Adamantus?

She would pay with her life.

CHAPTER FORTY-FIVE:
THE ORACLE OF HYLEA

Claudio-Valens Adamantus, Grand Legate

The skies had cleared; now, the sun shone bright against a blue sky.

Before him, down a hill, was the small settlement called Lornatium: a name Claudio had never heard before. Beyond it lay the rough blue waters of the ocean. It all lay in the shadow of Mount Hylea. Surrounded by a forest of oaks, dark green pines covered the jagged peak up to its snowy summit.

Milo walked beside him. A small dirt path broke off the road toward the lone mountain. Claudio looked at his friend and said, "Ready?"

"I think," Milo began, "that you should go alone."

"Why?"

"I don't know… I suppose I think you're the one the oracle needs to talk to. It just seems right…"

Claudio peered into his friend's dark eyes. He trusted his friend's judgment, but in truth, he did not want to go alone.

The mountain path wound round and round the peak up steep switchbacks and beside waterfalls. The air grew cooler and cooler, and despite it Claudio grew sweatier with every step. The air thinned, but he did not stop. It was more than an hour later when the path abruptly ended at a rocky meadow.

Two things immediately struck him: the ruins of a white pillared temple, and the sound of wild drums.

Claudio hesitated. He had commanded a battle, faced elephants, and gone deep into enemy territory; but he wondered if this oracle would undo him.

The drums continued. He took a few steps forward and stopped; then he swallowed his fear, and walked toward the temple with all the bravery he could muster.

When he reached the temple's broken pillars, the drumbeat quickened. As he stared at the destroyed temple, its roof collapsed and its stone floor now open to the elements, he got the sense someone was watching him. He touched the hilt of his sword.

"Ah, ah, ah," a woman's voice answered from behind.

Calmly, he removed his grip. Slowly, he turned around.

The woman's eyes were white and sightless. She wore a skirt and a brassiere, nothing more. A green snake had coiled around her legs and around her bare waist, and its cold reptilian eyes peered at Claudio from her shoulder.

"Claudio-Valens," she said. "I am the Oracle of Hylea. I have lived many lifetimes and I see all things, and yet—" She pointed to her eyes. "—in some ways I see nothing."

Her hair, dark and thick, hung to her hips.

"In some, I see imminent destruction. In others, I see long bitter life. In others, I see weakness."

"What do you see in me?"

The drums stopped and the silence felt strange. The snake flicked its forked tongue. "Why have you come?" the oracle asked.

"I have come because the Empire is in crisis. A rebellion has started and no one can defeat them. They have the god of the underworld on their side."

"What do I see in you, you ask," the oracle snapped. "Let me be clear, or vague. The emperor will wed a whore. The emperor will become a god. That much is clear. If it does not happen, the nation will crumble."

"There is no one on the White Throne. There is no emperor."

"The god of the underworld is on no one's side!" the oracle hissed. "The god of the underworld is a god of darkness and shadows.

If he grants power to the rebels, light must shine on them. I know what you must do, Claudio-Valens Adamantus! I will do the work. The goddess will call her Servant; but you must be brave. You must turn back, march to Imperial City. You must trust and believe in my words. Then, if you stand the test of bravery and faith, then, and only then, will the rebels falter, and the Empire find its rescue."

"Very well. I will turn back. What other choice do we have?"

"You say there is no emperor!" the oracle shrieked as if in pain. "That is why you must wed a whore!"

"What?" Perhaps she was insane after all.

"The emperor must wed a whore, as I said! You must become the emperor, and you must do as I said. If you fail, the Empire will falter."

"I don't understand!"

"Look!" the oracle screamed.

Claudio gazed beyond the madwoman. In the distance, near the path, someone was struggling through brush and vines: dark brown hair, olive skin. The Eloesian girl, the prostitute… Anthea Abantes. For once, the oracle's words made sense.

CHAPTER FORTY-SIX:
UNION

Anthea Abantes

The way he looked at her sent her heart fluttering. Those brown eyes held such compassion, and yet such incredible strength. Unwavering determination, perhaps imperfect like all humans; good, and yet strong.

The oracle turned around. Her wild dark hair and sightless white eyes caused Anthea to shudder. More than that, the snake twined around her body made her tremble. The yellow reptilian eyes, cold and murderous, betrayed an intelligence, or at least a kinship with the oracle: a shared soul.

A temple stood behind them, its roof shattered and its pillars broken. Perhaps, long ago, it had served as the earthly home of some ancient serpent god. "Claudio?" Anthea said.

The oracle took a few steps toward her. The snake exhaled and let its forked tongue loll. Anthea did not move. "Witness the wedding of the whore and the aspirant emperor! Witness it, Hermas!"

The snake twitched at its name. Claudio took a step forward: a weak, trembling step. His eyes were unsure. He cleared his throat. Here he was: Claudio-Valens, Grand Legate, brave-heart, a veritable god among men… awkward, nervous and utterly undone by a woman. It had always ever been. "A-Anthea—" He began with a stutter.

"Yes," Anthea responded. "Yes, I will marry you."

"Then it's done… I have wed her." His voice still trembled.

"No!" the oracle shouted. "A man has not wed his wife until they have become one. Let the marriage be consecrated on Mount Hylea, at the temple of the Trifold Goddess."

Nervousness. Anticipation. Claudio walked toward her and she felt weak.

CHAPTER FORTY-SEVEN:
VENGEANCE

Bruesio Lornodoris, August

At the morning meal, Bruesio stared daggers at his wife Flora. If she noticed, she made no fuss; any woman of proper breeding knew not to bring her problems to a guest's dinner table. Silvio made small talk, chatting endlessly about gods-know what. His sullen child Niccolo shoveled the stew into his mouth without regard for proper table manners. His wife, Marcia, went on and on about Dualmis' latest gossip. And Flora.

Flora. He had trusted her all these years. All he could think about was Flora, in a lover's embrace with Lucento-Valens. With an Adamantus. He couldn't abide the thought. He threw the napkin down and stood up. "Excuse me," Bruesio said, and left in a rush.

He followed the paved road, past the lofty palms. The rain had stopped for now. A while down a road was a town: one of those small, idyllic villages in the midst of wealthy enclaves. But even those would likely have what Bruesio looked for; and he had brought a pouch of gold coins enough to purchase it.

The apothecary was a square stone building. Inside, shelves full of powders, liquids, and jars of strange ingredients, greeted him. Behind the desk was a man of pallid complexion and light hair; perhaps a man of Gad, but Bruesio wouldn't hold it against him. At least, he wouldn't for now.

"How can I help you?" he said.

"I have a rat problem. A very, very *big* rat problem. I'm going to need poison… the deadliest poison you can get. I have human-sized rats in my house."

The man grinned. "A human-sized rat… I know what you want. I will get you the deadliest poison I have on hand."

That afternoon, Bruesio asked his wife to tea.

"Tea," Flora said, the sniveling shrew. "I didn't think you liked tea."

"I do now." Bruesio put on the best false smile he could muster. The more unprepared she was, the more shocked she'd be that her husband knew her for what she was.

Lucento-Valens… he shuddered.

Flora peered into his eyes. "All right, my dear."

The day was cold but not insufferably so, and dry. Bruesio had set the tea out in the garden, on Silvio's elegantly-chiseled stone table. He took a seat, and Flora sat across from him.

She put her thin fingers round the cup. She peered into Bruesio's eyes, and for the first time in nearly forty years of marriage, he saw distrust in them. "I thought you hated tea, husband."

"Things have changed." The words had more meaning than she knew.

The distrust in her eyes seemed to increase. "Husband, you don't look well."

He took his tea and sipped it. He remembered why he didn't like it, but swallowed it just the same. "I am fine, dear wife."

"I'm not sure…"

"I bought all this tea for you, and you won't drink it?" Bruesio glared.

"I…" She searched deeper into his eyes but she would find nothing; he was stone cold, now, and impossible to read. She put the cup to her lips, and drank.

Bruesio grinned a cold, joyless grin. "Tell me about Lucento."

She went white. Soon, she would go whiter. "I—I don't know—"

"You betrayed me. And not only did you make that most unfortunate mistake, you kept the letters. You *kept* them. Took them with you like a treasure. You let that arrogant man have you. Didn't you?"

"No!" Her eyes had grown moist. The poison was entering her, even now. Her life, *their* life, slipped away each second. "Those weren't mine…"

"No more lies."

"I'm sorry."

"Too little, too late."

"Haven't you ever made a mistake?"

"I've made plenty of mistakes," Bruesio said. His voice shook with anger. "But never once—not once—did I make the mistake of betraying you."

"I'm sorry!" she wept. "I'm so sorry! Gods, I'm so sorry!"

Bruesio shook his head. "I do not accept your apology. If you flung yourself off a high rooftop, if you crawled a mile across shattered glass… even then, I would not forgive you."

"I don't feel well," she choked through tears. Her stomach growled. "I feel…"

"Your life is a lie," Bruesio sneered. "The son of your lover marches across the Empire. Perhaps you gave birth to him!"

"No!" She retched.

"You have committed the ultimate betrayal against my name. You are no longer a Lornodoris! I divorce you! Let it be known that, before you die, you are no longer my wife."

She vomited blood. She had begun to grow white. She would die soon.

Like a statue, Bruesio Lornodoris stood there, hovering

among the myrtles, the fig trees and the lemon trees. Soon Flora had given her last spasms, and was still, lying in a pool of blood. And Bruesio was alone. Alone, like a ship cast adrift into waters unknown by man. He no longer had Flora… his companion. She had betrayed him. But what was he now?

Silvio burst into the garden, and went white: almost as white as Flora. "What is going on here? *What have you done?*"

"I poisoned her." Bruesio's honesty surprised him. But he felt numb. The threat of prison did not faze him. He had gone cold. He was empty, a spiritless body in this cruel world.

"Get out!" Silvio screamed.

"What?" Bruesio looked into his friend's bulging, irate eyes.

"*Get out!*" Silvio screamed. "*Get out, now!*"

Bruesio left the mansion with his luggage in tow. He had the box of his wife's letters. Perhaps he would read them. He walked through the cold day, detached from all worry. He walked along the beach and took in the salty air. At last he sat down on a rock.

He shivered. Through a veil of ocean fog lay Imperial City. As he sat there, thunder rolled across the narrow channel; a storm raged, but only within the city proper. Here, in Dualmis, he was safe. Safe from the rebels, but not from himself.

He buried his head in his hands, and cried.

CHAPTER FORTY-EIGHT:
NO RETREAT

Claudio-Valens Adamantus, Grand Legate

When Claudio told Milo about the marriage, his friend smiled and congratulated him. Milo, neither an August or a Knight, took no issue with his marrying a whore.

It was the other matter—the oracle's demand that they march to Imperial City on blind faith—that Milo would not accept. "Perhaps she *is* mad. Thought of that?" His voice rose above the rain pattering against the tent.

Claudio smiled wearily. "Of course I have. It is entirely possible. She worships a goddess I've never heard of. She lives in an abandoned temple. She lets a snake coil around her body, and she is blind. Madness is, perhaps, the best explanation. But what other options do we have, Milo? What else can we do, but take this chance?"

"We could leave. Move the capital to Bregantium or Brilium…"

"Retreat?" Claudio frowned. "You sound like you belong on the Imperial Council. If you wish to run, Milo, go ahead. I will march to Imperial City… alone if need be."

"You know me better than that." Milo knelt down on the tent floor. "You are my commander, and wherever you go I will follow… even to the Gates of Hell."

"And that, my friend, is where we are headed."

In the midst of an early morning storm, they departed. Minute by minute, hour by hour, Mount Hylea faded from sight. They found themselves again on the Path of Tidus with its wide breadth. The sound of eight thousand marching feet echoed as Claudio led them. Imperial City lay before him, and the time waxed late.

CHAPTER FORTY-NINE:
DARKNESS FOREVERMORE

Anthea Abantes

She could still feel him inside her. After the impromptu wedding, and the sudden wedding night, it seemed he had forgotten about her. But she had a feeling he had cast aside the cares of marriage for now; his resolve was indomitable, and she could neither ease his burden nor help him. But when he had accomplished his goal—as he had accomplished all else before him—he would remember Anthea Abantes, the lowly girl he wed. Then, when he sat on the White Throne, she would sit by his side as empress.

Empress! Never once in her life did the thought enter into her mind, not even in dreams. But the winds of fate are fickle, as the augurs well know. And somehow that madwoman, that oracle, had worked some magic on Claudio's mind, or perhaps convinced him with her mad blabbering.

She had climbed the mountain on a whim. She had slipped out of the camp, followed the trail as fast as she could. Who knew it would end up so impossibly in her favor? Anthea the lost girl… the daughter of a "sacred" concubine and an uncertain father. The girl whose father could be—and likely was—a vagabond, a wayfarer or diseased soldier-of-fortune. Anthea the Empress? She did not deserve it, and in truth, she still did not believe it all was real.

As she walked down the road, the sky darkened. The rain picked up and the winds howled among the brush and the scraggly pines. She remembered it probably would not come to pass at all.

The first hints of the coming metropolis greeted them: arches of triumph stretching over the path, and distant aqueducts ferrying water from the mountains. Towns—most abandoned—became increasingly packed together. At last night fell, and they had to sleep.

How strange it was to rest in the Grand Legate's tent. Claudio and his friend stayed up late, laying plans and discussing strategies. Anthea grew tired. She fell asleep with Claudio, sweet Claudio, in her view.

She awoke in a panic. A deafening groan filled the air, like a rift opening in the earth. Claudio, already awake, made a dash for the tent flap. Blood pumping, Anthea raced after him, out of the tent.

She cried out when she realized they were surrounded. The rebels in their blacks and reds had completely surrounded the Grand Legate's tent. Where were the soldiers? Where in gods' names were the soldiers? What had happened? It seemed that only Milo, Claudio, and Anthea were left.

The rebels in their black leather could hardly be distinguished from the darkness of the night. She looked around, heart racing, wondering about an escape.

Right in front of Claudio, two children stood. They looked similar, perhaps twins. Their pallid skin stuck out against the black clothing of their fellow rebels. Their dark, glassy eyes had a ghostly gleam: bewitching, perhaps demonic. Up above the rebels, wisps of gray darted about, moaning as they did.

"Fabius. Marcia," Claudio's words somehow distinguished themselves over the noise. "The Dark-Eyed Twins."

"Claudio-Valens Adamantus." The boy, Fabius, spoke first. "We killed your father. He tried to flee."

"Lies!" Claudio growled.

Marcia's eyes flicked to Milo, and the demonic gleam brightened. "Milo Furianus, a man of little birth and littler consequence. Your father was a poor freedman farmer. Your mother was the daughter of a tailor. I like you better than Claudio. You are neither Knight nor August. You may join our cause."

"Join your cause?" Milo took a few tentative steps toward the twins.

"Yes," the twins said in unison, and their eyes both fixed on him.

"Never!" Milo swept out his sword and charged them. "You underestimate my loyalty!"

In an instant, he fell to the ground dead.

The twins' hellish eyes flicked to Claudio. "He made a mistake," Fabius said. "We offered him his life, and he threw it away."

Claudio said nothing. Perhaps a wise choice, Anthea reflected.

"You are a Knight," Marcia said. "Highly-born, privileged, doubtlessly rich. You are so unlike the rebels… so unfit for our cause. To kill you now is unfitting; a torturous death would be most proper. But I worry."

"No more slaves." As Fabius spoke, the gleam of his eyes became torch-like. "No more poor. No more Knights. No more Augusts. Just darkness. Just darkness. Just darkness, forevermore…"

"Wait!" Anthea screamed and ran toward them, tripping into the mud. "Wait! Do not kill him!"

Their glassy, hellish eyes flicked to her.

"He is a Knight, but not in spirit. He loves the people… He…"

"You are lowlier than Milo!" Marcia smiled. "You sold yourself to make a living. Your mother was a sacred concubine; your father was an impoverished sailor, ravaged by lesions and sores. In time, his disease was the end of your mother—"

"Enough!" Anthea hissed. "I will take his place! Let me suffer for him! Without him, I have nothing to live for! Therefore, take all your hatred for Claudio and lay it on me!"

"Never!" Claudio roared. "I will never let that happen. She is my wife and she will *never* suffer in my place. I am a man of honor; I live for the Empire and I will die for it. Leave Anthea out of this."

For a while, the twins were silent, perhaps consorting with each other in their minds. At last they spoke in unison: "A Knight marries a whore. Strange. It does not exonerate the Knight of his privilege and wealth. It sullies the whore, whom we previously held in great honor. Therefore you are both condemned to die. Gogmor, the vicar of Yblis, wishes to judge you. It shall be done in Imperial Square, the center-point of unjust power and oppression."

Anthea walked up to Claudio. He held her hand. They began to walk in the dark storm. A great hole had opened up in the earth; perhaps that was where the soldiers had gone.

The morning was cloudy, heavily obscuring the sun. A chopping block stood in the center of Imperial Square. Blood stained the once-pristine tiles, and innards lay strewn all around. The people of Imperial City peeked through windows, and the intrepid watched from the side of the square. The rebels pushed Anthea and Claudio out into the middle of the wide space. Out of the darkness, Gogmor emerged.

The creature drove a dark coach. If a human, Gogmor was the largest who had ever existed; yet the question was impossible to answer. A dark gray cloak with frayed edges covered every inch of his enormous body, and a hood obscured his face. Muscular warhorses pulled the coach. Around its spiked wheels—themselves dripping with recent blood—a swirling chorus of ghosts flew.

When Gogmor spoke, his voice seemed to come from all sides, echoing not just in the air but also deep in Anthea's mind. "I have come to claim the upper world. Of all the sunlit races, only the *dweomer* know of Yblis' great domain. It is time that my god has claimed the upper world for Himself. And as I have promised the slaves—with my lord's consent—the tables shall be turned; the slave shall be the domino, and the domino, the slave."

"That is not justice!" Anthea screamed. Claudio looked at her, perhaps admiringly. "That is just reversal."

"Neither you nor your husband has any say," Gogmor said.

"You will be tortured before you die. You will pass from this world after infinite pain. That is my pronouncement."

All strength left Anthea's legs. She fell to the wet tile of the square, consumed with trembling. A group of black-garbed rebels appeared, holding garrotes and knives, hooks and other devices of torture.

Claudio drew his sword; Gogmor raised a gloved hand and the metal burst into a thousand scintillating shards.

The oracle was a madwoman. They had thrown away it all. The rebels had won. There would be no rich nor poor, no Augusts or slaves; just darkness, darkness, darkness, forevermore.

Claudio stood strong, statuesque as the rebels bound his hands. In the distance, at the edge of Imperial Square, two silhouettes appeared. Humans, a man and a woman; the woman muttering, the man with his arm slung over her shoulder. What was this?

CHAPTER FIFTY:
LAST HOPE

Marcus Silverus

Marcus had learned to trust Tivera. She was hopelessly crazy, but—at the same time—the sanest and the wisest person he had ever known. The supposed message from the goddess, the early departure, the winter journey across the sea… he had put all her faith in her. And he'd be damned if he would back out now: now that a group of men in black leather, wielding swords, were walking across the square toward them, and a cloaked giant riding on a hellish coach had turned to look at them.

"The goddess wants me to, but I can't do it! I will die!" Tivera screamed.

"Trust her! Trust the goddess, like I trusted you!" Marcus pleaded.

"I can't! I—"

The black-leathered soldiers were running at them now.

"Trust her!" Marcus shouted. "Do it! Trust the goddess, like I trust you!"

CHAPTER FIFTY-ONE:
SHINE

Tivera Marcianus

She loved Marcus. She loved him like she had never loved anyone before, like no one had loved her before. He didn't hurt her. He had a kind face, a face like the sun, like the Trifold Mother's face. Before she wandered into the garden she had been lost... she had no one, she had gone hungry in the horrible streets. Spent nights alone, starving. Yet always Mira's light lay in her mind.

The bad men in the leathers had stopped their movements, their eyes wide and their lips shaking. All the blood had left their face. She guessed it was happening. She thought that maybe it was already pouring out of her.

Tivera the Lamp—the goddess Mira had called her that in a dream. She didn't understand people; she never knew what they would say, how they would act. They were strange, and unkind, and violent. All light had left them, the light of kindness... they thought they were wise but they were blind.

Ah! She could see things clearer. It was coming out of her skin; the shadows retreated from the light.

These bad people in the black leathers wanted everyone to be the same—Mira told her. It had never been and never would be. Mira told Tivera that these "rebels" thought they were good, that they were wise and knew what was best—but all they had was envy and hatred. The light would expose them. The light.

Ah! It was happening now. It would consume her. The light would pour out of her, destroy her.

But she could see Mira's happy face. It was telling her to shine. Shine.

Shine!

CHAPTER FIFTY-TWO:
DAYLIGHT

Claudio-Valens Adamantus, Grand Legate

The girl's body had gone from fair, to bright, to blinding, to a living torch. Light brighter than the sun radiated from her. Brighter than the sun, and somehow better. The white light coursing from her pierced Claudio from within, untying the knots of weariness and struggle, undoing all the pains that the long march had inflicted on his body.

Gogmor, having turned to face her, tried to shield his eyes; but his gray cloak caught fire and began to burn.

Even the dark clouds in the sky fled from the light. As they peeled back, the open spaces revealed a bright blue expanse. The rebels screamed. A few covered their eyes. The girl—the living lamp—had blinded them.

The girl's light reached a zenith. The dark clouds above had all retreated and the sun greeted them in their place. The rebels fell back, their eyes now white and sightless. In the confusion, the people of Imperial City—now bathed in light—rushed to grab daggers and knives and weaponry. The rebels could no longer defend themselves.

The girl's light ceased; she fell to the floor dead. The man accompanying her fell down on her and began to weep. But the rebels, now blind, could not stand against the Imperial citizens. The sun now shone on the greatest city in the world.

As the rebels began to fall in the ensuing slaughter, Claudio ran and embraced Anthea, locking her in a passionate kiss.

The ensuing slaughter would undo the rebels' power. The wraith, Gogmor, had burned away. There was much still to take care of; but now there was only kissing, and celebration, and light.

CHAPTER FIFTY-THREE:
EMPRESS

Anthea Abantes

Two Months Later....

Anthea's husband Claudio stood before him, dressed in the robe of the emperor: purple silk, studded with rubies and gems, tied together with a golden belt. Often her husband remarked on how much he disliked it: the attire seemed so ostentatious, as he said, so opulent and, worst of all, southern.

She felt self-conscious in her own billowing dress. The sapphire blue dye, and the gold tissue embroidery made it expensive beyond the means of most anyone. But she had to remember, she was not here for show. She did not come to impress anyone. She came for only one reason: for Claudio, her great love. As those beautiful brown eyes met hers, she remembered all he had gone through. Not long ago he had been a provincial, a horse-rancher who was only noble in name. But now he had shaken the foundations of the Empire, punished its enemies; and still, there was work left to be done. Or so he said.

The Pontifex had come to Imperial City on the first ship available. Now the old man stood in the chapel, his blue-gold, diamond-studded miter glittering on his head.

Open windows let in the warm, fragrant spring air. And as she held Claudio's hands, staring deep into her eyes, the highest-ranking priest in the realm spoke: "Do you, Anthea Abantes, take Claudio-Valens Adamantus as your husband?"

She peered into his eyes and felt weak. He smiled at her, and she fumbled out her words like a fool: "Absolutely! Yes! A thousand times yes!"

"And do you, Emperor Claudio-Valens Adamantus, take Anthea as your wife?"

Claudio repeated her words with more calm than she had managed: "Absolutely. Yes. A thousand times yes."

"Then." The Pontifex smiled. "By the holy power of Hieronus and all the gods, and with the agreement of the god Imperium, and of the Imperial State, I pronounce you husband and wife. You may now kiss, Claudio and Anthea Adamantus."

They locked in a passionate kiss. A great celebration would take place through the streets of Imperial City. A grand reception with wine and food and the best musicians awaited them. But a wedding was a beginning; the beginning of a union and of a shared life, and she was determined to make it a good one.

CHAPTER FIFTY-FOUR: CLAUDIO THE GOD

Emperor Claudio-Valens Adamantus

In the months since his coronation, Claudio replaced every member Imperial Council. He picked the most patriotic and loyal members of the August class he could find. Those who had fought against him—the traitors, the cowards and the worms—were gone. Some had fallen to the sword; they were lucky. The remaining members fled across the sea to Khazidea, where they incited a rebellion. Once again a brother-sister monarchy ruled over Haroon; and the treacherous councilors lived in luxury. Chief among them, Bruesio Lornodoris, who had narrowly escaped Claudio's retribution. He had killed his wife in a fit of rage; over what, Claudio had no idea, but it would end in his death.

The fleet was ready, waiting in the harbor. The nascent springtime air greeted Claudio as he walked onto the balcony. It was time. The councilors would answer for their treachery, their disloyalty, their hatred of their own country.

"Emperor."

Claudio turned around. A page stood there in a white cloak, kneeling before him. "Yes?" Claudio said.

"The Council has a matter for you."

"I am terribly busy, signore… the navy is waiting for me."

The page looked up at him. "They say it is very important."

Claudio grumbled. "I suppose I can spare a few minutes."

In the Council House, the new members stood at rapt attention. A man with the dark curly hair and olive skin of an Eloesian stood before them, holding open a scroll.

"What is it?" Claudio said.

"A quick matter," said Marcello, the new Speaker of the Council. "A quick 'No' is all we need… more eastern superstition and decadence."

"Read it," Claudio ordered.

"A letter from the governor of Eloesus," the councilor said. "The men and women of Imperiopoli wish to erect a shrine to living emperors, and especially you. They wish to worship you, and your descendants, while still alive; and they seek your permission to build a grand temple."

"Yes," Claudio answered. "Let them worship me and call me a god. I grant them permission to build a temple to me."

A few councilors gasped.

"That would be a reversal of a thousand years of—"

Claudio cut Marcello off. "They would never rebel against a god. And if that is what I am in their eyes, so be it."

"Very well, Claudio!" the Eloesian messenger said. "Claudio the God…"

He boarded the flagship with as little pomp and as little notice as he could manage. The Council's proposition would be obscene to the virtuous men of the West and the North; but if the decadent and ancient East wished to worship him, then it could only ensure order. From Tarchon the Mad to vile Heidathra, the kings of the east called themselves gods, and the people rewarded them with absolute obedience. And if Claudio did not himself believe it, then he did no wrong; it was a matter of public order. But despite it all, Claudio knew the Empire had entered a new golden age. An age of peace achieved through strength, and wealth untold. No one would go hungry except the Empire's enemies.

Aboard the flagship, the fleet turned south toward those very enemies. The treacherous Imperial Council would pay, and Khazidea would be, irrevocably and unchangeably, a province. No longer would the despotic Fharese king own the productive fields. Now that the worms, the parasites that weakened the Empire, had faded from power, the nation's strength would go unchecked, and a better world would result: peace, against which none could rebel.

CHAPTER FIFTY-FIVE:
LAMPS

Marcus Silverus

Tivera.

Even months later, the name twisted a knife in Marcus's heart. The girl had changed him. Mad, yet wise beyond any he knew; kind-hearted yet helpless, vulnerable yet strong. Emperor Claudio allowed him to stay on as Guardian of the Wine Cellar, though—in his own words—it was a useless and costly position.

Marcus spent a lot of time wandering, enjoying the warmth of spring and the bright sun. He no longer wanted a mansion or a private island, or a pleasure barge. He didn't know what he wanted.

He spent a lot of time in temples, but no god or goddess had what he most wanted: Tivera's brilliant light. Hieronus, lord of honor and justice, was too stern and somber. Amara, kind Mother Goddess though she was, was unpalatably popular and widespread. Lorenus, another well-known god, spent too much time riding the sea-foam and waging war in the depths of the sea.

So who could shine the light in Marcus? Who could illuminate him like Tivera, the lamp long-extinguished?

Marcus spent a week in the records office, combing through births. The chance of finding Tivera was small since she was of low birth, and the records themselves were spotty. Most people went unrecorded. At last he gave up.

The next day he returned with a different goal in mind. He looked through the registry of temples. It struck him how the Imperial City was a veritable hive of gods and goddesses. Thousands, perhaps tens of thousands, of temples and shrines were listed. But with effort he found a small entry—the only one of its kind—for Mira, the Trifold Goddess of Light. The street was listed. Perhaps he would find a part of Tivera in the strange, ill-known deity she worshipped. What else of her remained?

The street ran along part of the harbor district, in sight of the gulls, the freight ships and the giant warehouses. The way seemed uncared-for; many pavestones had washed away to reveal dirt and the rest, worn by rain and time. Many of the houses lay empty: the windows boarded-up or left open, their dark insides doubtlessly skittering with rats and mice. He kept walking.

At last he came to the temple: a small stone building with a domed roof, hidden from the skyline by the much taller houses surrounding it. He hesitated at the open doorway. He gulped but at last walked in.

Within the stone walls, an altar stood beyond the pews. Upon it, a lamp cast light around it all; but the light was not like a torch. It did not flicker. And as Marcus stepped closer and got a better look, he realized that no flame burned within the lamp; instead, an orb of pure light shone from within.

"Among the Elders of the far north—"

Marcus jumped at the male voice speaking from behind.

"—these radiant jewels are called star-gems. Making them requires the magic of a lightbearer."

Marcus whipped around. A man stood there, dressed in a white robe: old and wrinkled, his face clean-shaven and his gray hair cut in a tonsure. In his right hand he held a staff.

"A pity, then, that lightbearers are so rare among men. With the death of the girl, perhaps they will be gone forever."

"Who are you?"

The old man smiled. "My name is unimportant. I am a priest of Mira, the Trifold Mother, Lady of Light. And who are you?"

"Marcus," he began. "Marcus Silverus… I came because my friend was a devotee. Tivera…"

"Tivera, savior of Imperial City. You knew her?"

"I was her friend."

The priest smiled. "Tivera was a gifted girl. She came into our care as an infant. A man and his wife adopted her, took her to their home. She became Tivera Marcianus, and for seven years they raised her in Eximenius."

He had never heard of the town.

"They had expected a normal girl. But Tivera was not a normal girl. She was not wholly 'there,' though she was very intelligent. Her parents abused her, tried to change her; she was an embarrassment to them and she suffered horrible treatment. We helped her escape but she was always afraid of them. Her parents took her happiness, and they took her childhood, but they could not take her gift… the gift of Light."

Tears formed in Marcus' eyes.

"She would have wanted to end her life like that: as a beacon of Mira, her mother and goddess. She saved the Empire, and all its citizens, but I have no doubt she is already forgotten."

"I cannot live without her." Marcus' voice trembled embarrassingly. "Her light shone in me, and it's gone now."

The priest smiled. He walked up to Marcus and laid a feeble hand on his shoulder. "I think Mira wanted you here today. I think she had a purpose in drawing you here. You are, perhaps, not a lightbearer like Tivera. But you can be her devotee. I will admit you into the Priesthood of Mira, if that is your wish. I am the last one left; if I die, the knowledge of her will pass from the world of men."

"Yes," Marcus said. "Yes, that is what I want. I will serve the goddess Mira and spread her light everywhere I can…"

Months ago, Marcus had lived only for himself. Now he had

something else: a purpose, a mission, and a brilliant light.

224

CHAPTER FIFTY-SIX:
WORMS

Emperor Claudio-Valens Adamantus the God

The red sandstone of Haroon lay across the sea. Informants on the ground and by water had explained the little they knew of the situation. The people of Haroon had taken in the eleven surviving members of the Imperial Council; and through some sort of deceit or empty promise they had secured for themselves a measure of power. The thought of those bickering cowards ruling a nation made Claudio laugh; but that was not entirely the case.

After all, they had shown their mettle: after setting up a new brother-sister monarchy and establishing themselves as advisors, they defected to Fharas and her new King of Kings. Even now, as the fleet sailed by, the Four-Pointed Star flapped on the turrets. Doubtlessly, the Lords of Fharas had brought all their forces to protect the province. The King of Kings and the treacherous councilors apparently called Claudio a 'devil,' a 'violent demon,' an 'untamed beast.'

Even if those descriptions rang true, the councilors were far worse. They were worms: cowardly, treacherous and weak; loving nothing except themselves and their nation's enemies, and hating the people. They were worms, and they would be made to suffer like worms.

The thought of the councilors made Claudio's teeth clench. The Lords of Fharas had brought all their vassals, their elephants, and their peasant-soldiers. But he had brought the whole forces of the Empire: a hundred thousand troops in total from every province, each soldier well-armed and well-trained.

They sailed a few miles from Haroon and deployed on the

verdant shore. It was nearly summer, and the desert sun burned Claudio's neck.

The one-hundred thousand troops assembled themselves in lush farmers' fields, and, wisely, no Fharese force tried to halt their deployment. Claudio led the march, and at the sight of the legions, the natives took shelter in homes or fled altogether. But the natives did not concern Claudio: he wanted only order, the submission of the province, and his captives.

The march to Haroon lasted several hours, but eventually, the red walls of Haroon rose above the lush greenery. The forces of the enemy had doubtlessly heard of their coming and taken refuge within. The Lords of Fharas would not return the province without a fight.

And so, Claudio ordered them to pitch tents around the red curtain walls. The gates had shut, and hundreds of Fharese archers waited on the battlements with curved shortbows. Haroon, an ancient city, had withstood many sieges. It would take much effort and— Claudio noted sadly—Imperial losses to claim it. The forty-foot walls stretched imposingly high.

The archers, with their conical steel helmets and their dark faces, did not attack. Claudio's men pitched their tents all around. No one could leave Haroon; and the Imperial fleet had already sailed back into the city's harbor, forming a complete blockade.

Claudio slept uneasily that night in his grand tent. It could all be undone so fast... he could lose the battle, lose the province to Fharas. The treacherous Imperial Council could live out their wormlike existences in luxury among the Khazidean palms...

The morning light woke him. Gently he rose. The smell of cookpots wafted through the fresh Khazidean air. The army he had summoned surrounded the whole city many ranks deep. Still, the Fharese archers refused to attack. Perhaps they knew better.

As the soldiers boiled meager pottages and stews, a legionary approached him: Metellus, Claudio recalled, a high ranking soldier relied-upon for information. "Your Worship!" he said, and knelt before him.

"Speak."

"There are sympathizers within Haroon, as we should expect…"

"Yes."

"They say they only have a thirty days' supply of food, and that is it."

Claudio smiled grimly. "And they have called for reinforcements, I presume…"

Metellus smiled. "I don't think they would risk it. You have—if I may be honest, Your Worship—completely humiliated the Fharese. You shattered their ideas of the King of Kings, proven he is not a god. Fharas is terrified of you, my lord emperor. I suggest you wait for them to run out of food. I am certain they will capitulate."

"I agree." Claudio nodded. "I will listen to your counsel."

Two weeks passed and the Imperial army remained well fed. In mid-morning of that day a trumpet pealed. The South Gate of Haroon opened. A few soldiers hollered, perhaps wanting to charge in. But Claudio called out for them to stop, and rushed out to meet them.

A horseman trotted out of the gate. His steed, covered in steel barding, had the large, muscular build of a charger. Its rider wore a suit of mail, and a scimitar dangled from his belt. Peering from an open-faced steel helmet, a set of dark eyes looked this way and that, perhaps searching for an opponent worthy of him.

Claudio walked out to meet him, feeling small in the shadow

of the high walls. "What is the meaning of this?" he shouted. "Who are you?"

"I am Darius," the horseman answered. "My grandfather was Archamenes, King of Kings. He is in the stars, now, with his brothers; you slew him." He smiled, his yellow teeth evident even through a thick black beard. "I am one of the Great Lords of Fharas. I thought I could retake our ancient province, but I erred in judgment. You are strong, Emperor Claudio. I have ridden out—alone, vulnerable—to discuss terms. I cannot promise you that I will not try to win Khazidea back." His smile widened. "But I can say that you have won, for now, and it is time for my troops and me to exit."

Claudio was careful not to return the smile. "Very well, Lord Darius. My judgment tells me to slay you all. But it takes courage to do what you've done. So here my terms: you will, without quarrel, hand the eleven Imperial Councilors to me; you will exit the land without taking any spoils, under threat of immediate retaliation; and you will renounce control over Khazidea."

Darius nodded. "I will do as you say, Emperor Claudio."

The Fharese had to physically drag the councilors out of the South Gate; bound in iron shackles and struggling in vain against the much stronger soldiers, kicking against the dirt of the road, they slowly but inevitably drew closer to Claudio. As he looked at Bruesio, his eyes darting this way and that in vain hope of escape, screaming as he tried to escape his captors' hands, Claudio saw a worm. He would ensure these eleven councilors—traitors not to Claudio, but to the Empire and their countrymen—would suffer a fate worse than any murderer, rebel, or escaped slave had ever suffered: for, as Claudio saw it, treason against one's nation was the lowest and most heinous of crimes.

CHAPTER FIFTY-SEVEN:
ECHOES OF THE PAST

Empress Anthea Adamantus, Wife of the God

As Anthea did each morning since becoming empress, she sat in front of the mirror and applied a modest amount of makeup. Not as much as she did in her former life on the streets, however; she wished to look merely presentable. Now, she was a married woman; empress, wife of Claudio, who still stole her breath whenever he walked into her view. He had left for several weeks and she yearned for him; but he said there were things left to be done.

She gazed into the mirror, peered into her own brown eyes. She now served as an inspiration to the girls and married women of the Empire. For their sake, she planned to live a virtuous—and long—life.

Someone knocked on the bedchamber door.

"Come in!" Anthea called out.

A handmaiden stood in the open doorway. "A woman is here… I'm not sure how she got in the palace. She says she wants to see you. She says she is an old friend, that she wants to say something."

The poor girl looked as confused as Anthea. "What is her name?"

"She didn't say," the handmaiden answered. "Shall I tell her to go?"

"No." Anthea's own words surprised her. "I will go see her with my bodyguard."

Who in Varda could it be?

A woman stood in the outer room, blocked by a group of Imperial Guards. Unarmed, she stood no chance against the tall, muscular warriors in their steel breastplates. But as she looked at the woman, her black hair half-hidden by an expensive silk cloak, Anthea's skin began to crawl with familiar goose bumps.

"Hello, Anthea," she spoke, and the shrill, commanding voice could only be Lady Ciutta.

"Restrain her!" Anthea's voice cracked as she shouted. Though now she was the empress, most powerful woman in the world, Lady Ciutta and the Order of the Red Hand still had a hold on her. She had no doubt they would try to assassinate Claudio, her dear husband.

The Imperial Guards held both of Ciutta's arms. She let her hood fall, baring her pallid skin and dark red lips to the light of the windows. At the sight of her harsh features, Anthea gasped.

"You will come with me," Ciutta growled. "You fancy yourself an empress, but you're street-trash. You're street-trash and that's all you'll ever be!"

She would respond harshly if anyone else said that. But she could not talk back to Lady Ciutta. She remembered the beatings and the humiliating, forced examinations of her health.

"Come back, street-trash. You belong to me!" Ciutta hissed. "I rescued you from your slime and filth. I fed you and looked after you when you were sick! I took better care of you than your idiot mother and the father who abandoned you—"

"Kill her!" Anthea shouted. Her strength surprised her. But it had to be done; not for her, but for Claudio and the stability of the Empire.

"No, street-trash!" Ciutta hissed. "You don't have it in you… You—" She drew in a shocked breath.

One of the Imperial Guards had slammed his dagger into her chest, and blood had begun to dribble down.

Tears formed in Anthea's eyes—tears she couldn't explain—and she turned and ran toward her bedchamber. She had removed an onerous yoke from her neck, yes; but the yoke had fed her and cleaned her, given a place to stay…

No. She had done the right thing. But she needed time to

mourn.

CHAPTER FIFTY-EIGHT: ETERNAL PEACE

Emperor Claudio-Valens Adamantus the God

Upon his return, Claudio had arranged a procession for the following morning. Now in the fresh air, he waited with a small, handpicked contingent of legionaries. They waited at the starting-point of the Walk of Triumph, where so many great conquerors and legates had gone before him. Just behind him, Metellus took care of the treacherous councilors: their feet, bound so tight in rope and chain they could not walk, and their hands tied behind their back, ensured they could only be dragged.

At a slow gait, Claudio rode his horse down the well-paved path. The councilors' cries of pain added much to the triumphal march, in Claudio's opinion, but soon the crowd—clustered tight along the perimeter—drowned them out.

The people, common and uncommon, rich and poor, cheered wildly as their emperor came into view. Many of them knew the councilors' treachery, and doubtlessly they welcomed the worms' pitiful state.

All along the Walk of Triumph, giant statues of national heroes—some forty feet high—loomed above Claudio. There was Anthans the Great, founder of Imperial City, riding on a horse with a helmet in his hand and his long hair flowing. There was Grand Legate Caro, slayer of vile "god-king" Heidathra! A few feet beyond lay the famous legionary Horatio, who risked certain death to recover the Imperial standard from the northern barbarians beyond the Wall.

But soon Claudio's admiration for these great heroes long-dead was drowned out: the closer he got to Imperial Square, the larger and denser crowd, the more deafening their cheers, and the more obvious their joy.

Claudio climbed the High Podium and took his place at the lectern. The people of Imperial City surrounded him like a sea. Just beyond, the eleven councilors had been tied in their place, securely-fastened and immobile, and their screams and pleas for mercy rose above the crowd.

"People of Imperial City!" Claudio shouted. "The King of Kings is dead, lying in a muddy unmarked grave. The province of Khazidea and all its wealth is ours… more importantly, it is *yours*. The Lords of Fharas dare not strike back, at least for now. The rebellion is no more. But if I want you to remember one thing today, it is this: the true, and most vile, enemy is not Fharas, much as I oppose them; nor was it the rebels, the servants of the Underworld. No, my friends, my people; the true enemy is here today. The councilors and all they represent: exhibiting treason, sedition and cowardice, and calling it compassion; despising the people of the Empire, governing them unmindfully, and calling it intellect; hating their own country's strength, and calling themselves wise. So let it be known, my dear people, that whatever punishment they receive, they deserve a fate a thousand times worse. May they remember their worthlessness as they perish in pain, and may they reflect on their lives in the fires of eternal Hell. Now, let the worms burn!"

A few legionaries tossed torches onto oil-soaked wooden posts. The flames quickly spread up their lengths, where, high-above, the treacherous worms of the Imperial Council were securely fastened.

"And so, my friends, begins a new age!" Claudio shouted. "An age of prosperity, an age of opportunity and of plenty: an age of eternal peace that none may take away. Long live the Empire! Long live liberty! Long live our country and her people, for ever and ever!"

CHAPTER FIFTY-NINE: WRITTEN IN FLAME

Adathra, Chief of the Magi

Adathra had no especial problem with Shapur, the new King of Kings and Archamenes' only son by his chief wife Roxana. He had ambition, charisma, intelligence, and a fiery—perhaps explosive—temper.

But—as Adathra stared into the crackling flame of the Fire Temple's brazier—he found himself unable to answer the king's question in a way that would not end in his own execution.

"What does it say?" Shapur hissed. "Read the omen! Will I avenge my father? Will I bring Claudio's devilish head back to Seshán?"

A welcome gust of ocean air wafted through the Fire Temple. Taifun, the greatest city in all the worlds, would take a collective breath of relief when the King of Kings left. "My lord king, God Manifest, we will most certainly take vengeance on the Empire. Whether it is Claudio or his successors, only Athra, Lord of Flame, knows."

"You are useless!" Shapur hissed in return. "I will remember your incompetence, Adathra."

In truth, the flame—lit with the holiest and most expensive of oils, on a rare wood that grew only in a faraway jungle—spoke more clearly than Adathra indicated: *Claudio will not die by Shapur's hand. The Empire will stumble but not by Shapur's hand. A grave foe will come from the east and trouble our kingdom, but not in Shapur's time.*

Adathra would not tell him, of course. Shapur's temper had already become legend. Claudio and his unclean, ignoble Empire would continue for now.

"But only for now," Adathra whispered as the train of Shapur's robe vanished through the door.

CHAPTER SIXTY:
HOMECOMING

Catalina Adamantus, Mother of the God

Catalina Adamantus, the empress mother. If she had anything to do with it, her friends around the Cipium ranch would never know. The news, however, had likely already gotten out.

She sat in a rocking-chair on the porch, knitting a glove and failing. The humid summer air had set in, and the skies hung above her, clear and blue.

She was now in her mid-fifties, an age that many of her childhood friends failed to reach. Just a while ago, she had her life planned out: Lucento her husband—gods rest his soul—would retire from the military forever; Claudio would marry a local girl and live near the ranch. Their family would thereafter retire from public life, and Catalina would live as long as the gods in Heaven willed, as a quiet country wife.

How things had changed.

She had taken up knitting, something to spend her idle hours. Claudio had sent many letters begging her to visit Imperial City. If she had her way, she would never enter that hive of hubris and immorality. If she had her way, she would never leave the ranch. She would be here, among the horses, forever.

One neighbor told Catalina that the people of the East and South worshiped Claudio as a god. At her words, Catalina had shuddered. Her son was not a god. If it ever got to Claudio's head, Catalina would sink forever into a deep sadness. If the station of emperor ever got to Claudio's head, the same.

As she sat there in the warm, humid air, the sound of pounding hooves echoed across the dirt path. Catalina looked up. Claudio was riding toward her, dressed in his plain boyhood garb. No escort of soldiers was in sight; but beside him rode a beautiful young

Eloesian woman who could only be his wife, dressed just as plainly as he.

Tears welled in Catalina's eyes. She dropped her half-finished glove and stood up. Her son had not changed, after all. He sat on the White Throne but he knew who he truly was: Catalina's son, Lucento's son; not a god, not an emperor, but a man. A citizen, like everyone else.

She would prepare the most delicious meal possible and open all the bottles of white wine. If her son, Claudio, had not changed—if he rode all the way to his family home dressed in plain clothes— perhaps Catalina could abide Imperial City; perhaps she could accept the position of Empress mother after all.

EPILOGUE

Valerio Lucullus, Emperor-Presumptive

Many years later…

Late Autumn, 1049

The emperor Claudio lay on his deathbed, as calm and stern at the end of his life as he had been in its prime. So much had happened in his reign: wars in the south; raids from the northern barbarians beyond the Wall; and famines and plagues without number. But Emperor Claudio-Valens, the unconquered son of Lucento, worshiped as a living god among his devotees in Eloesus and Haroon, had spared the common citizens from most of the trouble. Throughout his life he had fought at the vanguard, in battle and in life, in war and in discourse. He had not always been popular, but he had always ruled well; and Valerio Lucullus, veteran legate and adoptive "son," feared he could not match his predecessor. He feared that the Golden Age would end.

"Write," said the elderly Claudio-Valens. "I have last words; guidance for your reign."

Valerio nodded. "Yes, my lord emperor."

Valerio transcribed Claudio's words:

Dear Valerio:

In your reign, your goal should be peace. In peacetime, the citizens live long and happy lives. But do not confuse peace with passivity; for peace cannot be achieved except by strength, and by assertion of the Empire's might. Wolves abound in this world, leading the less civilized nations, and they must be deterred, defeated, and humiliated again and again. Nothing attracts these wolves like weakness does; and nothing aids them as much as sedition from within.

Therefore, Valerio Lucullus, veteran of many wars and dear friend, remember these words throughout your rule: Serve your people and your country, and lead at the vanguard like you always have. And, Valerio Lucullus, emperor of this great nation, let your goal therefore always be Conquest; and let your name be Empire."

Valerio set the pen down. He gazed at the former emperor, as his breaths even now grew strained and labored. What a man. What a ruler. What a long, a good and a thoroughly Imperial life.

Valerio would take the words to heart; he would read Claudio's words, and memorize them. His goal would be Conquest, and his name would be Empire.

GLOSSARY

Acronesis: An island off the coast of Anthania, near Peregoth.

Athra: A god of fire, favored in Fharas and especially by the magi.

Atman: A god of fertility, the male counterpart to Issa. His highest-ranking priests are called the Godlings.

Augusts: The higher of the two ruling classes (the other being Knights). They are the descendants of the original Peregothian families through the male line, and are the only people allowed to serve within the upper tier of the government.

Anthans: (1) Another name for Imperial City. (2) Anthans the Great, the last of the Sea Kings and the first emperor (having achieved the title with the ceding of Anthania).

Brilium: A lumbering town north of Bregantium. In the native tongue of Northern Gad, "Brill."

Cataphract: An order of heavy cavalry, originating in Fharas and—to some extent—mimicked in Eloesus. With the invention of the stirrup several hundred years ago, they became the padisha's favored shock troops, using devastating charges with the lance to full effect.

Empire: A large nation surrounding most of the Middle Sea. Their flag is a gold war-eagle on a red field.

Elders, the: According to legend, a race of mystical beings rumored to live "beyond the reach of the north wind."

Eloesus: An ancient land famed for its wealth and rich culture. Since the 500s YE, an Imperial province. Their flag is a laurel-wreath on a green field.

Fharas: An ancient empire centered in the plain of Gor Ilán. Their flag is a golden four-pointed star on a purple field.

Fingers of Barukh: An elite military order with origins in Kheroe, known for their mystically-conjured explosive arrows. The Empire values them highly, but they command a high price.

In general, they are apolitical, claiming to give no preference to the Fharese padisha or the "northern emperor"; and giving only reluctant lip-service to the king of Kheroe. Their name refers to their worship of Barukh, god of entryways.

Gad: The northernmost and least populous province of the Empire, known for its light-featured inhabitants.

Gor Ilán: A flat plain in the center of Fharas.

Godlings: An elite order of eunuch priests, worshippers of Atman. Their temple is located in Qabash, a region of Khazidea.

Haroon Spice: An intoxicant, currently banned in the Empire, which causes hallucinations and feelings of euphoria but—over the long term—afflicting the consumer with severe weight loss and, oftentimes, dementia. Crimson eyes are the telltale sign of long-term addicts.

Heidathra: A king of mixed Fharese and Eloesian descent who rebelled against the Empire in the late 400s and early 500s YE.

Hieronus: The god of justice and just war.

Imperial City: Also called Anthans. The de facto capital of the Empire, and the largest city in the known world.

Imperial Council: A body of thirty Augusts (see above), given certain governmental powers, including the ability to remove the emperor. They are elected by the people of Imperial City across its thirty districts.

Imperiopoli: A large city of Eloesus.

Imperium: The god of the Imperial state, represented as an eagle. His cult was founded in the 400s YE. The theologians of the Magisterium consider him a human invention.

Isle of Serpents: An island off the western coast of Anthania. According to legend, populated by giant venomous reptiles.

Issa: Goddess of fertility. Worshiped mostly in Khazidea and the southlands, she nevertheless has a large temple in Imperiopoli.

Korthos: An Eloesian metropolis.

Khazidea: A southern land along the Khazan River, surrounded by desert.

Kheroe: An area of greenery and rainfall, west from Khazidea across the desert.

Knight: (1) A mounted warrior, especially one wearing heavy armor; (2) A member of the lower tier of the Imperial upper class—the other being Augusts—officially tasked with the defense of the Empire. In actuality, not all knights serve actively as soldiers.

Lornatium: A small town near the Isle of Serpents and adjacent to Mount Hylea.

Lorenus: The god of the sea, favored by the city of Peregoth.

Magisterium, the: A large religious complex in Sanctum, led by the Pontifex, chief priest of Hieronus.

Peregoth: The founding city of the Empire, built on an island of the same name.

Peregothius: The first of the Sea Kings.

Orkus: The god of sharks, sea jellies, octopi and deep-sea chasms. Rumored to live in a deep rift within the Imperial Sea.

Saidoon: A city within the distant tropical jungle, considered exotic even by the Fharese who control it.

Seshán: A ceremonial city south of Haroon, the capital of Fharas.

Sur: A far-off land, nominally self-governing but heavily under the sway of the Fharese padisha. The region is highly valued for its large and fearsome elephants. The *bashaw* (great lord) of Sur and his family are said to live within the city of Janshi.

Tarso: A legendary city supposedly controlled by pirates.

Taifun: A large city of Fharas, south of Seshán on the shore of the South Seas. Its moniker is "the greatest city in all the worlds"—given by a magus who claimed to have traveled beyond the material world and through the various dimensions, and never found its equal.

Tiverium: The largest city of Acronesis with a population of about 14,000 persons, ruled by the Prince Maximo Valentus and his garrison of knights.

Tarchon the Mad: An Eloesian conqueror, prone to fits of insanity, who invaded and plundered Khazidea. He ravaged Gor Ilán, causing much destruction, but perished from disease on his journey to Seshán.

Wall, the: A large wall separating the Empire from the northern barbarians. Its origins are a mystery.

Zoar: The capital of Kheroe. Nicknamed "the City of Stone" because its buildings are carved from rock hill. The King of Kheroe and the Council of Elders rule it in name. Its lighthouse is famous across the world.

IMPERIAL CITY MAP KEY

Suburro: An ancient, poor section of town, flanked by the Equine and Aurean Hills. Though widely known for its poverty and shanty homes, many great Imperials found their origins here.

West Side: Arguably part of the Suburro, a poor section of town predominating much of the western two-thirds of the city. It is filled with parks and spice dens.

a.   **Armory District:** Once a center for the production of armaments and siege weaponry, this quiet district northeast of the Suburro is known for its charming shops and sprawling apartments.

b.   **Kings Terrace:** An ancient enclave near the center of the city, featuring the mansions and homes of rich councilors and government officials. Most of these mansions cannot be bought and are passed down through families.

c.   **Maxima:** Shops and theaters abound in this district, a center for drama and entertainment. Named for the war hero Adriano Maximus.

d.   **Villa Regis:** A wealthy section of town, built along the shores of the North River.

e.   **Bulus Wharf:** A section of town facing Imperial Harbor, a center of fishmongers and the fish trade.

Celsus Heights: A rich section of town built on a steep promontory. It is named for the infamous shipping magnate Celsus, who — rumor has it — burned down the area to build one of his mansions. Beside the rumor for arson, he was known for his unscrupulous business practices, charging exorbitant rents for those who stayed in his apartments, and was rumored to be a Strig, a kind of undead. Today, the mostly sumptuous apartment buildings overlook Imperial Harbor. Shops and music halls can also be found in abundance.

Harbor District: A sprawling district bordering the Imperial Harbor, featuring docks and warehouses.

Cloaca: The sewer district of Imperial City, flushing effluent into the South River. In ancient days, the first Cloaca broke and gushed forth water into the low-lying fields south of the river, creating the Palladian Swamp. The second Cloaca was built, much larger and stronger, after years of construction.

f. **Market District:** A vast district predominating the center of the city, featuring its eponymous markets as well as slum areas.

g. **Canyon Row:** Shops, apartments, temples and shrines predominate this central section of town. The Walk of Triumph begins here.

h. **Newmarket:** A quiet district of shops and apartments.

i. **Mud Bottom:** A dilapidated, ancient section of town, the most impoverished district.

Avediccus: A section of town facing the Palladian Swamp. Predominated by homes, shops, and small shrines, a concrete stairway into the swamp can be found here.

j. **Meridia:** A section of town bordering the Palladian Swamp and city bounds, featuring apartment blocks, shops and administrative buildings.

k. **Mystia:** A large section of town featuring markets, shops and homes, as well as the garrison for the city watch.

l. **Villa Maris:** A section of town bordering the South River, highly developed, known for its taverns along the river's shore.

Emporia: Markets and shops predominate this central district.

m. **Loud Surf:** A section of town built along cliffs, featuring often more pleasant weather than the city below. Its inhabitants call this section of town the city's most blessed area.

n. **Perrine:** Named after the Emperor Perrius, this section of town has a mixture of wealth and poverty. It is a favored home for members of the military, as it connects to a road to Fort Mettius several miles away.

o.   **Gaboline:** Named after the Emperor Gabolus, originally built around a fort then outside of city bounds, this district is known for its quaint stone streets and temples.

p.   **West Limes:** A border area facing Wagontown Settlement, it is nonetheless highly developed and features vast theaters and gladiatorial arenas.

q.   **East Limes:** A border area featuring many gladiatorial arenas. It abuts a section of cemeteries outside city bounds.

r.   **Terrentian:** Named after the legate Terrentius, this section of town is known as a site of public executions. Shops and homes can be found here.

s.   **Majorian Markets:** Named for two sprawling indoor market complexes, it is rumored that anything in Varda can be found here on sale.

The Ricci: A walled-off, closed section of town that houses the city's ratling population.

t.   **The Strand:** A highly developed area of town known for its lighted roads, specialized taverns and bookshops.

u.   **Meletus**: A section of apartments, shops and temples bordering the North River.

v.   **Urubus:** A vast section of town below Celsus Heights, relatively impoverished, where the smoke of the city often settles. City administrators consider it a public health nuisance.

About the Author

Cursed at birth with a wild imagination, Andrew Cooper spent his youth dreaming of worlds more exciting than Earth.

He is a graduate of the Odyssey Writing Workshop. His stories have appeared in Morpheus Tales, Fear and Trembling, Residential Aliens and Mindflights, among others.

CONTACT THE AUTHOR

Visit **www.aj-cooper.com** to sign up for the newsletter and stay up-to-date on new releases.

Find him on Facebook at:

www.facebook.com/AJCooperauthor